# THE RIPLEY EFFECT

## THE HOUNDS OF ZEUS MC
## BOOK 7

### BY FAITH GIBSON

THE HOUNDS OF ZEUS

Copyright © 2023 by Faith Gibson
Published by: Bramblerose Press LLC
Editor: Candice Royer
Proofreader: Kerstin Meier
First edition: July 2023
Cover design: Jay Aheer, Simply Defined Art
Cover photography: © Wander Aguiar Photography
LLC www.wanderbookclub.com
Cover model: Soj M
ISBN: 978-1736890066

# Dedication

One balmy summer afternoon on a lake in Tennessee, I met this young woman who was full of life and cute af. After spending the day listening to her story, I knew she was going to be in a book. I asked her permission before using her name, and she graciously said yes. While the real Glory's story would make an exciting book, I did not include it here. The story in these pages is from my own crazy mind, fitting the narrative that is The Ministry. There are similarities in their personalities and looks, but I changed my Glory to make her Ripley's perfect mate. (He likes his women a little plump.) If any of you reading this know the real Glory, you know how special she is. This one's for her.

# PROLOGUE

GLORY CHOKED BACK bile as her stomach rumbled again. She never got sick. She would chalk it up to everything she'd eaten that day, but it had been hours since she'd had any food. Using her forearm, Glory wiped the sweat from her brow. She had one shot at taking the man down when he entered the barn, and she didn't need her vision impaired. Glory had a moment of doubt about stabbing someone, but the man was evil. He wanted to make a trade – Glory for her new friend, and after learning about the woman's gift, she had no doubt the man wanted her friend back for his own gain. Glory couldn't let that happen.

The doorknob turned, and Glory took a deep breath. *Jacob* stepped into the barn, and Glory didn't hesitate. She sliced across the back of his knees, bringing him to the ground.

"What the fuck?" he cried. Jacob turned and pointed the pistol her way, but Glory had the advantage. She jumped across his body, slashing his wrist as she went. He dropped the gun, but he wasn't done. Even with his legs and arm bleeding, Jacob twisted. "I'll fucking kill you!" he raged.

"Not if I kill you first." Glory kicked the weapon across the floor. She didn't want to alert the guards

1

with a gunshot, so her knives would have to do.

"You're not going to kill me, Glory of God. You don't have it in you," he taunted.

Glory gripped both knives tightly, but before she could attack the man, her stomach rumbled again, and this time, there was no holding back. Glory threw up, and it landed on Jacob's face. She stumbled away from him as he thrashed about, swiping the mess away with his good hand. While he was preoccupied, Glory wiped her mouth with the hem of her T-shirt, careful not to cut herself with the blade in her hand. She was weak from whatever had been used on her earlier but still standing. Glory walked behind him, and stabbed him in the side with the hunting knife. Jacob cried out for the guards. He called out to God. He cursed Glory. He grabbed for the knife, but Glory was faster. She used her serrated weapon to slice through his bicep and jumped back. Forward, slash, jump back. She continued her assault until he no longer attempted to dig the knife out of his side.

Blood trickled out of the side of his mouth as he glared at her. "Y-you'll go to H-hell for th-this," he stammered.

Jutting her chin, she told him, "Save me a seat." Glory kept an eye on the man as she went to the cabinet and got another knife. Shouts outside the barn had Glory scrambling to the ladder. She climbed as quickly as possible carrying two weapons, but she wasn't waiting for one of the guards to come in and shoot her. Glory had never been in the loft, so when she got to her feet, she looked around. The small area was filled with crates. Glory stumbled over to the closest one, finding it empty. The next three were also bare, but the last one held at least a dozen weapons like the guards used. Glory had never fired a gun, and these large, black rifles were daunting. Ignoring them, she made her way to the window. It was smudged with years of grime, so Glory wiped away a small section so she could peek outside, then wiped her hand on her shorts.

Then the most beautiful sight ever appeared below. Glory banged on the window and yelled, "I'm up here!" A rifle blasted behind her, and the window shattered, raining glass everywhere, ending her short-lived moment of joy.

# CHAPTER ONE

## Glory

GLORY KNEW BETTER than to stab harder than necessary, but she was upset. No, she was pissed. That wasn't a word she would ever utter aloud lest she get thrown into solitary. Solitary sucked. Another word she would never say aloud. Taking a deep breath, she steadied the knife and sliced into the deer's pelt, careful not to cut the meat. Skinning the animal was second nature now that she'd been doing it so long. Her first time had been the result of talking back to her parents in front of Brother Josiah. He felt learning to prepare an animal was both a punishment as well as a good life skill to have. If she lived out in the real world and was a hunter, sure. But she didn't, and she wasn't. At least the doe had already been gutted and bled before it was brought to the barn. Glory prayed she hadn't been a momma with fawns left to fend for themselves. The men of Haven didn't care about things like that.

"Looking good, Glory."

Glory was tempted to stab again, but this time not the deer. William had brought the animal in while Glory was in Bible study. He often stood around watching while she skinned the animals, even though it wasn't allowed. Single men and women were never to be alone without a chaperone, and even then, they were only supposed to be together if they were what the elders considered dating. She and William were not. Glory knew William wanted that, but she found nothing about the older man desirable. Not that it mattered. Women weren't given a choice in who they were paired with. In a small community like Haven, it was hard to find any of the single men attractive. If she had been born within the fences of the compound, she wouldn't know any different, but Glory had been a teenager when her parents uprooted their lives. She and her three younger sisters had been taken from a somewhat normal environment to one which didn't allow any freedoms. No phones. No television or movies. No running outside to play in the yard after chores and homework were finished. No boyfriends who... *Don't go there.*

It wasn't as bad for Splendor and Majesty since they had been ten and eight at the time. Her next youngest sister, Hope, had been fifteen, so she too remembered what life was like before. Hope was meek and never questioned anything their parents told them. At least not aloud. Where Glory hated life behind these prison walls, Hope adapted much easier. Her demure nature caught a lot of attention, but luckily for her, she had been paired up with a soft-spoken man her age. They were expecting their first child in the fall. She seemed happy enough, but it wasn't something Glory wanted for herself. Not with a man like William or any of the others who had requested her hand.

Ignoring him never worked, so she muttered, "Thank you." What she wanted to say was, "leave me the hell alone," but she didn't. Once she'd made the necessary cuts to the hide, Glory cracked the animal's four legs and cut them off at the knee joints, tossing the limbs into the nearby bin for disposal. The first time she had watched Rhetta show her the process, Glory had thrown up. Thankfully, the older woman had been sympathetic and didn't chide her for her "weak constitution." Instead of helping Glory attach the legs to the bars that would allow her to raise the deer into the air, William leaned against the wall with his arms crossed over his chest. Whatever. She didn't need his help.

"What's going on in here?" Brother Thomas stormed into the barn, but instead of yelling at William, he pointed a finger at Glory. "You know the rules."

"I do, Brother Thomas. I assure you I am only doing my job. I'm not sure what he's doing though," she said, pointing the knife in William's direction. If looks could kill, she would be dead five ways to Sunday.

"I apologize, Brother Thomas. I only stopped by to tell Glory she will accompany me to the market tomorrow. Her father agreed with my request to pursue her hand in marriage, and we will use that time as part of our courtship. I realize my error in not asking for a chaperone. I'll take my leave now." William stalked off but not before he leered her way. This was bad. So very bad. If her father agreed, it was all but a done deal. Glory's hands shook as she gripped the hide and pulled.

"I will let the infraction go this time," Brother Thomas said. "Only because William is an honorable man. You're lucky he's interested."

"Very lucky, Brother Thomas." Glory felt anything but. Her gut churned, and she had to take several deep breaths to keep the bile down. She knew she wasn't the prettiest woman at Haven. She was on the plump side. Always had been. She would rather be a little overweight than starve herself. Glory was a meat and potatoes kind of girl. Salads were okay as a side item but not as a whole meal. Her mother was also on the larger side, but she once told Glory they had good breeding hips. She didn't understand what that meant until she was older.

The elder, who was Brother Josiah's second-in-command, left her alone. Once the barn door was closed, Glory dropped to her knees. No way was she marrying William or any of the other men at Haven. There were only a handful of men her age, and they were already married. The ones interested in her were old enough to be her father. Speaking of fathers, Glory was going to have a talk with hers. She bit the inside of her jaw to keep from yelling out. It would only call attention to her, and that was the last thing she wanted.

By the time she finished skinning the deer and cutting the meat into pieces, Glory was ready to scream. Or run. If only she could disappear the way Anna had. Glory didn't know what happened to the pretty woman, but she prayed wherever Anna was she was happy. Glory made her way to the cabin she shared with two others and headed straight to the shower. She didn't have much time until she was required in the kitchen. Dinner would be served soon, and one of her jobs was to wash dishes. She didn't get to eat until after the men had their meal.

The second Bible study of the day happened in the evening. Married couples ate first, then went to the chapel. While they were there, the single men ate. Then it was their turn to hear the nightly sermon while the single women had their meal. Since no one was excused from Bible study, some of the single men returned to clean up while the women went to the chapel. Later, as Glory was walking to the largest building at Haven, her father stopped her. "Come to the cabin after chapel. We need to talk." He didn't give Glory time to respond. Since William had already spilled the beans, Glory didn't have to wonder what Father wanted to tell her.

It was all she could do to sit still while Brother Thomas ranted about proper Godly behavior and the sins of the world outside of Haven. For as long as Glory and her family had been there, Brother Josiah had been the one to preach, but one night, Brother Thomas informed them that Brother Josiah was out in the world searching for lost souls. She wasn't stupid, though. You didn't bring lost souls to a place like Haven that was guarded heavily. If he was only teaching God's word, he wouldn't be raising an army.

The boys who grew up at Haven were taught to shoot at a young age, and they weren't all out hunting game like William. He carried a hunting rifle, while the others were strapped with what she'd learned were assault rifles. If they were doing God's will, who were they assaulting, and why would they need to defend their home? For a while, right after Josiah disappeared, some of his guards did as well, and those who remained began dressing in regular clothes. Then about a month ago, the guards returned to patrolling the perimeter. More than once, she'd overheard William ask Brother Thomas to put him on guard duty, but for whatever reason, he was denied the position.

Speaking of William... The final amen was chanted, and Glory rushed from the chapel to the small cabin her parents lived in. She didn't bother waiting after she knocked. Her father stood when Glory closed the door.

"I will not marry William."

Father's face turned dark, the same way it had before she was taken from her home. "It is your duty to Haven but more especially to God."

"I understand my duty, Father. But I will not marry William or any of the other men who are as old as you are. I would rather die first."

Glory didn't see the fist coming. The blow was so hard it knocked her to the floor. Her mother rushed over, but her father shouted, "Leave her be." Mother glared at her husband, something Glory had never witnessed in her twenty-four years. Not even after that night six years ago. Mother helped her to her feet and stood between the two of them.

"That was uncalled for, Father. We do not strike our children." Mother kept her eyes averted from Glory, because she knew that was a lie.

"She's being insolent." Her father pointed his finger at Glory. "You will marry William and have his children."

9

"I won't. I will cause so much trouble Brother Thomas will keep me in solitary."

"You'd rather spend your days alone and shaming our family?"

"Yes. I hate it here. You know I do. Please, I'm begging you. Just let me go."

"Go? Go where? Back into the world of sinners? Is that what you want?"

"I'd rather take my chances out there than marry someone I don't love."

Her mother took Glory by the arms, her eyes filled with tears. "You really mean that, don't you?"

"Yes, Mother. Please, let me go."

Mother looked over her shoulder. "Amos—"

"Absolutely not. The girl has no life skills. She wouldn't make it a day," her father scoffed. He took a menacing step toward them both. "Your life is here at Haven, and you will do what is needed for the good of the community. As part of your courtship, you are being allowed to accompany William to the market tomorrow. You will have a chaperone, so don't get any ideas in that fool head of yours about escaping. Now, get out of here." When Glory opened the door hard enough for it to hit the wall, her father rushed forward and grabbed her bicep, squeezing. "If you do something stupid, you will still go to the market tomorrow, and then you'll be tossed in solitary after. Do not do something stupid. Do I make myself clear?"

"Yes, Father." Glory was seething, but kept her eyes down. He could think she was submitting. Once he turned loose, she calmly walked back to the opposite side of the community where she shared a

10

cabin with two other women. The fourth bed had been Hope's until she married Scott. Why couldn't Glory have been matched with someone her own age? She already knew the answer to that. She was too plain. Too plump. Too sullied.

Melinda and Lisa Ann were both knitting when Glory walked into their cabin. They made and sold baby blankets at the market where Glory would be helping William the next day. Glory didn't have any type of skill such as sewing. Her only talent was singing, but that wasn't something that could be sold to make money for the community.

Melinda tossed down her project and rushed to Glory. "What happened to your face?"

"Father." Glory grabbed Melinda's hand before she could touch Glory's cheek. "I found out he's agreed for William to court me."

"Oh, Honey." Lisa Ann was older than both Glory and Melinda. She had been at Haven longer than Glory, but for whatever reason, she remained single.

"I told my father I would rather be dead than marry William, and he got upset. The good news is I will be going to the market tomorrow as part of our courtship. It will be the first time I've left Haven in all these years. While I'm not happy for the reason, I am curious to see what the outside world looks like now."

"I'm so sorry, Glory," Melinda said. She had only been at Haven a few months, but there was something about her Glory couldn't figure out. Something secretive about the woman.

"Thanks. I'm going to lie down. My head is throbbing."

Both women gave her sympathetic looks but didn't say anything else. After Glory changed into her sleep clothes, she crawled under the covers and closed her eyes. Her cabin mates were quiet as they continued with their knitting, but the silence was too much. It allowed Glory's mind to fixate on William and what he would do to her when they were married.

"Melinda, will you please sing for me?"

"Sure." Instead of a hymn, Melinda sang a tune Glory wasn't familiar with. It talked about someone the singer used to know, asking if she could take his picture. It wasn't a love song, more like a song of what could have been. When she was alone, Glory often sang songs she remembered from before, and if she had been out in the real world then, this song would have been something she listened to. Glory fell asleep and dreamed of standing on a sidewalk, taking photos of random people.

The next morning, Glory was excused from kitchen duty since she was going to the market. She ate breakfast with the other women, then met those who were traveling to the next town at the gate. The women were transported in one van, while the men were transported in another. Most of the men were only there to watch over the women and answer any questions customers might have. Glory wasn't sure exactly what she would be doing other than standing with William. Lisa Ann had explained the set-up process that morning while they were getting dressed. Her cabin mate loaned Glory a dress since she didn't have one of her own. It didn't fit properly, and Glory wished she were allowed to wear the plain cotton pants and top that was their daily uniform. Winter was the only time they were allowed to wear thicker clothing, and since the weather was milder, they were back to the thinner garments.

Haven rented three stalls where they sold things like blankets, quilts, baked goods, and deer jerky. Glory had no idea the animals she prepared were used for anything other than food for their community. She wondered who made the jerky. Who packaged it to be sold. There was a lot about their world she didn't know, like where the money for guns came from. Where did the guards get their black clothes? The women who sewed the daily uniforms surely didn't make those as well.

Once they were underway, Glory forgot about those things and enjoyed the breeze coming in through the lowered windows as she watched the world go by one mile at a time. The scenery was glorious even if it was nothing more than woods with a few houses dotted here and there. A deep longing for their old home took hold of Glory's soul. As bad as things had been, it was still better than Haven.

The ride took about forty-five minutes, and Glory hummed to herself for most of that time. Thankfully, the others didn't mind. She'd never dealt with silence well. When they arrived, the women remained in the van while the men set up the three booths. Once ready, Glory and the others piled out of the vehicle. William was waiting on her, and with him was one of the elders.

William glanced at the bruise on her cheek but didn't ask how it got there. "You'll be at the stall with me selling jerky. You are not to speak to any of the customers. If they ask you a question, I will answer them. Your job is to keep the table stocked. If someone purchases one bag, you replace it with another. If they purchase three, you add three to the table." When Glory didn't say anything, William stopped and glared at her. "Well?"

"Don't speak. Restock. Got it." It wasn't rocket science.

"Let's go." Brother Zachariah gestured to where the other women were already stationed behind their tables with men of their own watching over them. Glory took in the other stalls and the people selling their wares. There were fresh fruits and vegetables. Homemade jams and jellies. Soap and lotions. Glory wished with all her heart she could walk around the market and take it all in, but she knew that wouldn't be allowed. They weren't there to buy things but to sell their own items to make money for Haven.

All three booths saw plenty of customers. Glory kept theirs stocked without William having to remind her. Time passed by quickly, and soon it was noon. Someone had packed sandwiches and bottles of water in a cooler for their lunch, and Glory devoured hers in between customers. A shadow fell over Glory, and when she looked up, a gorgeous man was standing on the other side of the table.

"Do you make the jerky?" he asked Glory.

"No, I just skin the deer," Glory said, even though she'd been told not to speak to the customers.

The man winked at her. "Now that's a fine skill to have."

14

William stepped between Glory and the table, almost knocking her down. "That'll be fifteen dollars."

"How much for three packs?" the man asked.

"Can you not add?" William asked, his tone scathing. "Three times fifteen is forty-five."

"Yeah, smartass. I can add, but most places give discounts for multiple purchases." He tossed the pack at William's chest. "You can keep it." While William was replacing the pack in the row it belonged in, the man caught Glory's eye and winked again before striding off on long legs encased in worn jeans. Glory only stopped watching him walk away when William grabbed her arm. She jerked away from him, and Brother Zachariah intervened.

"Glory, if you don't want to be confined to solitary when we return to Haven, you'll behave."

Of course she was the one at fault. She didn't want to be punished, but it was hard for Glory to keep her mouth closed. Needing a moment to herself, she turned to William. "I need to use the restroom." Glory had seen some of the other women leaving their stalls, so she didn't think it would be an issue.

"I'll take her," Brother Zachariah said. That made sense considering she and William weren't allowed to be alone together. She followed the elder past all the booths to where a concrete building sat off to the side. Brother Zachariah waited right by the door as Glory went inside. The facility was surprisingly clean, and Glory went into one of the open stalls. She took her time peeing and sat there for a few extra minutes to delay having to return to the booth and William. The outer door opened, and Glory felt foolish sitting on the toilet without actually using it, so she stood and pulled her panties up. She flushed with her foot, not wanting to touch the handle. When she came out, a woman with short, lavender hair stood by the sink.

In a foreign accent, the woman whispered, "Hello, Glory."

# CHAPTER TWO

## Ripley

AN EAR-PIERCING SHRIEK woke Ripley. Sitting on the ground with his back against a tree, he opened his eyes in time to see Major running past, buck naked. He couldn't help but grin at the kid. Right behind the blond whirlwind was his mother, clutching Major's clothes in her fist.

"Major Lazlo, get your bare ass back here," Natalia yelled. When she passed by Ripley, she muttered, "Sorry, Ripper."

"No problem," he responded. It wasn't like he hadn't been around the twins long enough to know a nap anywhere in their vicinity was likely to be short-lived. Major running around naked was a regularity in their world. The dire wolf chasing after Natalia was not. Nikita, Kayos's adopted daughter, was taking advantage of being out in the middle of the woods where she could safely shift into her Wolf without fear of anyone other than their family seeing her. Another high-pitched squeal rent the air, followed by Major's cute-as-fuck laughter. A few minutes later, Natalia strolled back by, shaking her head.

"That kid…," she mumbled, but Ripley knew Natalia loved Major as much as she did Marshall. The lavender-haired, former Russian mafia princess adored her two boys, even if she hadn't given birth to them.

Ripley rubbed his chest, the longing always bubbling right below the surface. Pushing to his feet, he decided a walk farther away from the campsite would do him good. As he made his way deeper into the woods, Major's giggles got louder. Ripley found out what had him laughing when Nikita strolled by in her fur with the now clothed boy riding her back. He had one hand in her thick pelt and the other was circling the air like a bull rider at a rodeo.

"Where ya going, Rip?" Major asked as Nikita stopped.

"Just taking a walk. I won't be long." Ripley ruffled Major's hair, then took off along a path. The June weather was perfect for camping as well as riding. Being a Gryphon, the cold temperature associated with winter in Upstate New York didn't bother him, but he preferred taking his bike when he didn't have to worry about ice on the roads. While Ripley preferred fall, spring was nice too with the trees filling out, the flowers and plants blooming, and the temperatures not too cool or too warm. The area where they were camping was private property, and the Hounds felt safe there. The vast acreage was surrounded by wooden fences and No Trespassing signs. They didn't shift into their Gryphons, but they did let their Lions out while others stood guard. Their Eagle forms were much easier since they were commonplace, and a human sighting one didn't cause chaos. Ripley's own

18

beast was itching to be turned loose, but Ripley didn't feel like stripping down. After witnessing both Nikita and her mother, Quinn, shift without shredding their clothing, Ripley wished he had that same type of magic. Then again, if he had their magic, he wouldn't be a Gryphon.

*Would that be so bad?*

His beast had been a surly bastard for the last twenty years, ever since life as he knew it was tossed on its ass. Ripley met Sara Beth the night he and his family were celebrating him passing his bar exam. Everything was perfect. Ripley had a job at his parents' firm and a sweet woman who thought he hung the moon and stars. He bought Sara Beth the home of her dreams right on the beach. They had been living together close to three years when Ripley bought a ring. Before he proposed, he came clean about what he was, thinking enough time had passed and his female would be okay with his truth. He was wrong. Sara Beth freaked out when he shifted. She passed out, then when she came to, she lost her shit again. Inconsolable, Ripley had no choice but to let her go. Before he did, he used his Gryphon voice to erase her memories of that night. He convinced her she no longer loved him, and with a broken heart, Ripley let her walk away. When being in the same town as Sara Beth was too much to bear, he moved far away from the Florida coast, finding his new home with the Hounds in Upstate New York. It didn't take Ripley long to go from a clean-cut male who lived in suits and ties to one who wore ripped jeans and a kutte, acquiring a myriad of tattoos. Since then, he had guarded his heart, only bedding females when the itch to fuck was too strong to ignore. But Zeus, how he longed to find someone to share his life with. To have kids with. Ripley's life should be a charmed one. He was a Hound of Zeus, one of the chosen ones, after all.

Ripley found a best friend in Asher "Ace" McMurray and a family in the motorcycle club. Unlike the Lazlo brothers who were mercenaries, Ripley preferred helping their father, Sutton, track down members of The Ministry, the cult who had caused the near apocalypse thirty years prior. While working as an attorney, Ripley invested his earnings wisely, so he wasn't hurting for money and could go about his days not worrying that Sutton wasn't paying him for his time. Finding the cult leaders and getting them away from their flocks was payment enough. Ripley had gotten his license to practice law in New York, but now he did pro bono work, mostly for those the Hounds rescued from The Ministry.

Ryker's loud whistle indicated it was time to load up, so Ripley turned and headed back. By the time he arrived at the campsite, all the tents were down, including his. Ace tossed a grin over his shoulder, and Ripley smiled back.

"Thanks, man." Ripley helped gather the equipment and store it in the back of the SUV Ryker had driven. With Rhiannon pregnant and due to give birth within the next few weeks, Ryker rarely let his mate ride on his bike. Ripley didn't blame him. They may be experts at handling two wheels, but too many drivers didn't watch out for motorcycles. Quinn, on the other hand, who had only recently announced she was

20

also expecting, demanded she ride with Kayos until she started showing.

"There's a market not far from here that Rhi wants to check out," Ryker said after everything was packed.

"It's a beautiful day for it," Natalia said as she helped the twins with their helmets.

When Ace raised an eyebrow, Ripley nodded. "Fine with me." He wasn't sure what the market had to offer, but he had no place to be other than with his family. Once everyone was loaded up, Ryker led the way. If he had been on his bike, Ryker would have led the formation. Since he was driving, Maveryck took the lead position with Sultan next as sergeant-at-arms. Ripley and Ace brought up the rear, putting them as a buffer between the precious cargo in the middle and any vehicles that came behind. They traveled at a slower pace with the kids riding in their sidecars. The normally wild Major was the perfect passenger, remaining still and with his arms inside where they belonged.

The group stuck to backroads, so the trip took a little longer, but the scenery was worth the extra time. When they arrived, heads turned as the bikes rumbled into the parking area. Ripley dismounted his bike and rubbed his hands through his hair after removing his helmet. The group strolled toward the gated entrance, taking in all the market had to offer. Various food scents wafted through the air, mingling with the smells of essential oils.

"Something smells yummy," Major said, patting his tummy.

"Then let's go find out what it is," Natalia said,

ruffling his hair. Major grabbed one of her hands, while Marshall took the other. It did Ripley's heart good to see the two little dudes with their mom. For being a retired assassin, Natalia had taken to motherhood easily. Ripley fell in line with the others as they made their way through the outdoor market, stopping when the females did to check out the items for sale. Natalia and the twins met back up with them. Major's face was covered in chocolate, and Marshall was nibbling neatly on his treat.

They were headed toward a booth that sold quilts when Rhi froze, grabbing Ryker's hand. She turned her back to the stalls. "Those are people from Haven," she whispered.

Ripley glanced over at the booths. One female in particular caught his eye, and his beast pushed against him.

*Mate.*

The female was cute, but her dress didn't fit well, so he couldn't ascertain her body type. Not that it mattered. Ripley was one of the least shallow males in existence. Still, he pictured her as a slightly plump pixie, and that turned his crank. She definitely caught his Gryphon's notice if it was declaring she was their mate with one glance. Ripley had thought he found his mate before in Sara Beth, but he'd been wrong. His eye snagged the bruise on her cheek and the stiff way she held herself. Ripley observed as the man next to her talked to customers while the female didn't make eye contact with anyone. She replaced items that had been purchased quickly before stepping back.

"Ripper?" Ace nudged Ripley's shoulder, so he

turned his attention to his best friend. "What has you glaring?"

"The pretty female with the bruise on her cheek."

"That's Glory," Rhi said. "The man with her is William, and the other one standing at the back of the booth is Brother Zachariah. He's one of the elders. If I had to guess, she's with William because she's been promised to him, and Zachariah is acting as their chaperone." *Glory.* The name suited her, as in Ripley found her glorious. He wanted to stalk over there and demand to know if William had put the bruise on her face.

"She doesn't seem thrilled to be with him," Natalia stated, and Ripley agreed.

"No, she wouldn't be," Rhi said. "I didn't interact with her all that often, but I do know she wasn't happy when her family arrived at Haven. Like me, she was a teen who had lived a somewhat normal life, then was dragged off to a completely different world. She was tossed in solitary on more than one occasion for being difficult."

"Then we need to rescue her," Ripley said as he took a step toward the booth.

Ace's hand on his shoulder halted his feet. "Rip, you can't just go over there and kidnap her. First, we need to make sure she wants to be rescued."

"I'm only going to check out the jerky. Everyone likes deer jerky, right?" Ripley removed his kutte and handed it to Ace, considering the men from Haven knew it was the Hounds who had rescued Rhi. He broke away from their group and sauntered toward the booth, keeping his eyes on Glory. He perused the selections and picked up a packet, waiting until William was busy with another customer. "Do you make the jerky?" he asked Glory.

"No, I just skin the deer," she admitted in a sweet voice.

Ripley winked at her. "Now that's a fine skill to have." Glory smiled, but it was short-lived. William placed himself between Glory and Ripley.

"That'll be fifteen dollars," the man said.

Ripley didn't want to fund Haven's cause, but he also didn't want to walk away from the pretty female. "How much for three packs?"

"Can you not add?" William sneered. "Three times fifteen is forty-five."

"Yeah, smartass. I can add, but most places give discounts for multiple purchases." Ripley tossed the pack at William's chest. "You can keep it." While William was replacing the pack in the row it belonged in, Ripley caught Glory's eye again. By her smug grin, she wasn't judging him the way William had. Ripley winked again before rejoining their group.

"What a dick. I want to get Glory away from him on principle alone."

"This might be our chance," Natalia said. "Look." Glory was leaving the booth accompanied by the older man. "They don't know my face, so I'll follow and see if I can get her alone." Natalia handed the twins off to Maveryck and took off at a quick pace. Ripley couldn't wait. He set off after them, doing his best to stroll casually, while his Gryphon was clawing at him to go after William instead. Ripley ignored his beast and continued after Natalia. As luck would have it, Glory had gone into the restroom with Natalia close behind. Zachariah stood sentry just outside the doorway. Ignoring the man, Ripley went into the men's restroom, where he used his shifter hearing to eavesdrop. He entered one of the stalls and closed the door.

*"Hello, Glory,"* Natalia whispered after several minutes.

*"H-how do you know my name?"* Glory asked, also whispering.

*"A mutual friend pointed you out. Do you remember Rhiannon? Oh, wait, she went by Anna when she was at Haven."*

*"Anna? She's okay?"*

*"She's doing great. My brother-in-law, Ryker, rescued her, and now they're happily expecting their first child."*

*"Glory?"* a man's voice asked. Must be Zachariah.

*"Crap. I gotta go."*

*"Wait,"* Natalia said. *"Are you happy at Haven?"*

*"Not in the least, but unless you have another brother-in-law who rescues women, I need to get back to the stall."*

*"Maybe not a brother-in-law, but I've got a whole family of bikers out there who would gladly get you away from Haven if you want. You saw one of them back at the booth."*

"Glory? You've been in there long enough."

"I'm pooping. Hang on to your hat," Glory called out, and Ripley shoved his fist in his mouth to stifle his laugh. Dropping her voice, she continued, *"How, though? I can't waltz out of the bathroom and just go with you."*

*"Why not? They can't keep you there against your will."*

*"I don't want to cause you or your friends any trouble."*

Natalia laughed, and Ripley could imagine her

rubbing her hands together. *"We've had our eye on Haven for a while. Let's just say once my family gets their hands on Josiah, the man is toast for what he did to Rhiannon. And whoever put that bruise on your face won't be lucky either. So, what do you say? Want to leave that life behind?"*

*"And do what? I don't have any identification. I can't get a job without it."*

*"You let us worry about that. We're good at helping those who want out of the cult life. I'm Natalia, by the way."*

"Glory! If you're not out in thirty seconds, I'm coming in after you."

Ripley needed to give Natalia more time, so he exited the restroom and strode up to the older man. "Dude. Chill the fuck out. Does someone put a timer on how long it takes you to shit? No, so leave the woman alone. As a matter of fact, you shouldn't stand outside the women's room like a creeper. Should I call the police? Tell them you're getting your jollies by spying on the women here?"

"I'm not spying," Zachariah spit out. "I'm waiting on one of my workers."

Ripley took a couple steps away, snagging his phone out of his pocket. "Sounds sensible. Like a *worker* can't go to the restroom by herself. What are you really doing? I think the police would like to know. And while you're explaining that, you can also tell them how she got the bruise on her face." Ripley waved his phone and pretended to dial the cops. He stepped even farther away, hoping to draw Zachariah away from the door. Placing the phone to his ear, he said, "Yes, I'm at the farmer's market on Highway 28.

26

There's an old man creeping on the women's restroom."

"Now wait just a minute!" Zachariah made a grab for the phone, but he was no match for Ripley's size and strength. Ripley kept moving away from the restroom with Zachariah following. He continued the ruse long enough for Natalia and Glory to exit the building and rush behind it, headed away from the booths where the Haven people were set up.

"Yes, thank you." Ripley pretended to disconnect. "The cops are on their way. I'll wait here with you until they show up."

"I'm not a stalker." Zachariah's face was mottled.

"Could've fooled me." Ripley tapped out a text to Ace, giving him a heads-up. When he received a response that Glory was safe with Ryker and Rhi, he shoved the phone in his pocket. Ripley wanted to go to the female, but he also wanted to make sure Ryker had time to get Glory away from the market before the old man realized she was gone.

Zachariah huffed off back to the booth with Ripley on his heels. "We have a situation," the old man told William.

"Where's Glory?" William asked.

"Still in the restroom, but that man called the police on me for standing outside the building." Zachariah pointed at Ripley, who leaned against the booth with his arms crossed over his chest.

"And you left her alone?" William started to walk toward the restroom, but Ripley gripped his bicep.

"What is it with you men thinking a woman can't pee by herself? Are you another creep? Likes to watch

27

unsuspecting women with their panties down?" Ripley was drawing a crowd and not the kind the men of Haven wanted at their booth.

"No, I'm not a creep. We just want to make sure our women are safe. Is that so wrong?" William asked.

Ripley pointed at Zachariah. "No, but that one was threatening to go in after the woman. Who does that? Like I asked your buddy, is there a time limit on how long it takes to do your business? And you call her bruised cheek safe?"

William frowned at Zachariah before turning to one of the women at the next booth over. "Sandra, please go check on Glory."

The woman nodded and rushed out from behind the booth where she was selling quilts and knitted baby blankets. Ripley released William's arm and strolled over and perused the items. Were these what Rhi had wanted to look at? Probably, but now that she knew who made them, Ripley doubted she would want to purchase one. There were plenty of other places to get items for their baby. A whistle sounded on the air, and Ripley casually looked around. Ace nodded, and Ripley moved to the next stall down from the quilts. He continued browsing until he could turn a corner, out of sight from William and Zachariah. Ripley met Ace beside a taco truck, and his stomach rumbled. He had skipped breakfast at the campsite.

Ace handed Ripper his kutte. "We need to get out of here before they realize Glory's gone."

Shouts came from the direction of Haven's booths, and Ripley muttered, "Too late." He and Ace took off jogging toward their bikes with Ripley sliding his vest on as he went. Everyone else had already loaded up and taken off. Ripley slid his helmet on and cranked his Harley. Easing out of the parking lot, he checked his mirror, sending up a prayer of thanks when he didn't see anyone chasing them. He pulled up alongside a grinning Ace.

"That was fun," Ace said.

Ripley had to agree. His beast urged him to ride harder and faster so they could get to wherever Glory was. He knew what had the Gryphon so riled up – it considered Glory their mate even though their interaction had been brief. Ripley wanted someone in his life. A female to come home to at the end of every day. Someone to ride on the back of his bike and share his tent when the Hounds went camping. Someone to give him kids like the twins. A female he could take to visit his parents. Whether or not Glory was that female remained to be seen. At least they had rescued someone from Haven who didn't want to be there. That was the important thing.

# CHAPTER THREE

## Glory

NATALIA LED GLORY behind the restrooms and took her the long way through the market to where a group of people waited. As they escaped, Glory noticed the guy from the booth arguing with Brother Zachariah. He glanced her way, and she swore he smirked. When they reached Natalia's friends, Glory couldn't help but stare. The woman hadn't been kidding about the bikers. Glory should have been leery, but seeing the women and kids with the badass men set her nerves at ease. As soon as Anna – Rhiannon – took her hand and smiled, Glory knew she was going to be okay.

"We need to hurry," Rhiannon said, keeping a tight grip while also holding onto a tall, dark-haired biker, whom Glory assumed was her husband since they were expecting a baby together. The man led them to an SUV while everyone else climbed on bikes. Glory stared in amazement as Natalia helped two of the cutest little boys she'd ever seen into a sidecar. Once she was seated behind her man, all the bikes rumbled to life. Rhiannon climbed into the backseat of the vehicle with Glory, and her husband started the engine, leading the procession out of the parking lot.

Glory turned and looked out the back window, expecting William to come after her. Rhiannon tried to get Glory to relax, but she couldn't. Not until she knew the handsome biker was safe. At least, Glory assumed he was with them. He was dressed the same as the others except for the black vest they all wore. When he approached their stand and winked at her, she about fainted.

"I promise you're safe now. Even if William comes after you, the Hounds won't let him near you."

"Hounds?"

Rhiannon gestured at her husband. "That's the name of their motorcycle club – The Hounds of Zeus. You couldn't ask for a better group of men to watch your back. Ryker here is their president," she said proudly.

"There was a man who came to my booth. Was he with you?"

"Yes, that was Ripley. I noticed the stalls were manned by people from Haven and pointed it out so we didn't approach, but as soon as Ripley saw your bruised cheek, he made a beeline for the booth."

Not only was he handsome but chivalrous too. And what a cool name – Ripley. Glory sighed internally. There was no way someone like him would truly be interested in someone like her, but a girl could dream.

"Natalia mentioned something about you all getting people out of cults."

"Yes. Ryker's father, Sutton, has been going after The Ministry for many years. Some of the Hounds, like

31

Ripley, help in that endeavor. If people want to be there, that's fine, but for those like you and me who are held there against our will, they move heaven and earth to see it done. They have housing set up where the rescued can live and get acclimated to being back in the real world. Ryker's niece is a whiz with computers, as is one of the Hounds, and they obtain things like birth certificates. Ryker's mom, Rory, has a group of helpers who figure out what type of jobs are fitting for each person. You're welcome to stay at the home as long as you need to. If you want to go to college, that's also an option."

"I wouldn't even know what to study if I did." Glory didn't want to admit what her true dream had been, so she told Rhiannon, "When I was in high school, I had thought about being a music teacher, but we moved to Haven before I got my diploma, and the education at Haven is lacking, as you know."

"The good thing is you were older and almost finished with high school. You should be able to get your diploma easily. You might have to take some remedial classes first, and there are plenty of Hounds willing to help you study. As a matter of fact, Ripley is super smart. He's an attorney. Just something to think about."

"Are you going to college?"

"No. I have a job at a cute floral shop called The Blooming Boutique. It's owned by one of the Hound's girlfriends, Charlie. I've always had an affinity for plants. Being pagan, you could say I'm grounded by the earth. It's where I get my gift."

"Your gift?"

Rhiannon held out her hand. "May I?"

"May you what?"

"Heal your bruise."

"Heal it? How?" Glory knew Rhiannon was different. It was why she was always being put in solitary, but laying on hands should have been celebrated, not shunned.

"It's something I've been able to do all my life. I can send a warm energy into your skin and help the healing process speed up," Rhiannon explained.

"Oh. Sure." Glory held still as Rhiannon placed her palm against Glory's cheek. Sure enough, warmth spread across her skin, and the pain instantly eased. "Wow. That's amazing."

"It is now that I'm not being used against my will. My father installed these chips under my skin, and when the remote was pressed to activate them, I lost sense of myself. Josiah would take me to the clinic and make me heal newcomers. I would lose time, thinking I had dreamed about healing people. When I escaped, the chips were activated, showing up as a GPS of sorts. My father found me and kidnapped me, but I managed to get away from him. Ryker rescued me a second time."

"That was all you, Angel. You used your power to put David on his knees. Literally." The pride in Ryker's voice was evident. Glory was happy for Rhiannon. Escaping, finding a man who loved her, making a life for herself outside Haven. Would Glory ever find that for herself?

"Tell me more about where you're taking me. How do I pay for it?"

33

"You don't. Think of it as a women's shelter. It's set up free of charge to help you get on your feet. You can cook if that's something you enjoy, or you can clean. Everyone does their own laundry. Clothes will be provided for you. No more pajamas twenty-four seven." Rhiannon rolled her eyes, grinning. "Our first order of business is getting you out of that dress. No offense, but it's hideous."

Glory couldn't help returning her smile. "Lisa Ann loaned it to me since I didn't have one of my own. Skinning deer didn't require me to dress up. I don't suppose this home kills its own food?"

"Goddess, no. That's just... Ew." Rhiannon scrunched her nose, and Glory laughed at the other woman. "I remember when Josiah sent you to Rhetta as punishment."

"It was awful. I threw up when Rhetta broke the deer's legs before chopping them off. I broke out in a cold sweat the first few times I had to do it, but after a while, it became second nature. I do like to cook, so I'll at least be helpful." Glory sneaked a peek at Rhiannon's clothes, glad to see she wore something close to what Glory would choose for herself. "I cannot wait to get a pair of jeans and a T-shirt. And a hoodie. God, how I miss hoodies." Not that she'd ever had one of her own, but she had worn Chad's during school.

"Then hoodies and jeans you shall have. And whatever type of shoes and boots you want too. And maybe some shorts. It's warm enough for them."

"Maybe I'll get some capris, but I'm not sure about shorts." Glory's legs were white from wearing pants all the time, plus she felt self-conscious in shorts.

"Whatever you want, but remember, money really is no object, so we'll take you shopping to get everything you want. And underwear. Real underwear," Rhiannon whispered. "So much has changed in the last few years. TVs are bigger. Phones are smarter. Clothes are pretty much the same though. Tell me, before you went to Haven, what did you like to do?"

"I wasn't allowed to do typical teenage things like go to the movies. I did get to spend the night with other girls, but only if they attended our church and their parents were friends with mine. There was no playing video games or listening to music. I didn't do overnights often because it was boring. Since my best friend, Sheri, didn't attend church, I wasn't allowed to hang out with her. She had an old MP3 player she loaned me so I could listen to music at night when I went to bed. I had to use earbuds so my parents didn't hear it. I was in chorus at school, which I liked. I also sang in church, but it wasn't because I wanted to. My parents were super religious if you couldn't tell by mine and my sisters' names. We were at church every time the doors were open." Glory didn't want to tell the truth of why her parents uprooted their lives, so she gave Rhiannon part of it. "When I was a senior, I had a boyfriend. He and I were close even though we only got to see each other at school. We made plans to be together after graduation, but Father found out about Chad. He decided we were too close, and that's when he sold all our stuff and moved us to Haven. He didn't let me go back to school. I didn't get to say goodbye to Chad or Sheri."

Rhiannon took Glory's hand and squeezed. "I'm so sorry your life was uprooted. I know what that's like. But now you have the chance at a new normal, one of your choosing. The good thing is you can take all the time you need to figure out what that looks like."

"Sorry to interrupt," Ryker said. "Do you ladies want to stop by the mall on the way home? Or would you rather get settled at Providence House first?"

Glory really wanted to go shopping, but she hated the thought of not having her own money. Not only that, but what if William was following them? Rhiannon must have read her mind because she squeezed Glory's hand again. "First off, don't worry about William. He's not getting anywhere near you. And secondly, don't think about the money. The Hounds really do have more than enough to get the things you need. It'll take a while to get used to how nice everyone is, but you will. And I don't want you to think you'll be stuck at the house once you get there. I only work part-time, and I can always use another friend. Ryker's brothers all have women in their lives, and they took me under their wings. They'll do the same to you if you let them. You've already met one of them."

"Really? That sounds nice."

"It is. The first thing I had them do was take me to a salon. My eyebrows were out of control." Rhiannon wiggled her manicured brows, and Glory grinned.

"Are you trying to tell me something?" Glory pointed at her own face.

"Yes. Your gorgeous eyes are being overshadowed by a couple of caterpillars."

Glory huffed, but she wasn't offended. Rhiannon was correct. "Then how about we go to the mall first? They still have salons there, right?"

"That they do. I would suggest Ryker dropping us off so we could make an afternoon of it, but with William possibly following, I would feel better if he and some of the Hounds came with us. I know one in particular who would love it if William showed up."

Glory felt her cheeks burning. She wasn't exactly innocent, but she doubted Ripley would want someone frumpy. He was a god among men, and she was, well, nothing special. "I don't want any trouble."

"One thing you'll learn about us Hounds is we welcome trouble," Ryker said. "Especially from anyone involved with The Ministry."

"I studied about them in school before we moved, but I didn't realize Haven was part of them."

"Sadly, it's true," Rhiannon said. "My grandmother is married to the leader. She's the main reason my father moved me to Haven after my mom died. Then you have men like Josiah and his brother, Gideon, who oversee the branches. I guess I should say *was* in Gideon's case. He's in jail."

"Speaking of Josiah, have you seen him lately?" Ryker asked.

"No. He hasn't been around in a while. Brother Thomas said Josiah is out recruiting new members."

Ryker drummed his fingers against the steering wheel. "Is there anyone else there against their will?"

"There are kids brought in like I was who hate it, but as for the adults, I don't think so. I have a question. Why do they need guards with guns?"

"They have guns now?"

"Yeah. They stopped patrolling for a while, and the guards stopped wearing black, but about a month ago, things returned to normal."

"That's good to know, and as for the reason, they aren't the God-loving people they claim to be. They are a totalitarian group hoping to take over the world one community at a time. They almost succeeded back in the early 2000s. That's when my Pop decided to go after them."

"Thank you for getting me out of there. I was this close to having to marry William against my will," Glory said, holding up her thumb and index finger. "I was ready to make a run for it. I even told Father I would rather be dead than to marry someone I didn't love. He didn't take it well."

"Your father put that bruise on your face?" Ryker growled.

"Yes. It's only the second time he's struck me. The first was before we moved to Haven." Glory didn't want to reminisce about why he hit her the first time.

"Then I'm glad I wanted to visit the market today." Rhiannon patted the huge swell of her stomach. "I figured there were homemade baby blankets and such, plus I knew the twins would love to see all the stalls with food."

"They sure are cute. What are their names?" Glory wanted to find out all about the group she was with. The ones who had saved her from a life of misery. She listened as both Rhiannon and Ryker told her stories about Major and Marshall and how they came to be in the Hounds' lives. Before she knew it, they were at a mall. Ryker parked the SUV at the far end of the lot, and soon several of the bikes were parking as well.

Glory unbuckled and asked, "Do you do everything as a group?"

"Every chance we get. There are quite a few Hounds, so it isn't always the same ones getting together each time, but with Ryker having four brothers, it's usually the same core group. Now, come on. Let's get you some clothes."

Once everyone was unloaded, they stood together as Ryker explained why they were there. Glory cast a glance around the parking lot, searching for a certain biker. Not seeing him anywhere, she moved with Rhiannon toward the entrance. It had been years since Glory had been to the mall. She didn't recognize many of the stores. Before moving to Haven, her parents didn't let her and her sisters shop at the popular retailers, instead getting their clothes at either thrift shops or second-hand stores. The mall visit was only allowed on her birthday, and then she had to shop at the bigger retailer that had plain clothing instead of the more fashionable choices.

"I'm hungry, Lolly," one of the twins said. Glory grinned at the nickname.

Natalia ruffled his hair. "You're always hungry." To the group, she said, "We're going to hit the food court while you shop for clothes." She held out both hands, and the twins grabbed one with their dad following close behind. Glory always wanted kids, and having been responsible for her sisters when she was younger, she knew she'd be good at it. Seeing how cute the twins were had Glory longing for a child of her own, but without a man in her life... It was better to think about things she could control, like clothes.

A shop with graphic tees came into view, and Glory pointed it out. "There, please." She had always wanted to visit that store when she was a teen, but her mother assured her it was of the devil. When she stepped through the doors, Glory was inundated with T-shirts everywhere. The walls were filled, top to bottom, displaying bands, TV shows, and logos of products. Some she had heard of, but there were plenty she hadn't. Glory didn't know where to start. The hair on her neck stood on end when someone stepped close to her back, and a familiar voice said, "Can't go wrong with the classics." Glory looked back, then up at Ripley. Where had he come from? Not that she wasn't glad to see him.

Finding her voice, she nodded. "Yeah, a lot of these aren't familiar. But I do remember that one," Glory said, pointing out a Cyanide Sweetness tee. Their music was hard rock, and she'd only heard it when a classmate played it during study hall while the teacher was out of the room. Most of the music she had liked before Haven was considered pop, but she and her sisters weren't allowed to listen to it at home.

"The lead singer, Desi, is a friend of a friend. I can probably score backstage passes if you'd like to go see them."

Glory gasped. "Are you serious?"

Ripley grinned, morphing his face from handsome to over-the-top gorgeous. "Yep." He stepped around her and dug through a bin, pulling out the band's shirt from a cubby. "Do you want it to fit or be a little

40

loose?" He held the tee in front of her chest. She wasn't about to tell the man she didn't really listen to rock. If he was willing to take her to a concert, she'd learn to like it.

"I like my shirts to fit, but I prefer hoodies to be a little big."

Ripley put the shirt back and got the next size down. "Okay. What else catches your eye?"

*You.* Of course she didn't say that aloud. Rhiannon, who was standing next to her, winked. "I'm going to look over there." She thumbed behind her, then walked off with Ryker, leaving Glory alone with Ripley. He led her around the store, telling her about the bands or shows she wasn't familiar with. From there, they went to a store where she could choose jeans and tees. Rhiannon and Ryker were with them the whole time, but it still felt as though Ripley was her own personal shopper. It should have felt weird having this strange man help her with styles and sizes, or have her show him each item she tried on, but it didn't. Ripley was comforting as well as comfortable, like they'd known each other forever. His attention was never creepy either. Sure, he was eyeing her ass in each pair of jeans, but not once did he make a lewd comment or look at her as though he wanted to get into the jeans. After he paid for her things, Glory slipped back into the dressing room and traded the hideous dress for some of her new things.

While looking for shoes, Ripley insisted she have a nice pair of black leather boots for riding. She certainly wasn't going to argue, having already imagined riding on his bike with her arms wrapped around his waist.

When it came time to pay in every store they visited, he handed over his own credit card. Glory didn't know what to think about that. Rhiannon had said there was money for clothes, but Glory thought Rhiannon or Ryker would be the one to pay.

When she assured Ripley she had enough clothes, Rhiannon ushered Glory into a salon. She didn't have an appointment, but luck was on her side, and one of the stylists – Treena – had time to do her hair as well as her eyebrows. She sat down in the chair with the stylist asking what she wanted. Glory looked at Treena's reflection in the mirror and told her, letting out a deep breath after doing so. Being free from Haven never felt so, well, freeing. This was the first step in taking back her identity. Treena took care of Glory's eyebrows first, then started on her hair. Glory sighed with contentment at having her hair shampooed and her scalp massaged. Back in the stylist's chair, she kept her eyes closed as the comb tugged and the scissors snipped. She didn't peek when Treena was drying her new style. She was equal parts excited and sick to her stomach. Years of being told how to dress and wear her hair were hard to let go of.

The dryer turned off, and Treena asked, "Well, what do you think?"

Glory finally opened her eyes and grinned. Gone was the long hair Father insisted on. "I love it."

Rhiannon stood over her shoulder smiling. "That's awesome."

Glory thought so too. Now, there was another opinion she wanted.

# Chapter Four

## Ripley

RIPLEY IGNORED THE looks Ace gave him while he followed Glory around the mall. Was he going overboard? Yep. Did he give a flying fuck? Nope. Something about the female called to him, but he wasn't going to examine the longing too closely. His beast was content for the first time in years, and that sense of peace settled deep within Ripley. Instead of allowing Ryker to pay for her clothes from the foundation's funds, Ripley handed over his card at each store. His Gryphon had insisted. Providing basic items for Glory felt like the right thing to do, even if nothing came of the gesture. While Glory was in the salon, Ripley stepped down the mall and purchased a leather jacket for her, fully intending she wear it one day while riding with him on his Harley. He needed to get her a helmet as well, but she would have to try it on to make sure it fit. Baby steps.

Mayhem and Havyk left a couple hours into the shopping excursion, wanting to get their mates and kids home. Natalia and Sadie promised to get together with Glory in the next week for a girls' day out.

Before Ace left soon after, he clapped Ripley on the shoulder. "I hope you know what you're doing."

"I'm being nice is all," Ripley responded, but his best friend knew it was more than that. Asher knew better than anyone how much Ripley wanted a mate. Ace inclined his head, then took his leave. Ripley stepped next to Ryker outside the salon, waiting.

"Something you want to tell me, Rip?"

"It's just... Something about Glory calls to my beast, and for the first time in years, I have hope." Ripley lowered his voice, knowing his Pres would have no trouble hearing him. "I thought I found my mate once, but when I revealed my true nature, she freaked out. I had to wipe her mind. Broke my heart in the process, so I left her with the house I'd bought her and moved up here."

"Then I hope it works out this time," Ryker whispered.

Before he could say anything, Glory and Rhiannon strolled out of the salon. Ripley couldn't believe the difference in the before and after. Gone were the bushy eyebrows. Also gone was half the length of Glory's hair. It was now cut in an asymmetrical bob that accentuated the female's heart-shaped face. He took the few steps between them and snagged a strand of hair, tugging gently. "Very nice."

Glory blushed, but at the same time, glowed under his approval. "Thanks. One day I'd like to come back and have some color put in it."

Ripley shifted the bag with her jacket to his left hand so he could offer his right to Glory. She glanced at it for a beat, then took it, lacing their fingers. Her

44

smaller hand fit naturally in his bigger one. Ryker and Rhiannon both noticed, but Ryker placed his arm around Rhi's shoulder and turned her toward the exit. Ripley and Glory followed as he asked, "Yeah? Like red or...?"

"I was thinking something bolder like blue. Might as well go all out while I'm being rebellious."

"Is blue your favorite color?"

"Hmm, it used to be. I guess I haven't really thought about it in so long. At Haven, everything is bland. Most everything is beige except for the guards' uniforms."

"I think you'll rock blue hair, just like you're rocking your new clothes."

"You're really good for my ego," Glory muttered.

"I'm only being truthful." Ripley figured Glory didn't hear many compliments if any. Knowing what he did about Haven from Rhiannon, Glory probably didn't hear many positive words at all. And if someone like William was who she had been promised to? Zeus, he couldn't imagine what she had gone through. He thanked his god Rhi wanted to stop at the market, or Glory might have had to marry the older jerk.

"What's the plan now?" Ripley asked. "Are you headed straight to the manor or stopping to eat?"

"Sutton and Rory are waiting for us, and Mom cooked. You're welcome to come with us," Ryker said.

Ripley wanted to say yes, but he also didn't want to overwhelm Glory or intrude as she was getting settled in. "I appreciate the offer, but there's something I need to do tonight." Glory tensed, and Ripley glanced down at the female. She gave him a smile, but since he

45

didn't know her well, he couldn't be sure if it was real or not. He smiled back, and Glory's face lit up. Now *that* was a real smile.

Exiting the mall, Ripley and Ryker searched the parking lot for any sign of William. They continued to where the SUV and Ripley's bike were with no sign of trouble. Ripley held out the bag. "While you were getting your hair cut, I got you something."

Glory stared at him with wide eyes before looking in the bag. She pulled out the jacket and dropped the bag, immediately shoving her arms in the garment, running her hands down the supple leather. "It's... Ripley—"

"It's perfect." Ripley tucked a strand of hair behind Glory's ear. "You deserve nice things, and if you decided to ride with anyone, you'll need to be protected."

Glory looked up through her naturally long lashes. "Are you offering?"

"I am, but we'll need to get you a proper helmet. How about I give you a few days to get settled in, then I come get you for lunch and a trip to the bike shop?"

"I'd like that. Thank you, for everything." Glory launched herself at Ripley, wrapping her arms around his waist. He hugged her back, kissing the top of her head before turning loose. He opened the back door to the SUV and helped her inside.

"I'll see you soon," Ripley promised before closing her up. He patted the side of the vehicle, then strode to his bike. As he tossed his long leg over the seat, he glanced back to find Glory watching him. He smiled, unable to help himself. Ripley wasn't unaccustomed to females ogling him. Hell, he even caught men staring sometimes. Personally, he didn't think he was all that handsome, but being a Gryphon, Ripley exuded natural strength and confidence. He might look like a badass biker, but deep down, Ripley was kind and caring. He was a nurturer at heart. That was probably the reason he'd insisted on paying for Glory's clothes.

*It's more than that.*

*We'll have to wait and see.*

*We've waited fifty years.*

*We're not fifty yet. Don't rush it.*

Granted his birthday was coming up in a few months. Being a Gryphon, he would live at least a couple centuries barring any unforeseen incidents like the men at Haven shooting him. Speaking of... Ripley took another look around the parking lot before firing up his bike and heading to New Troy.

Ripley rode home, but instead of sitting around moping until he could see Glory again, he hopped in his Camaro and drove to the local bike shop where he found a cool helmet with blue flames. He purchased it in three sizes, sure one of them would fit Glory. Was he getting ahead of himself again? Yep, but again, he didn't give a fuck. He knew next to nothing about the female, but that wouldn't change unless he spent time with her. After loading his purchases in the trunk, he shot off a text to Ryker.

Ripper: *Did Glory get settled?*

Ryot: *Rhi is still with her. They're washing all her new clothes. Sutton and Rory are here, and Pop wants to talk to you.*

Ripper: *Should I come there?*

Ryot: *They're getting ready to leave. Pop said to meet him at his house.*

Ripper: *Will do.*

He angled into the driver's seat and blew out a breath, wondering what Sutton wanted to talk about. Ripley figured it had to do with what happened at the market. At least he hoped it was and not the older Hound warning him away from Glory because that wouldn't go well. As he drove the short distance to Sutton and Rory's home, he took deep, calming breaths. The older Lazlos were normally calm and level-headed. Outside Ripley's parents, those two were the steadiest couple he knew. They were relationship goals. By the time he parked behind their SUV, Ripley was at ease. Mostly.

Sutton opened the front door before Ripley could knock. "Ripper, come on in, Son." Once inside the living room, Sutton offered him a drink, which Ripley gladly accepted.

With high-ball glasses in hand, Sutton gestured to the sofa. "Thanks for stopping by. Ryot told me a little of what happened at the market, but I'd like to get the full story from you."

Ripley took a sip of the expensive whiskey, relaxing against the cushions, and recounted the events of the afternoon, leaving nothing out.

"Those motherfuckers." Sutton stood and refilled both glasses. "Glory's father is the one who bruised her face when she told him she'd rather be dead than marry a man like William. She told us Josiah hasn't been around in a while, and that someone named Thomas has taken over. She also said she isn't aware of

48

anyone else other than some of the kids who don't want to be there."

"What's the plan then? Are we going to continue waiting on Josiah? Because I have to tell you, I'm ready to go back and string her father up by his neck."

Sutton handed the refilled glass over. "Ryot mentioned you bought all of Glory's clothes instead of letting him pay with the foundation's funds."

"Is that a problem?"

"Not at all if there's something between the two of you. Is there something there?"

"I'd like to know the same thing," Rory said, walking out of the kitchen with a cup of coffee. Ripley could smell the strong brew across the room.

"There's something about Glory that caught my beast's attention the moment we laid eyes on her. I thought it odd considering we don't have fated mates, but it wouldn't rest until I got to the mall and saw she was okay. Spending time with her as she shopped felt… natural."

Rory crossed the room and wrapped her free arm around Sutton's waist. "Sometimes you just know, and she sure is smitten with you." Rory's eyes sparkled as she took a sip from her mug. "But seriously, think about it this way. You just happened to stop by the market the first day Glory was allowed to step foot outside Haven since she was taken there. Coincidence? I think not."

Sutton kissed Rory's temple. "I agree. We might not have someone predestined to be ours, but Zeus seems to put us in the path of those who are perfect for us."

49

Ripley didn't know how Sutton and Rory met, but with the way they still seemed completely in love after close to a century, he bet it was something similar to how he met Glory. Then again, he hoped not. He never wanted anyone to be held against their will the way Glory, Rhi, Sadie, and Kerrigan had been. Now that he thought about the other mates and how the Hounds found them, thinking of Glory being meant for him didn't seem so far-fetched.

"Did Glory give you any usable intel about Haven?" he asked Sutton.

"She did. Unlike Rhi, Glory was an integral part of their society. She worked in the kitchen when she wasn't skinning animals. She is going to sit down tomorrow and draw a picture of the compound. Even though we've been there, I'm hoping she'll have some better insight into weaknesses in their defenses. We'll keep an eye out for Josiah from the sky, but for now, there's no reason to barge in."

"Except to find her father and beat his ass," Ripley muttered.

"Except that," Sutton agreed. "If it's something you feel the need to do, just be careful."

Ripley didn't need Sutton's permission to seek revenge on Glory's behalf, but it felt good to have it. "As for Glory, I promised to give her a few days to get settled. I offered to take her out for lunch and to shop for a helmet, but I went by the shop and bought three different sizes."

"A little advice?" Rory didn't wait for permission before she gave her opinion. "Don't wait too long. Maybe give her tomorrow to find her feet with the other residents, but that girl is strong. She won't need to wait days, and the sooner you see her, the sooner you can begin wooing her."

Ripley laughed. "Is that what the kids are calling it these days?"

Sutton kissed his mate's temple again. "I happen to think wooing sounds so much better than courting. I wooed the fuck out of this one."

"That you did." Rory turned her face up for a better kiss, and soon the older couple was lost in one another. Ripley softly placed the tumbler on the coffee table and showed himself out the door before he got an eyeful of Ryot's parents making out. He was glad they were still that in love, the same as his parents were. Ripley always made sure to call before going to visit his folks, and even then, he didn't use his key to walk into the house unless he texted first to make sure the coast was clear. One incident of seeing them getting busy was one too many.

Driving home, Ripley thought about Rory's advice. He would give her the next day, and then he was going to begin wooing her. Chuckling aloud in the car, he shook his head at the old-fashioned construct. No matter what it was called, though, Ripley planned to spend as much time with Glory as possible so they could get to know one another better. It had been so long since he tried dating. Not since Sara Beth. He had taken her to nice restaurants, to plays, and concerts she chose. But Glory wasn't Sara Beth. He needed to find out what interests she had before Haven. Thinking back to their conversation at the mall while Glory was looking at T-shirts, a plan took form. Not one that would happen quickly, but he would make it happen.

The need to see Glory again, to make sure she was okay at the manor, pressed against his chest. No, that was his beast trying to break free. His hands tightened around the steering wheel, and it was all Ripley could do to push his Gryphon back. He couldn't remember having to fight against the other part of him when he was with Sara Beth. Even when they made love, his Gryphon stayed firmly in the recesses of his mind. Maybe it had known she wasn't meant for them. If so, Ripley wished it had spoken up before he went to the trouble of buying her a house and a ring. It would have saved him a lot of money and heartache. The money he didn't care about, but it took a long time for his heart to get over the betrayal of her denying his true nature. Would Glory be the same way? Would she freak out if he revealed what he was?

*No, she won't.*

*How can you be sure? We don't know her.*

**Glory is strong. She's a fighter, and besides that, she isn't interested in your money. You saw that at the mall when she shopped the bargain bins.**

*Are you saying Sara Beth was?*

When his beast didn't answer him, Ripley assumed that was answer enough. Was it right? Had she only wanted Ripley for what he could give her? Rip tapped the button on his steering wheel, and when the female voice instructed, he said, "Call Mom." He was close with both parents, but his mother would be honest with him where his dad would try to spare his feelings.

"Rip! How are you?"

"I'm well, but I have a question, and I need an

honest answer."

"Of course."

"Do you think Sara Beth only wanted me for my money?"

"Yes, Son, I do," Regina responded with no hesitation.

Ripley slapped the steering wheel. "Then why didn't you warn me?"

Regina sighed. "We did. Your father and I both cautioned you in the beginning, but you were so taken with the female and wouldn't listen."

"I don't..." Ripley was going to say remember, but he did. He hadn't understood why his folks, more than once, brought up the fact that Sara Beth looked out of place that night at the restaurant. "Shit, Mom."

"What brought this on, Rip? Why think about the past all these years later?"

"I met someone. It's new. We rescued her from The Ministry, and my beast claimed her instantly."

"I see. And did your Gryphon ever claim Sara Beth?"

Ripley blew out a breath. "No. I just don't want to trust that she's my mate only to have her freak out like Sara Beth did."

"Tell me more about how you met."

Ripley pulled into his garage just as he finished recounting his day. He shut the engine off and angled out of the car, switching the call to his phone. He entered the house through the kitchen, flipping on lights as he went. It was modest considering the amount of money he'd amassed over the years. Nothing like the beach house he'd bought for Sara

53

Beth.

Regina's steps sounded through the phone, then a door opened and closed. He imagined his mother on the covered patio. She loved sitting outside. "The good news is Glory has someone else in her corner. Rhiannon was rescued as well, and she's now mated to a Gryphon. Don't spring the truth on Glory until she's had time to see the other mates with their Gryphons. She sounds like a strong female. She took a chance on getting away from Haven, trusting a group of strangers. Granted, she already knew Rhiannon, but it took guts to go with Natalia. Trust your beast, Son."

Ripley grabbed a beer out of the fridge and popped the cap off. He took a long swig before saying, "I will. Thanks, Mom."

"You're welcome, Rip. And once you've spent some time with her, your father and I would love to meet her. Whether that is here or in New York, just let us know."

"Sounds good." And it did. Ripley would love nothing more than introducing Glory to Conrad and Regina, the two most important people in his life.

# CHAPTER FIVE

## Glory

PROVIDENCE HOUSE WAS huge. Glory expected it to be filled with people like her who had been rescued from Haven. Instead, there were only a handful of others there, and most of those were caretakers, for lack of a better word. Ryker's parents, Sutton and Rory, were waiting for her when she arrived, welcoming her as though she were one of their kids. After laughing in all their faces, because come on, Sutton and Rory didn't look any older than Ryker, Rory assured her they just had good genes. Glory side-eyed them all, but it was Rhi, as everyone called Glory's new friend, who convinced her they were serious.

"You'll get used to it," Rhi whispered.

Glory was then introduced to Branson and Lynette Miller, a couple who oversaw the home. Glory figured Branson was one of the bikers because both Sutton and Ryker referred to him as Brick. He was dressed much the same as the other men in his faded jeans, white T-shirt, and black boots. Lynette was about Glory's size, which meant her husband towered over her. What was it with all the men in Rhi's life being so tall? And muscular? And downright sexy?

After introductions, Rory explained that most of those who had been brought there before had already moved on with their lives after being trained in how to get by in the real world again. There were two other females, but they had gone out to eat together. Glory took that to mean they were getting along well in their training or therapy; whatever it was they were going through.

Glory was expected to keep her room clean, wash her own clothes, and if she felt like it, cook her own meals. The kitchen was stocked with more food than Glory had ever seen. Even at Haven, they didn't have the variety Glory found in the pantry. Haven was all about being self-sufficient, and that meant eating a lot of wild deer and vegetables grown from their gardens. Someone did purchase flour, rice, and beans as staples, but that was about it. She couldn't wait to make macaroni and cheese. And have pizza. And a hamburger. All the things she missed from before. When she found several different kinds of soda, she squealed aloud. Rhiannon had commiserated with her.

Rhi helped Glory with her laundry while Rory and Sutton sat with Ryker, Branson, and Lynette in a comfortable-looking room at the back of the house she thought of as the den. Glory didn't know what it was referred to, but it wasn't the main room that sat at the front of the large house. Even though it was late, she and Rhi spent a couple hours talking about Haven and their experiences there while getting Glory's new clothes washed, dried, and put away in her new bedroom. A room she didn't have to share with others.

One that had a nice bathroom attached with endless hot water and fancy toiletries. It was even stocked with pads and tampons which Glory almost cried over. Having to wear rags during your period and washing them in the bathroom had been the pits.

Rory gave Glory her own smart phone, showing her how to access all the contacts already in it as well as how to browse the internet. The phone had unlimited access, so she didn't have to worry about using it too often. Glory hugged Rory tightly, thanking her for the gift. Even though it was an essential item, Glory was overwhelmed with the gesture. The whole day had been a roller coaster of mostly ups. The only down was that Ripley wasn't there. He offered to come by in a few days to take her to lunch, and Glory was looking forward to it. She prayed he didn't change his mind.

Rhi, Ryker, and his parents said their goodbyes, and Glory was left to roam the large house on her own. The only other rule she'd been given was to respect the privacy of anyone else who lived there. Their bedrooms were their sanctuary, and no one was allowed in unless given permission. Glory liked that. After checking each room, she found herself in the kitchen. No one else was around, but she'd been told to make herself at home. Rory had cooked for everyone, but Glory had been too nervous to eat much, so she went to the pantry and chose a box of pasta. She gathered the ingredients to make mac 'n cheese. Before Haven, Glory made the dish often for her sisters. She had just put the dish in the oven when the back door opened, and two women entered. They stopped short upon seeing Glory.

Lynette appeared out of nowhere, startling Glory. "Welcome home, ladies. I'd like to introduce you to Glory, our newest resident. Glory, this is Helen." Lynette gestured to the older of the two, standing closest. She was gorgeous and probably mid-thirties with long black hair and bright blue eyes. She smiled brightly and said hello. "And this is Julia." Lynette motioned toward the younger woman who was closer to Glory's age. Julia was rail-thin with blonde hair cut in a bob. She quickly raised and lowered her hand, muttering, "Hi."

"Hello. I was making some mac 'n cheese. You're both welcome to some after it's finished. I only know how to make enough for a big family."

"That's wonderful, Glory. If Helen and Julia don't want any, Branson will help you eat it. It happens to be one of his favorite dishes."

"Did I hear someone was making mac 'n cheese?" Branson hollered from somewhere in the house.

Lynette rolled her eyes. "I swear, that man has the hearing of a bat." Ignoring her husband, she approached the two women. "How was your outing?"

"It was nice. We went to Martina's place. She was there with her baby, so we visited a while after we ate, and then we went to see a movie," Helen said.

"Aww, how is little Patrick?" Lynette asked.

"Cute as a button. He's got four teeth, and when he grins... Gah, so precious," Helen replied. Her eyes were misty, and Glory wondered if she wanted kids of her own.

"Cute if you don't mind all the slobber," Julia

added, shuddering.

Helen laughed. "There is that. Tank had to change his bib twice he was drooling so much."

Lynette grinned. To Glory, she said, "Tank is a member of the Hounds MC, and Martina is his wife. She owns a Mexican restaurant not far from here. If you like authentic Mexican cuisine, you'll love her place."

"I've only ever had tacos from a fast-food chain, but I'd be willing to try it. Heck, I'm ready to try all the foods as long as it's not deer or rabbit."

"You didn't have cows where you lived?" Helen asked. "I mean…" Helen glanced at Lynette.

"Yes, Glory was rescued from Haven, one of The Ministry's locations."

Glory leaned against the counter, clasping her hands in front of her. "We did, but they were mostly for milk. We had a few for slaughter, but that meat was reserved for the elders. I haven't had beef in six years."

Helen's smile fell. "I'll never complain about Sanctuary again. And if you want to go to Martina's, I'll be glad to take you."

"Thank you." The timer beeped, and Glory turned to remove the cheesy dish from the oven.

Lynette opened a cabinet, pulling down several bowls. "Branson isn't the only sucker for mac 'n cheese."

"I hope it's edible. I haven't made it since before Haven, so it might not be any good," Glory said.

"It's noodles and cheese." Branson entered the kitchen, patting his flat stomach. "Can't really screw that up."

It was more than that, but Glory wasn't going to correct the huge man. "Then I hope you enjoy it."

Lynette filled three bowls when Helen and Julia declined, stating they were still full from their dinner. Helen remained in the kitchen, while Julia excused herself to her room.

"Julia's still finding her feet," Lynette explained as she retrieved forks from one of the drawers. "When she first arrived, she barely came out of her room, but Helen has been a big help in getting her out of her shell more. She's really a sweet young lady, but she was at Sanctuary almost her whole life. She doesn't remember anything from the outside world, so it's taking her longer to become acclimated to all the differences."

Glory blew across the bite of noodles on her fork. "I can't even imagine, except that would be my two younger sisters if they ever escaped. I wasn't taken to Haven until I was eighteen. Even though it's been six years, I didn't see much that was different when we stopped at the mall earlier other than new bands and TV shows I didn't recognize."

Helen opened one of the cabinets for a glass and filled it with water from the door on the refrigerator. "I didn't go to Sanctuary until I was nineteen. I was still living at home while going to college. I lived a sheltered life, not really learning the skills I needed to be alone and function as an adult. My dad always paid the bills, and as long as I was in school, I didn't have to work. My mom did all the household chores and cooking while I was at school, so even the most basic task like feeding myself didn't come easy. I lost both my parents when they died in a car wreck, and I was honestly a little lost. I had no siblings, and my parents were only children, so there were no aunts or uncles to help. My parents lived on my father's income, so when they died, the meager life insurance policy he had wasn't enough to cover the cost of the mortgage."

She stopped to take a sip of water. "Long story short, I was approached by a man one day when I was just getting back from classes. He said he was a friend of my dad's, knew about my situation, and wanted to help. I was so lost I didn't even question his sincerity. He convinced me to sell the house and move to Sanctuary. He told me all my basic needs would be taken care of. I asked about college, and he said I could return at some point if that's what I truly wanted. So, I went with him. Talk about culture shock. I knew I'd made a mistake after the first few days, but I had nothing and no one to return to, so I felt stuck."

"How did you get out?" Glory asked, her mac 'n cheese forgotten.

It was Branson who answered. "That's a long story, but the short answer is Josiah's brother, Gideon, was the leader of Sanctuary, and he kidnapped the wrong woman. Two of Ryker's brothers, Warryck and Maveryck, were out riding when they overheard about a missing woman, and they traveled around searching for her. War found her when she managed to escape from the compound. He and Kerrigan are now together, so that part of the story has a happy ending. Sutton and some of the other Hounds returned to the compound to confront Gideon, and when the congregation found out what kind of man he truly was, they were offered the chance to leave if they wanted.

Helen was one of those who chose to leave."

Glory had scooped up a bit of food, but her fork hung slack as she digested what Branson said. "They kidnap women?"

Branson pushed his empty bowl away. "From what we've gathered, it doesn't happen often, but once is one time too many. Josiah also kidnapped Ryker's first wife a long time ago and 'gave' Juliette to Gideon because he had a thing for redheads. Since we've yet to locate all the Ministry camps, we can't be sure the other leaders aren't doing the same thing."

"Man, that sucks." Glory took a bite of her food, and after swallowing, she asked Helen, "Were you never promised to someone to marry? I mean you're a beautiful woman, and if you'd been at Haven, you'd have been paired up quickly."

Helen's hands tightened around the glass. "I was married. I..." She brushed a tear off her cheek and cleared her throat. "When I first arrived at Sanctuary, I lived in Gideon's house as one of the chosen. He kept four women at his home at all times. He would allow them to live there while he decided whether he wanted to marry them. When he tired of them or basically decided they weren't the one he wanted for his wife, he found them husbands. I was there almost a year when he collected me one day and introduced me to a man named Kyle. Kyle was older, but he was gentle. It was more than I expected, honestly. We spent several months courting before getting married. Things were okay for the first year, but then we started trying for a baby." The tears fell, and Helen turned her back. Lynette stood from the table, wrapping her in a hug

62

from behind.

"Helen had several miscarriages," Branson whispered. Glory's heart broke for the woman. When Helen composed herself, she thanked Lynette and turned back to Glory. "I was considered a failure. Kyle asked Gideon for a different wife, and I was sent back to live in one of the cabins with the single women. There was no divorce as far as I know. I was just tossed out of the house I'd lived in with my husband for years as though I'd never mattered. In the end I guess I hadn't. He married someone else, and they had two kids together."

Glory was out of her chair and hugging the woman before she could second-guess her actions. "I'm so sorry." Helen returned the embrace, and they held onto one another for a while.

"I'm okay now," Helen said, pulling away. "Lynette said you were rescued. Do you feel like telling me about that?"

"Yes. Let me clean up the dishes first."

"You two go ahead and chat in the den," Lynette said. "Branson and I will clean up in here."

Branson pulled his bowl closer. "After I eat the rest of the mac 'n cheese. This is delicious, Glory. Feel free to make it anytime you want. You know, daily."

Lynette slapped her husband's arm, but she was grinning. Something squeezed Glory's heart. It wasn't exactly jealousy, but a feeling of longing. Wanting what the couple had. What Rhi had with Ryker, and Rory had with Sutton. In the few hours she'd been away from Haven, Glory was seeing how couples could be together. How they *should* be together, unlike

63

all the relationships she'd witnessed at Haven. Like the one Helen had where she was tossed aside so easily. And the fact that she'd not been given a divorce before Kyle married another woman? How was that legal? It probably wasn't, so the marriage might not have been valid either.

Glory and Helen sat together on a comfortable sofa, then Glory told her with a smile how the Hounds showed up at the market. She left out no details save the ones where Ripley paid for her purchases at the mall. She didn't know if it meant anything special, and she didn't want to feel like a fool later if it turned out he was merely being nice. When Helen excused herself to bed, Glory remained where she was, allowing herself to daydream about the stunning biker. She was roused from her musings when Lynette stuck her head in the room.

"Oh, I was just coming in to turn off the lights. It was so quiet I didn't realize anyone was in here."

Glory rose and stretched. "Sorry, I was lost in thought."

"No need to apologize. You've had a full day."

"That I have. I'll see you in the morning."

"Goodnight, Glory."

Glory made her way to her new bedroom, closing the door. It was going to be odd not having two others in the room with her. She didn't think she would miss their soft snores or shuffling on their hard mattresses. Thinking of the soft bedding, Glory couldn't wait to test it out. First, she wanted to try out the shower. She couldn't wait to stand under hot water and not have to hurry. Having toiletries not made by women at Haven was going to be a luxury. She turned the water on, and while it was heating, she brushed her teeth. She then flossed for good measure. She hadn't done that for six years, and it made her gums bleed. She couldn't imagine what a dentist would say if she got the chance to go for a checkup. Then again, she didn't eat sweets, and her teeth didn't have any apparent cavities, but who knew what they would find?

The shower was wonderful with its heavy pressure. Since her hair was shampooed earlier at the salon, Glory did her best to keep from getting it wet while she shaved her legs and armpits. Razors weren't allowed at Haven, probably because they could be used as weapons. After bathing, Glory remained under the hot water a few minutes longer, humming to herself as she thought back over everything that had happened since she woke that morning. She couldn't believe her luck. Just when she thought all hope was lost, a savior with lavender hair appeared out of nowhere along with knights in leather vests and worn jeans. Instead of horses, they rode motorcycles. Maybe her past sins hadn't been as great as her father insisted they were.

Not wanting to use up all the hot water, Glory turned the water off and wrapped up in a luxurious towel. She put on deodorant before combing her now shorter hair. She still couldn't believe it when she stared at her reflection. Glory grinned as her hair bounced around her face. Rhi had convinced Glory to buy some soft pajamas, so she changed into them before sliding beneath the covers. It was heaven. Glory turned on her side, her head sinking in the fluffy pillow. She couldn't stop the sigh from escaping as she closed her eyes. For the first time in years, she sent up a prayer, thanking God for the Hounds.

As expected, the room was too quiet, and Glory couldn't sleep. She never thought she'd miss Lisa Ann's snoring. Glory hummed for a bit, but that didn't help. Eventually, she pushed back the covers and decided to head downstairs for a glass of milk. Before Haven, her mother insisted having a glass before bed helped her younger sisters sleep, so she decided to try it. She turned on the bedside lamp, then padded quietly down the stairs to the kitchen. Flipping on the light, she found a glass in one of the cabinets. Having the freedom to do something as simple as getting a drink this late was mind-blowing. After pouring the milk, Glory walked through the house into a room where a piano sat in one corner. She placed her glass on a side table before sitting on the bench. She ran her fingers over the keys, wondering if she would even remember any of the songs she learned as a teen. Glory stood and strode to the door, closing it. She didn't want to wake the others, but the urge to play was too strong.

Glory placed her hands in the middle of the keys and closed her eyes, letting muscle memory take over. It took a few tries, but soon she was playing a pop song she'd taught herself when her parents weren't home. She quietly sang along, and the joy at doing something she once loved was overwhelming. With the last note echoing in the room, she placed her hands over her face and sobbed.

Glory jumped when strong arms encircled her shoulders. Lynette's voice was gentle when she apologized. "I didn't mean to scare you."

"I-I'm s-sorry if I woke you up."

"You didn't. Branson and I read for a while before we sleep. I'm sorry for imposing on your privacy, but I heard this amazing voice and had to come take a listen. You didn't tell us you could be a pop star."

Glory swiped at the tears. "I don't know about that, but I do love to sing."

"You can sing as often as you like here." Lynette squeezed Glory's shoulder. "I noticed the milk. Trouble sleeping?"

"A little. My room is too quiet. I'm used to my cabin mates snoring and shuffling around on their beds."

Lynette scooted off the bench. "I have just the thing. One of our other residents had the same trouble, and when she moved out, she left behind a white noise machine. Let me run and get it." Glory blew out a breath as she ran one finger over the keys. She couldn't wait until it was daytime so she could play without worrying about waking everyone. When Lynette returned, she was holding a box. "Come on. I'll show you how to work it." Glory followed the woman to her bedroom, and Lynette plugged the device in after placing it on the nightstand. "There are a bunch of settings. There are thunderstorms, rainfall on leaves, soft music, and even the sound of a fan. Just push this button to scroll through them to find the one you want."

Glory blinked back another round of tears. "Thank you. Not just for the machine, but for everything."

"You're welcome, Sweetheart." Lynette squeezed

Glory's arm before walking out and shutting the door behind her.

Glory scrolled through to the thunderstorm and flipped off the lamp. It was the perfect solution to the quiet room, and within minutes, she drifted off.

# Chapter Six

## Ripley

RIP STARED OUT the back door drinking his fifth cup of coffee. With thoughts of Glory plaguing his mind, he'd been unable to sleep well, so instead of lying there, tossing about, he'd showered and dressed before the sun rose. At some point, maybe around his third cup, the darkness had eased into light. Now, the dew glistened on the grass in his backyard. His thoughts were still on the pretty female his Gryphon insisted was their mate. Rip was going to take Rory's advice and not wait to go see Glory. He wasn't even giving her an extra day. He knew Branson and Lynette wouldn't have a problem with him showing up early, but the ass crack of dawn might be frowned upon.

The other women at Providence House knew Ripley since he'd helped get them away from Sanctuary. Helen had no problem with Rip, but Julia was still shy whenever he stopped by to see Branson. That didn't bother him. He wasn't going to visit her. It was the cute-as-fuck Glory who had his insides twisted.

"Fuck it." Ripley tossed back the lukewarm dregs,

then placed the empty mug in the dishwasher. He slid his boots on and grabbed the keys to his Camaro. To give the occupants of Providence House more time, Ripley stopped by his favorite bakery, ordering enough sweets for everyone. He had no idea if Glory even liked sweets, but if she didn't, he would make her bacon and eggs. The residents were encouraged to cook, but there were times Ripley and the other volunteers stepped in when the newcomers were still finding their place.

Rip sent a text to Branson saying he was on his way with pastries, then drove the short distance with the radio tuned to his favorite rock station, singing along with every song. Ripley loved music of all forms, from heavy metal to rap to classical. He admired those who could take random words and put them together to form thought-provoking lyrics. Or those who could pick up an instrument and put random notes together to form intense or beautiful melodies. Rip didn't have a talented bone in his body when it came to the arts. He couldn't play or write or even sing well, but that made him more appreciative of those who could.

When the gates rolled back after Ripley punched in his code, he eased the Camaro down the long driveway, his pulse ramping a few notches. His Gryphon was practically vibrating at seeing Glory.

*Down, boy.*

**I am not a boy nor a dog to be commanded.**

*No, but you are a pain in my ass. We can't go barging in scaring Glory. She's had enough overbearing men in her life. We have to be gentle and subtle. If she wants us, she will let us know.*

**Fine.**

Ripley rolled his eyes at the petulant beast. He parked in one of the designated spots, then grabbed the pastries. The front door opened, and Ripley turned to say hello to Branson, only it wasn't the male standing in the doorway. Glory was there wearing a new pair of jeans and a hoodie, even though the temperature didn't warrant one. She had on socks with no shoes, and her smile had his steps faltering.

"Good morning," he husked, clearing his throat.

Glory made grabby hands. "Morning. Branson said you come bearing gifts of the sweet kind."

Ripley wanted to pout. She was only happy to see him because he had treats. Instead, he put on his brightest smile and handed the top box over, not allowing her to carry all the containers. "I didn't know what you liked, or if you even like pastries, so I got an assortment."

Glory stopped just inside, and once Ripley closed the door, she sniffed the box in her hands, exhaling with glee. Cute as fuck. "I love pastries. And donuts. And pie and cake. Anything sweet. It's been six years since I had something loaded with sugar, so you just became my favorite person in the world."

"Good to know." Ripley winked, and Glory blushed as she turned and headed toward the kitchen. Branson and Lynette were sitting at the island drinking coffee. "Good morning," he greeted the couple.

"Morning, Ripley. Thanks for the pastries," Lynette said, toasting him with her mug.

"My pleasure."

"I had already started cooking bacon for breakfast, but when Branson mentioned you were bringing pastries, I didn't make biscuits. I figured that would be overkill on the carbs," Glory said, placing her box in front of Lynette. "Coffee?" she asked him.

"Yes, please. Black." He had already downed enough caffeine earlier to make a human jittery, but with his Gryphon metabolism, it didn't bother him. And if his pretty female was offering? Who was he to turn her down? He took the mug from her, allowing their fingers to touch. Glory's freckles glistened in the morning light, and Ripley wanted to stare, but he also didn't want her to feel uncomfortable. "If I had known you were planning on biscuits, I'd have waited until tomorrow to stop at the bakery. Please tell me you can make gravy too."

"Sure can. My granny on my mother's side taught me how to make it, but she used bacon grease instead of sausage. Is that a problem?" Glory teased.

"No. No problem here. I grew up in the South where I'm pretty sure bacon grease was a staple in most households."

"Yeah? Where in the South?" Glory asked as she pulled plates out of a cabinet and set them beside the now opened boxes. Branson hadn't waited on a plate. He had already demolished a bear claw and started on a chocolate-covered donut.

"Florida on the Gulf Coast. My parents are still in Florida, but now they live on the Atlantic side."

Glory passed Ripley a plate before picking out a couple of different pastries for herself. Ripley was glad she wasn't a female who shied away from eating. He would much rather love on a woman with a few extra pounds than feel their ribs and hips when he held them. Instead of moving away, she remained standing beside Rip.

"I bet that was amazing. I always wanted to see the ocean, but we never went on vacations. Father said it was a waste of money." Glory took a bite of her glazed donut, moaning as she chewed. Ripley's dick took notice, but so did Lynette and Branson. The couple was watching him closely. "This is so freaking yummy," Glory said before taking a sip of coffee. It was probably a good thing they had chaperones, or else he might have been tempted to lick the sugar off her lips. Branson was smirking, but Lynette narrowed her eyes, so Rip chose his own treat and begged his body to behave.

"It was amazing when I was younger, but the shine wore off after a while. It was no longer an indulgence. I think for some, it becomes part of your everyday culture instead of being something to look forward to." He didn't want to tell her the real reason the shine wore off. Ripley loved the ocean, but he needed to put distance between him and Sara Beth. "Kind of like those people who live in the desert or areas where it's mostly hot year-round and take a vacation up north to see the snow. Snowfall is beautiful, but when we get storms with several feet, it's not as enticing."

Glory cocked her head to the side. "So, you wouldn't want to live somewhere like California where you could surf all the time?"

Ripley tore the donut in half. "I've never tried surfing. The water is different around Florida. The waves aren't as big as they are out West."

"This one used to surf," Lynette said as she handed

Branson a napkin, pointing at his face. The Hound wiped his mouth as he grinned at his mate. "As a matter of fact, it's how we met. I grew up in the Midwest, but my grandparents lived in Fresno, and I spent every summer with them. One year, I took off driving up the Pacific Coast Highway and stopped off in Monterey for lunch and to take some photos. Here I was, sitting on a picnic table with my camera aimed at a boat in the distance, when suddenly, the image blurred. I had been so focused on getting the perfect shot that I forgot to stay aware of my surroundings. When I look up, this big brute is standing in front of me grinning like a loon."

"What did you do?" Glory asked.

"I threw my camera at his head and screamed *my* head off." Lynette knocked Branson's shoulder with her own. "Thankfully, he had good reflexes and caught my camera before it could fall to the ground and smash into a million pieces. He handed the camera back, apologized for scaring me, introduced himself, then asked me on a date. We've been together ever since."

"Wow. Just like that?"

"Just like that," Lynette told Glory. "When you know, you know."

"Good morning," Helen said, entering the kitchen with Julia hovering in the doorway. The brunette smiled at Ripley. "I thought I heard you down here."

"Morning. I brought some pastries." Ripley gestured to the open boxes.

"Oh, those look amazing, but I really shouldn't." Helen sighed dramatically, smoothing a hand down her flat stomach, then grabbed a jelly-filled donut,

74

laughing. "This is nice. Thank you." Helen bumped his arm with hers.

Glory tensed up, and Ripley took a step away from Helen, putting himself closer to Glory. "I wanted to welcome Glory properly," he said, and his cute female blinked up at him with wide eyes.

"Of course. Just like you welcomed me. You're such a sweetheart."

Ripley hadn't done anything special when Helen and Julia arrived. He didn't like the negative vibe coming from his right, so instead of waiting to give her the helmet, he decided now would be a good time. "I have something else for you. I'll be right back." Ripley sucked the glaze from his fingers, and Glory's eyes tracked the movement. Ripley licked his lips, and Glory coughed, covering her mouth with her fist. When he knew she wasn't really choking, he headed out to the car for the helmets he'd bought her. He felt Branson's presence as he opened the trunk. "I went ahead and bought Glory a helmet. Since I didn't know her size, I got three for her to try on."

"You're smitten," the Hound stated.

Ripley rubbed the back of his neck. "My Gryphon insists she's our mate."

"Then you should listen to your beast. Mine took one look at Lynette and claimed her."

"And you didn't argue?"

"If a female threw a camera at you, wouldn't you argue?" Branson chuckled. "But no, I didn't. She caught our eye from across the water. I was getting ready to put my board in the water when my beast kicked up a fuss, demanding we go take a closer look at the female sitting alone by the rocks. I listened, and I'm glad I did."

"I thought I found my mate when I was younger. We were together three years. Bought her a house and was set to propose. When I showed her my true nature, she freaked. Badly."

"You could have wiped her memory. Made her forget what she saw."

"Yeah, I know, but…" Ripley gripped the edge of the trunk and looked at his friend. "Would you want to be mated to Lynette if she didn't know you were a Gryphon? If you had to hide what you are?"

Branson rubbed at his chin, staring past Ripley. "No, I don't guess I would, but thank Zeus she accepted me fully."

"Exactly. I did wipe Sara Beth's memory, but I also made her think she'd fallen out of love with me. What if Glory feels the same way?"

"What if she doesn't? Wouldn't you rather take a chance that she's as strong as my mate?"

Ripley blew out a breath. "Yes, but if she rejects me, I swear to all that's holy I'm giving up on finding someone to spend my life with. It tore me up once, but twice?" Ripley shook his head.

Branson reached in the trunk and grabbed a couple of the helmets. "Yeah, I'd probably feel the same way. But if you're already buying Glory a helmet…" Branson raised his eyebrows, waiting.

"I'm ready to try again," Ripley said, lifting the last box and closing the lid. Neither one mentioned Helen's actions, but Ripley would talk to his friend about it if she continued. He followed the other Hound into the house. Ripley had hoped Helen wouldn't linger, but no such luck. He couldn't help that he wasn't attracted to her. Sure, she was gorgeous, but she wasn't Glory. Julia was nowhere to be seen, but that wasn't unusual.

Branson set his two helmets on the table, so Ripley added the third, then turned to Glory. "I mentioned getting you a helmet." He gestured toward the assortment. "Since I didn't know your size, I bought three so you can try them on and see which one fits. That way, when we go to lunch, you'll be set."

Glory rounded the island and picked up one of the boxes. "You got blue," she whispered.

"You did say it was your favorite color." Ripley took the box and opened it, pulling the helmet out, then settled it on her head. He fastened the strap, then wiggled the helmet to see how it fit. "Hmm, it's a little loose. Let's try a different size." The next one didn't fit quite right, but the third one was perfect.

Glory shook her head, then bobbed it up and down, doublechecking the fit. "Yep, this one. You'll have to teach me how to sinch the strap."

Ripley took her by the hand and led her to the small bathroom in the hall. Standing behind her in front of the mirror, Ripley unfastened the strap, then showed her the proper way to thread the vinyl through the double loops. It only took one time until she did it herself.

"You did it."

"Yay!" Glory pumped a fist in the air, and Ripley grinned at her reflection. "Thank you."

"You're welcome." Ripley turned Glory to face him and efficiently removed the helmet, placing it under his arm. "If you'd like, you can ride with me to the store to return the two that don't fit."

Glory brushed a hand through her hair. "I'd love to go with you, but I need to check with Lynette to make sure there isn't something she needs me to do here first."

Ripley backed out of the bathroom and held out his free arm. "After you."

When they entered the kitchen, Lynette and Branson were still sitting at the island, drinking coffee, but Helen was absent. "We have a winner." Rip placed the helmet on the table, then repacked the others into their boxes.

"Ripley asked me to ride with him to the bike shop. Is there anything you need me to do this morning?" Glory asked Lynette.

The female slid off the stool and stepped closer to Glory. "Not chores, and you can say no, but Branson was sad he didn't get to hear you play last night."

"Play?" Ripley asked.

"Glory can play the piano, and she has an amazing voice." Lynette reached out and grasped both Glory's hands. "I don't mean to put you on the spot."

Glory smiled at Lynette. "You're not, and I don't mind. It's the least I can do to repay you all for saving me." She turned to Ripley. "Keep in mind I haven't played in six years, so I'm a little out of practice."

Ripley couldn't wait to hear Glory play. He followed her through the house with the other couple close behind. When they reached the room where the baby grand piano sat in the corner, Ripley wasn't sure whether he should stand close or sit in one of the chairs

78

where she couldn't see him. Glory slid onto the bench and ran her fingers over the keys in what he figured was a warm-up. Lynette and Branson chose to sit on the loveseat across from him.

If Glory was nervous, she didn't show it. She moved easily from the warm-up into a song. When she hit a wrong note, she didn't apologize. Instead, she continued from where she was, choosing not to start the song from the beginning. After running through it once, she started over, this time singing along. He recognized the song as an older pop tune. It made sense she didn't play a current hit since she'd not had access to a radio in six years. He sat mesmerized by her talent at both playing and singing. Lynette was right; Glory had an amazing voice. Ripley didn't know whether she was considered alto or soprano or whatever the term was for in between, but she hit low and high notes equally well. Regardless of her voice type, Glory nailed the song, and when she was finished, he whistled and clapped, while Branson and Lynette praised her with their own whoops of enjoyment.

Glory glanced over her shoulder at Ripley, and this time it was she who winked at him. Fuck, he was in trouble.

Going to the bike shop was forgotten as Glory continued performing for them. Not long after she'd begun, Helen and Julia joined them. Helen sat off to the side, but after a few songs, Julia surprised them when she added harmonies to an old hymn Glory played at the female's request. Since Julia had been raised at Sanctuary, she wouldn't have known any secular

79

music. From what Ripley understood, there was little singing at The Ministry compounds, but at some point, the female had learned at least one gospel song. She was timid at first, but the further she got into the song, the louder she projected her voice, and the way it melded with Glory's was something of beauty. Ripley wasn't into religious music, but he could appreciate the talent both women possessed.

"Where did you learn that song?" Lynette asked Julia once it was finished.

"From my mom. When it was just the two of us in our cabin, she would sing to me all the time. As I got older, she taught me to harmonize with her. I miss it. Not Sanctuary, but singing."

Glory turned on the bench, facing the other woman. "You're welcome to sing with me anytime."

Julia blushed as she admitted, "I'd like that."

"As would I." Lynette put her arm around Julia's shoulder. "Because I can't carry a tune in a bucket, but the two of you were amazing. I bet you could put an act together and go on the road. You'd be selling out arenas in no time."

"Hear, hear."

Julia let out a squeak at the deep voice. At some point, Ryker and Rhi had snuck in, but Ripley was so focused on Glory, he hadn't noticed.

"Don't mind us. We came to see how Glory's first night was, but from the sounds of it, she's settling in nicely," Ryker said from the doorway. Rhiannon left his side and waddled over to Glory and Julia.

"I didn't know you could sing like that," Rhi told Julia.

"Yeah, uh. I need to get ready for church." With that, Julia rushed from the room with Helen following.

After watching them leave, Rhi turned to Glory. "And you? Just wow."

"You know, Angel, you have a set of pipes on you too. Maybe we have the next big trio on our hands?"

Rhi shook her head at her mate. "I'm perfectly happy working at BB's."

"Come on, Rhi. Let us hear you. One song." Glory faced the keys and played a few notes, then nodded to herself. "I bet you know this one," she said with a smirk, and the familiar notes from "Rhiannon" by Fleetwood Mac filled the air. Rhi rolled her eyes, but when it came time for the lyrics, she sang to the tune she was named after. When Glory lent her raspy voice to the chorus, it was nothing short of perfection. Ripley was proud of the female he hoped to one day call his mate.

# CHAPTER SEVEN

## Glory

GLORY HAD NEVER felt more alive. Playing piano came naturally to her the moment her mother taught her simple songs. She learned all the classic church hymns because that's all that was allowed in their home. If her parents ever found out she played for the chorus, they'd probably have made her quit. She had been lucky they weren't interested in what she did at school. It was only what she did after they kept an eye on. The applause from everyone at Providence House was thunderous, and Branson was calling for an encore.

Lynette held up her hands, and the room quieted. "Let's not overwhelm Glory. Besides, she and Ripley have somewhere to be. Glory, thank you for indulging us, but I can speak for the room when I say you are welcome to serenade us anytime."

"It really was my pleasure." Glory stood from the bench and stretched her back. "Did you need me for something besides being your accompanist?" she asked Rhiannon.

"I wanted to come see how you were settling in, plus we need your information to apply for a replacement birth certificate. I forgot to get that last night."

"Let me ask Lynette for paper and a pen."

"Or you could just text it to me," Rhi offered.

It had been so long since Glory used technology that she forgot that's how things were done now. She dug her phone out of her back pocket and held it to her face to open the screen. It took her a second to figure out how to send Rhi a text, but Rory had done a good job of explaining the device. "There."

Having such an unusual middle name had been the brunt of many jokes and taunting when she was younger, and she expected Rhi to at least react negatively. Instead of making fun, she asked, "Do you like your middle name?"

"Would you like it?" When Rhi shook her head, Glory said, "I hate it. If I could change it, I would."

"You can change it, if you really want to."

"Oh, I would love to, but won't that cost money?"

Rhi looked over to where Ryker was talking with Ripley. He nodded at Rhi as though they were having an unspoken conversation. She took Glory's hand and pulled her across the room and out into the hallway, not stopping until they were alone in the den. "Bishop can change it for you. And before you ask, no, it's not exactly legal. If you prefer to do it the legal way, you'd need to fill out an application and appear before a judge. It might take a couple months for that to happen."

"Are you talking about hacking the system?" Glory asked.

"We prefer the term manipulation, but sure. He'd

be hacking the system. It's up to you."

Glory chewed her bottom lip. She'd never broken the law except for speeding the few times she'd driven her father's car, and that had only been a few miles above the limit. And technically, she wouldn't be the one breaking the law if she agreed. "Does Bishop do this a lot? I don't want him to get in trouble on my account."

"I can neither confirm nor deny what Bishop does," Rhi said, grinning. "But he won't get in trouble."

"Then yes, I would like for him to change it. I would say I don't know what my parents were thinking giving my sisters and me the same middle name, but they're both fanatics when it comes to religion."

Rhi's eyes widened. "No," she exaggerated.

"Yep. Glory of God, Hope of God, Splendor of God, and Majesty of God. You want to talk about being teased." Glory felt bad for her sisters, but at Haven, there was less chance of being ridiculed since most of the adults there were fanatics as well.

"Do you have any idea what you'd like your new name to be?"

"Can I have time to think about it?"

"Take all the time you need. I'll have him get your birth certificate with your current name, then once you figure out what you want it changed to, we'll let him know so he can get you a new one. Now, let's get back to the guys. Did I hear you and Ripley were going somewhere?" Rhi hooked her arm through Glory's as they returned to the parlor.

84

"He bought me a helmet. Well, three actually, since he didn't know my size. We're taking the two that don't fit back to the bike shop."

Rhi patted her round belly. "I miss riding, but Ryker's a little protective now that I'm pregnant."

"And for very good reason, Angel." Ryker held open his arm, and Rhi released Glory, going to stand in front of her husband. Ryker circled his arms around her, cradling her stomach. "You're carrying precious cargo."

Ripley joined them, and Glory craned her neck to look at him. "You ready?" he asked, his minty breath invading her senses. He must have found gum or candy somewhere after coffee and donuts.

"Yep. I just need to put on shoes and grab my jacket. I'll be right back." She slipped away from the group, rushing up the stairs to her bedroom. She did a lot of walking at Haven, but she was still winded after taking the stairs quickly. Glory caught her breath as she slipped on the new boots Ripley bought her. She pulled off her hoodie since it was warm outside and chose one of the T-shirts Ripley helped her pick out. She then went to the closet where she'd hung her jacket. The weather was turning warmer, but it was still cool at night, at least it was to her, and Glory didn't know what time she'd be returning. Plus, she wanted to show Ripley how much she appreciated the gift. When she reached for it, her hand froze in the air. Rhi had helped Glory put her clothes away the night before, and Glory noticed Rhi hung them all with the front of the garment facing toward the closet door. The jacket had also been facing forward. Now, though, the zipper was away from her. Had someone been in her room? Surely not, as that was the most important rule at Providence. Removing the jacket from the hanger, she checked it over. For what, she wasn't sure, but it didn't appear to have been bothered other than facing the wrong way.

Not wanting to keep Ripley waiting any longer, Glory put the issue out of her mind and rejoined the others. Ripley eyed the jacket Glory had cradled to her chest. When his blue eyes met hers, she shrugged, and he grinned. Yep, glad she decided to bring it with her even if she didn't really need it.

"Ryker and Rhi are going with us, if that's okay."

"Yeah, that's great." Glory was a little nervous about being alone with the biker, so having her friend as a buffer was welcomed. Branson and Lynette said they would see her later, but Helen and Julia weren't there. Glory hadn't seen them upstairs, so she figured they had gone to church together. Glory wanted to make friends with the two women. Having been through similar experiences, she felt they had something in common. Ripley carried both helmets under one arm and placed his free hand on her back as he directed her to a sharp Camaro. A memory of another sports car sprang to mind, and Glory stumbled.

"Are you okay?" Ripley asked, his hand gripping her arm to keep her upright.

"Yeah. Uh, nice car." And it was. Nicer even than the one—

"If you'd rather ride with Rhi, I'll understand."

Glory put on her best smile when she faced Ripley.

"No. This is fine. I just wasn't expecting you to be in a car like this," she lied.

"No? What *did* you expect?"

"I guess an SUV like Ryker drives." Glory waited as Ripley put the helmets in the trunk. When he opened the door for her, she lowered herself onto the smooth leather. At least that was different. When Ripley was seated next to her, he started the engine, and the motor rumbled even above the loud music. Ripley turned the volume down, apologizing.

"Sounds like a lotta horses."

"You know about engines?" he asked as he put the car in gear and rolled down the driveway.

"Not really. I had a… a friend in high school who had one of these. It was an older model and not nearly as nice. Or powerful. I think it was a V-6 or something like that."

"Six cylinders. Still has some get up and go, but I had this one modified with a Corvette engine. More horses. Vettes are sleek, but I've always preferred the body style of the Camaro, and this way, I get the best of both worlds."

Glory strapped on the seatbelt and settled in for the ride. She clasped her hands in her lap to keep from chewing her cuticles. Her nails already looked bad enough from the work she'd done at Haven. Maybe now she could grow them out a little.

"Do you know how to drive?" Ripley asked.

"I do, though I don't have a license."

"Never got one or it was taken when you moved?"

"That. My father said I didn't need any paperwork like my birth certificate or license when we moved.

Maybe after Bishop changes my name and gets my birth certificate, I can get another license. I'll need it for work, won't I?"

"It's usually required, yes. What's this about changing your name? Bishop is a hacker, not a lawyer."

"Oh, my sisters and I all have the same crazy middle name, and Rhi said Bishop could change it if I wanted to." Glory squeezed her hands together. The need to chew on her fingers was like an itch that needed scratching. That and Ripley was driving one-handed. The other dangled over the side of the console where his forearm was resting. His fingers were close to her thigh, and she wanted to touch them. It had been years since she felt someone else's touch besides her sisters', and hugging them wasn't the same as being held by a lover. She longed to be held. Kissed. Made love to. Would Ripley be gentle? Or would he be rough and demanding? He let out a huff, getting Glory's mind off things best left alone. She turned to see if he was angry. "You don't approve?"

"Is your name that offensive that you can't take the proper steps instead of having Bishop change it illegally?" Ripley practically growled.

"Sorry," Glory whispered, returning her gaze to the side window.

"For?" Ripley reached over and laid his large hand over both of hers. "Glory?" he prodded.

"I don't know. Making you mad?" Ripley eased her hands apart and threaded his fingers with hers. Okay, so he wasn't angry with her, but something had made him growl.

"I'm not mad, but I do tend to lean toward staying

on the right side of things. If you need your name changed quickly, for a reason other than you merely hate it, then I can understand having Bishop change it."

"I guess I don't need it changed quickly. Or at all. I didn't know it was even possible until Rhi mentioned it."

Ripley jiggled her hand. "Is it that bad? Your name?"

"I think so. It's of God."

"Ovgod?" Ripley asked as he flipped on his turn signal, then hung a right. Glory wanted to take in the scenery since she was in a new town, but the scenery in the driver's seat was much more enticing.

"Of God, two words. As in Glory of God. My parents are religious fanatics."

Ripley squeezed her hand. "I can see why you would want to change it. Any ideas of what you'd like it to be?"

"Not really considering I never knew it was possible. Maybe I'll get one of those baby name books and see if something calls to me."

"How about we get Bishop to order your birth certificate as-is so you'll have it, then when you decide on a new name, I'll file the paperwork for you?"

"You'd do that?"

"I'd be honored. You mentioned your parents are fanatics. How did you feel when they moved you to Haven?"

"Pissed." Glory wouldn't tell him why they moved abruptly, but she'd give him the basics. "My parents spent all their spare time at church. It was my responsibility to watch after my sisters if they were at

89

meetings. We weren't allowed to have a television or radio at home. I wasn't allowed to spend time with anyone outside of school whose parents didn't also attend church. But I still had friends, and I enjoyed school because it was normal. I played piano and sang in the school chorus. It was the only time I was truly happy."

"Is that where you learned to play? At school?"

"No, my mom taught me the basics, but I can hear a song and just know it. My best friend would let me borrow her MP3 player at night so I could listen to music when I went to bed. We had an old upright piano at home, and when my parents were out of the house, I'd play the songs I'd listened to the night before. Majesty and Splendor were too young to know I wasn't playing hymns, and Hope enjoyed the pop songs, so I got away with it."

"That's amazing. I admire anyone who can play or sing. I love music of all kinds. It's one of those things that can make a bad day better. Have you ever thought of playing professionally?"

Glory swallowed hard, biting back tears. That had been her dream before she'd been uprooted. She was going to get out from under her parents and move to Tennessee. When she could talk without crying, she answered softly, "Yeah. I thought about it."

"But then Haven happened," Ripley finished for her. "The good news is you're still young, and you have your whole life ahead of you. You can follow that dream now."

Glory didn't get a chance to ask how since they'd arrived at the bike shop. Motorcycles lined the front of the store, and several people, men and women, were checking them out. Ripley came around and opened Glory's door, holding his hand out for her. She took it, letting him pull her to her feet. Ryker and Rhi pulled in next to the Camaro, and while they got out, Ripley retrieved the two helmets from the trunk.

The two couples made their way inside, and Glory stopped just through the door. She shouldn't think of herself and Ripley as a couple. Helen had said Ripley welcomed her to Providence House too, so maybe he was just a really nice guy. It surprised Glory that Ripley wasn't with the pretty woman.

"You okay?" Rhi asked.

"Yep, just taking it all in," she lied. She found herself lying more than she was comfortable with, but she didn't feel right asking Rhi about Ripley's past girlfriends. Rhi took her hand and led her to the women's clothes. They browsed the many rows of shirts while the men were at the counter. One long-sleeved tee in particular caught Glory's eye, and she held it up in front of her. It was a pretty lilac but had a white skull emblazoned across the chest.

"Ooh, that's nice." Rhi picked up the same shirt in a different color. Hers was pink.

"I always imagined biker shirts would be black," Glory muttered as she refolded the shirt and put it back before picking up the next size up.

"They used to be," Ryker said as he and Ripley joined the women. "But over the years, more women started riding. I guess they wanted to look pretty and badass at the same time."

"Makes sense." Glory went to put the shirt back,

but Ripley touched her arm. "Do you like that one?"

"Sure, but I don't ride."

"You will be. Why do you think I got you a helmet?" The corner of his eyes crinkled when he smiled down at her.

"Are we dating?" she blurted. Ryker coughed, and Rhi smacked his chest before pulling him away.

Ripley took the tee from Glory. "I prefer to call it getting to know one another. You might not enjoy my company." Glory snorted, then promptly covered her mouth. Ripley tugged her hand away, grinning. "You're too damn cute for your own good, but why the snort?"

"I think it'll be the other way around," Glory admitted. "You're a successful lawyer with friends and family who love you. I no longer have a family. I didn't finish high school, because no matter what Haven calls it, their education is nothing more than Bible study. Sure, the younger kids learn to read and how to do math, but that's about it. I was almost ready to graduate when my parents uprooted us."

"Let's look around at the clothes and table this discussion until we're somewhere with a little more privacy."

"I can't let you buy me any more clothes, Ripley. You've already spent too much money on me." Glory tried to take the shirt from him, but he held it out of reach.

"You let me decide what's too much. Consider it birthday presents for the last six years."

Glory wanted to consider it gifts for the last twenty-four birthdays. No one other than Sheri and

92

Chad had ever given her real gifts. Her granny had tried, but her father wouldn't allow it. Glory's parents didn't celebrate the way most parents did. She and her sisters weren't given gifts at Christmas other than new clothes for church.

Ripley placed his hand on her upper arm. "Glory?"

Leaning into his touch, she protested, "You've already bought more than six years' worth of presents."

"No, I'm only at one with the helmet," he argued with a big grin, his one dimple popping.

"And all the clothes and the boots and the leather jacket," Glory countered, waving a finger in his face.

Ripley grabbed her finger, leaning down to nip at it. "Nope. All those were necessities. Technically, the helmet is a necessity too, but that's more for me since I really want you riding behind me. So, you can either get five more items here, or you can save them for other things you might want."

Glory punched his arm with her free hand. "Are you always this stubborn?"

Ripley released her finger and rubbed the area where she hit him. "Yes. Remember, I'm an attorney. I'm an expert at arguing and making people come around to my way of thinking." He arched one thick eyebrow, daring her to disagree.

Glory didn't want to argue. It was selfish, but she wanted him to buy her things, so she huffed out, "Fine. Five more things, but that's it."

"Fine." Ripley tapped her on the nose. "Five more here or...?"

Glory wanted makeup, but she wasn't going to ask

him for that. She would ask Rhi if she could borrow some of hers until Glory had a job and could get her own. "Let's keep looking." Ripley smiled like she'd agreed to buy *him* presents. By the time they left the store, she had chosen the tee and a shirt that snapped up the front. Glory couldn't help herself. When Ripley paid for the items, she stood on tiptoes and kissed his cheek. "Thank you."

Ripley winked at her. "My pleasure."

# CHAPTER EIGHT

## Ripley

RYKER RECEIVED A text from Quinn about a job, so he and Rhi said their goodbyes after promising to meet up with them later. Once Ripley and Glory were back in the Camaro, he broached their earlier conversation. "What were you planning on doing after high school? Did you want to go to college?"

Glory chewed the side of her thumb, something he'd noticed she did when nervous. He reached over and laced their fingers so she didn't harm herself. "College wasn't really in my future since my parents didn't have much money. I..." Glory sighed, looking out the side window. There was something she wasn't telling him, and he didn't want to push, but if this was going to work between them, she needed to trust him.

"Whatever it is, you can tell me. I want us to be friends, and that means sharing the good and bad."

Glory turned to look at him, her eyes glistening. "Is that all you want? To be friends?"

Ripley brought her hand to his mouth and brushed his lips against her knuckles. "No. I want to see if we can be more than that, but it's important that we're friends first. That means trusting each other with our truths."

"Have you ever been married?" she asked.

Well, fuck. Ripley had hoped to be further along in their relationship when they talked about his past, but if he wanted her to open up, he'd have to do the same. "No. I had a girlfriend when I was younger who I planned to propose to, but in the end, she decided we weren't meant to be."

"And she was the only one? Girlfriend, I mean?"

"Yes. I won't lie and say I've been a saint since then, but I've not found anyone I wanted to get serious with."

Glory stared at him, and he didn't think she was going to be honest with him. She let out a breath as she leaned her head back. "I had a boyfriend in high school. With the way I was raised, I wasn't allowed to date, so it was hard spending quality time together outside of school." Glory gazed out the window, or maybe she was thinking about this boy, but she wasn't looking at Ripley. "It was serious, this thing between us. He had a job with his dad's construction company, so he already had a little money saved up. After graduation, we were going to move in together. I was going to get a job somewhere while I figured out what I wanted to do with my life. He was so patient with me. Promised he could wait. We only had two months until graduation, but..." Glory swiped under her eye with her free hand. "It was the night of our senior prom. I just wanted to be a normal girl for once. I told my parents I was spending the night with a girl from church, and instead of going to her house, I went to my

96

best friend Sheri's. She had an old prom dress she let me borrow, and she did my makeup. Chad picked me up, but instead of going to the dance, we went riding around and listening to music. We ended up parking by the lake on his grandpa's land and..." Glory cleared her throat. Ripley didn't have to hear the words to know what happened then.

Ripley squeezed Glory's hand, offering support. "He was your first, then."

"Yeah, and my only. I was so stupid," she whispered. "Not because of what we did, but because I thought I'd get away with it. I don't know how my father found us, but after we... We'd just righted our clothes when bright lights shined in the window, and my father was there with the Sheriff. If I hadn't already turned eighteen, my dad would have had Chad arrested. Since I was of age, there was nothing the Sheriff could do. If I'd only waited two more months, I'd have been free. Instead, my father made me get in the car with him. He didn't say a word until we got home, but once we were there, he made me take off Sheri's dress, and he beat me with a belt while calling me a sinner and a whore. He beat me so badly I couldn't get out of bed for days. By the time I could walk, my parents had arranged to leave for Haven. I never saw or spoke to Chad or Sheri after that night."

Ripley's beast growled, begging to be turned loose so it could go after the man. Glory narrowed her eyes at the sound. It took all his might to keep the Gryphon at bay. Ripley placed a kiss on her palm, praying she didn't think he was mad at her. "I'm so sorry that happened to you. I have to ask, are you still in love with him? Chad?"

"I guess a small part of me will always love him, but it's been six years. Those feelings have faded, and I just hope he found someone else to love. What about you? Do you still love your ex?"

"Not at all. Like I said, that was a long time ago." Ripley really hoped she didn't ask how long. That wasn't a discussion he wanted to have yet. She had laughed upon meeting Sutton and Rory, seeing how they didn't appear much older than Ryker. To get her mind on something more pleasant, he asked, "What about Sheri? Would you like to get in touch with her?"

"Could I?" Glory turned in her seat, facing him. "That would be amazing."

"Sure. All I need is her name and the address from when you were younger, and I'll find her for you."

Glory leaned over the console and hugged him awkwardly. "Oh, thank you. Consider that one of my birthday gifts."

Ripley buried his nose in Glory's hair. "Let's wait and see if I find her first." Ripley's dick was plumping from having the female in his arms. "Are you hungry?"

Glory returned to her side of the car, her smile bright. "I could eat, but do you think I should check in with Lynette?"

"No. Providence isn't a prison, Sunshine. She knows you're with me."

*Sunshine.* Glory melted a little on the inside. "Okay, then. Yes, I'd love to get lunch."

"How about Mexican? I know a great place not far from here."

Glory put on her seatbelt. "Is it the one Tank's

wife owns?"

"Yes, it is, but how do you know that?" Ripley fastened his own belt and put the car in gear.

"Helen and Julia went there last night and were talking about it when they came in."

"Gotcha. Martina's food is amazing." Ripley exited the parking lot and reached for Glory's hand. "What do you think about getting your GED? I can help you study for it."

"I would like that because I'm going to need to find work. But what kind of job am I going to be able to find? All I have experience with is working in the kitchen or skinning a deer. Doubt there's much need for the latter."

Rip didn't want to imagine his pretty female with a knife, slicing through deer hide. He also didn't want to think about her doing kitchen work. Not that there was anything wrong with it, but she was too talented not to pursue a musical career. "Why don't you do something with your music? You're exceptionally talented."

Glory shrugged. "I wouldn't even know where to start. I do love to play and sing, but don't you have to live in a big city for something like that?"

"I guess it would depend on whether you want to just play locally or if you wanted to get a record deal. I bet we could call Desmond Rothchild, the lead singer for Cyanide Sweetness, and he could put you in contact with the right people if that's the case." Whatever Glory decided, Rip would be there every step of the way to make sure she wasn't taken advantage of. He wasn't an expert with those types of contracts, but he could read it over and decide if they needed to hire a different attorney.

"How is this my life?" Glory's words were so soft he would have missed them if he weren't a shifter.

"Karma, my little nightingale. Your life was stolen from you, and it's time for the good kind to be given back."

Lunch turned into a long visit with Tank, Martina, and baby Patrick, who took an instant liking to Glory. Having three younger sisters, it wasn't surprising she was good with the little tyke. It also didn't surprise him when his Gryphon nudged him.

*She'll be good with our young.*

*You're getting ahead of yourself.*

The beast didn't respond, but it didn't need to. It planted the seed of hope, but he didn't know if Glory even wanted kids of her own. It was too soon to be thinking such things. He'd only met the female the day before.

*She's our mate.*

Okay, maybe his shifter wasn't finished. Glory narrowed her eyes at him again. She was good at sensing when the beast was rumbling. He kept his focus on Patrick, who had a strong hold of Rip's finger. If he'd been alone with Tank, he would have made a crude joke.

Martina had the cooks prepare a variety of dishes for Glory since she'd only ever had fast-food tacos. She expertly ate one-handed while holding Patrick. Glory had attempted to hand him off to his papa, but the baby wanted Glory. Rip knew the feeling. After a couple hours of Glory and Martina getting to know one another better, sharing their histories with each other, they left the restaurant after promising the females could visit again soon.

"Martina's great," Glory gushed once they were back in the car.

"She said the same about you. I'm glad to see you making friends with the other Hounds' females. When you meet the rest of Ryker's brothers and their women, you'll have a sisterhood at your disposal."

"You're so sure they'll like me?"

"What's not to like?" Rip reached over and tucked a strand of hair behind Glory's ear. When she leaned into the touch, he left his hand on her cheek. He figured his female was touch-starved. Growing up with the type of parents she had, they probably hadn't offered much comfort. Then spending six years at Haven, well he could only imagine the loneliness. At least he'd been able to hook up when his own loneliness became too much. "What would you like to do now? We have several hours before we meet back up with Ryker and Rhi."

"I have no idea. Maybe a movie?"

Rip opened the internet browser on his phone to see what movies were playing, but the device vibrated in his hand. Seeing it was his mom calling, he glanced at Glory. "Sorry. It's my mom."

"Well, answer it. Unless you don't want to talk to her."

Ripley always wanted to talk to her, but not with Glory sitting beside him since she was going to be the topic of conversation. "I'll call her back later." He sent his mom a text explaining he was going to take Glory to a movie and would call her back. "Okay, what kind of movie do you want to see?" When he pulled up the listings, Rip leaned on the console and held the phone out for Glory to look at. She rested her arm against his, and used her finger to scroll through the choices.

"Most of these are sequels. Since I haven't seen the previous ones, I'll probably be lost."

"Then I have a suggestion. What do you think about going to my house and watching the first in whatever series you're interested in? I promise to be a perfect gentleman. Watching movies only." Glory stiffened next to him. So maybe he was moving too quickly. He was practically a stranger after all. "Or we can do something else."

"No!" Glory leaned back and turned so she was facing him. "I mean, no, I'm okay with going to your house. I would love to watch movies with you. As long as you have popcorn, that is." Her smile said one thing, but her eyes said another. Ripley wasn't a fool. He was good at reading people. And the look on his female's face told him everything. She wanted him. Maybe being a perfect gentleman wasn't what she needed.

They had both eaten their fill at Martina's place, but he wouldn't deprive his female of the salty snack if that's what she wanted. Ripley would give Glory anything she desired. "I have popcorn, but we'll need to stop at the store for something to drink with it. I only have beer, coffee, or water, none of which go well with popcorn."

And that's what they did. Shopping was usually a perfunctory chore, but with Glory, it was enjoyable if not a little heartbreaking. Glory lit up at all the different types of chips and dips. She marveled over

102

the chocolate selections, but the true delight was when she took fifteen minutes deciding what soda she wanted. When it looked like she wouldn't be able to choose, Ripley put five different varieties in the shopping cart and then grabbed his own favorite root beer.

Rip's nerves jangled the closer they got to his house. He'd never brought a female home. All hookups happened at either the woman's place or a hotel. His home was his sanctuary. He decorated it with only himself in mind when he bought it all those years ago. The other Hounds visited on occasion, but it was rare when he wasn't alone there. Now it would be filled with Glory's scent. Hopefully her laughter. Just her presence would imprint on the air, and that would linger once he took her back to Providence.

*Then don't take her back.*

Ripley chastised his beast – again – for jumping the gun. They couldn't ask Glory to move in after a day. That way lay madness.

Ripley encouraged Glory to look around his home while he put the sodas in the fridge and the snacks on the island. He wanted her to see what he'd made of the structure after having it built to his specifications. Four bedrooms, the master on the bottom floor, a game room, which opened to a stone patio at the back. A large yard, fenced and full of tall trees which offered plenty of shade in the summer. Next to the patio was a hot tub, which sat outside his master suite. He'd thought about covering it, but Ripley loved nothing better than to enjoy the jetted water while gazing at the stars. When he met with the architect, Ripley avoided

103

the man's questions about why a single man wanted such a large house. Ripley spent a few years getting over Sara Beth's rejection, but deep down, he wanted a family, so he built a house worthy of one.

The game room held a massive TV across from a comfy sofa, a bar in the opposite corner, and space for a pool table he never got around to buying. Now that Glory was in his life, Rip thought it would be the perfect spot for a baby grand piano. He would have to research how to make the room more suited to the acoustics, if that was something she needed to play well.

"Wow," she muttered from one of the other rooms. "This place is ridiculous, but he is a lawyer." As he listened in to her monologue while exploring, Ripley got the popcorn going on the stove. No bagged stuff here. He loved the process of shaking the kernels in the pot as the steam did its job of puffing each piece until the lid was balancing precariously.

"That is so cool." Glory moved to his side, leaning around his arm, her chest brushing his bare skin. She'd removed her hoodie as soon as they entered his home, and her T-shirt and bra offered little barrier.

"Have you never seen popcorn cooked this way?" Ripley continued moving the pan back and forth, scooting over a few inches so he wasn't coming off as a pervert.

"Nope. The only time I had it was at a sleepover, and it was microwaved."

"Then you're in for a treat." Ripley took the pot off the hot eye and dumped it into three waiting bowls. "We have options. Buttered, ranch, and parmesan." He poured melted butter over each bowl, added a little salt to one, some ranch seasoning to the second, grated cheese to the third, then mixed them with a spoon to coat as many pieces as possible. "Go ahead."

Glory grinned as she tried the ranch first. She hummed her approval before moving to the parmesan. Her eyes widened as she took another piece. "This is the shi-uh stuff," she amended.

"You can say shit. I won't be offended." Ripley went to the fridge and pulled out one of each soda, placing them on the island next to a glass of ice. "I'll take these to the game room while you make up your mind what you want to drink." He placed one bowl in the crook of his arm, then picked up the others and carried them across the house. When he returned, Glory was staring at the cans, chewing the side of her thumb.

"I can't choose. Why is this so difficult?" Her expression was one he never wanted to see on her face again. He never wanted her to be anything other than happy and sure of herself. Ripley couldn't imagine being denied the small joys of life for so long that it made something as simple as choosing which soda to drink difficult. Glory leaned forward, thunking her head against the island, and Ripley slid his hand between the granite and her skin.

"Want me to pick for you?" he offered, gently raising her head and rubbing his thumb across the redness.

"Yeah. Uh, yes, please. God, I'm such a loser." She wrapped one arm around her waist while chewing on her other thumb.

Ripley reached out and took her hand, kissing her knuckles. "None of that." He released her so he could pour a grape soda into one of the glasses before pouring his root beer. He gestured toward the hallway, and Glory made her way to the game room. She sat on the sofa, and Ripley eased down close but not where their legs would touch. He placed both glasses on the coffee table, then handed her the bowl of parmesan popcorn before picking up the remote.

"What kinds of movies do you like?" Ripley held his breath. Not that her choice would be a dealbreaker, but he prayed to Zeus she didn't want a rom com. Those had been Sara Beth's favorites, and Ripley sat through them because he'd loved her. He would do the same for Glory. Not because he was already feeling that depth of caring, but because he knew he could.

"I was never allowed to watch television, and the few times I did watch shows or movies at a sleepover, they were geared toward little kids." Glory took a bite of popcorn, chewing and swallowing before she continued. "I always wanted to see *Star Wars* because I imagined escaping to a distant planet and having my own little droid that followed me around."

"We can absolutely do *Star Wars*. All the movies as well as the series that followed if you'd like. That'll keep us busy a while." Ripley lifted the remote and said, *"The Phantom Menace."* When it popped up on the screen, Ripley didn't immediately start the movie. "Did you know they filmed the first three movies long after four, five, and six were released?"

"Yeah. I couldn't watch the movies, but I did read about them whenever I had a free minute in the library

106

at school. Our computers allowed us to research, but I made sure to wipe my searches before I logged off. I'm sure the administrators could track our usage, but I was a good student, plus I didn't abuse the privilege."

"Then you know these are the crappy ones. At least I think they are. I prefer the latter ones, but *The Mandalorian* series is my favorite." Ripley leaned back after grabbing the bowl of buttered popcorn and started the movie. While Glory's attention was on the screen, Ripley's was on his female. He liked being able to give her something she'd never had. He wanted to be the one to show her the world and help her experience everything it had to offer.

They had just started watching the second movie when his phone pinged with a text. Upon seeing Ryker's name, he hit pause and read the message. "I totally forgot we're supposed to meet Ryker and Rhi."

"I might have ruined my appetite for supper with all the popcorn," Glory said.

"Me too. Let me tell him we'll meet up another time."

Glory stood and left the room without saying anything. While texting Ryker, Ripley used his shifter hearing to listen. When the bathroom door closed, he gave her some privacy. His phone vibrated, and Rip groaned when he read Ryot's text.

Ryker: *Rhi told Natalia about singing with Glory. The twins were there and want a show of their own.*

Ripley waited until Glory returned from using the bathroom. She took her seat on the sofa, and he said, "The twins heard Rhi talking about the two of you singing together, and they want a private show."

107

"Oh, those two are so flipping cute. I'll have to practice up on kids' songs."

"You'd do that for them?" Ripley shouldn't have expected any other reaction. He could already tell Glory had a good heart.

"Why not? I think it'd be fun, and if I can get them to sing along, all the better. Is it okay if I text Natalia and ask her what kind of stuff they'd like?"

Ripley reached over and lifted Glory from her spot, settling her on his lap. She let out a squeak, grinning. "Is this okay?" he asked.

Snaking her arms around his neck, she played with the hair at his nape. Ripley's beast rumbled low, and Glory narrowed her eyes. "You do that a lot."

"Do what?"

"Rumble. Growl. Something. It's like you have a big cat inside you. Not that I know what a big cat sounds like, but it's what I imagine a lion sounding like when it's ready to pounce."

"Yeah? And that doesn't scare you?" Ripley's heart sped up, afraid of her answer.

Glory tugged at his hair. "No. It's kind of sexy, to be honest."

Ripley's Gryphon rumbled again, this time louder, and Glory's eyes widened. "What the hell? How do you do that?"

"It's a little trick I learned a long time ago." Changing the subject to get her focus off his shifter, he said, "As for you texting Natalia, I think she'd love it. She'd do anything to make those boys happy, and if you can learn a few songs for them? She'll become your new best friend. I can get her number from Maveryck."

"Oh, I have it. Rory put a bunch of numbers in the phone she gave me, and Natalia's is one of them. So is yours. What did you tell Ryker about meeting up? I don't want to disappoint Rhi."

"If I tell them we're watching movies and would rather get together another night, I'm sure they'll understand."

"Then do that, please. I'm having fun."

Ripley was too. Just being around Glory was better than anything he'd done in so long. He kissed her on the nose, then returned her to the sofa, only he placed her next to him. He sent off a text asking for a raincheck, and when Ryker agreed, Ripley pushed play on the movie. Only this time, they watched it with his arm around his female and her leaning against his side, her text to Natalia forgotten.

# Chapter Nine

## Glory

GLORY WAS IN heaven. Surely, she was dreaming because here she was with this hot-as-sin biker who could have any woman he wanted. So, what was he doing with Glory? When Ripley pulled her onto his lap, she expected things to get hot and heavy, thinking that was what he wanted from her. But true to his word, he was a gentleman, returning her to the sofa before things got out of control. Sitting cuddled up was just as nice and probably wiser than jumping right into sex with someone she just met. Glory never expected to feel so comfortable around the biker, especially one with money. She had no idea how much he had, but he must do well for himself to have such a large home. And what a house it was. While he was getting the popcorn ready, Glory walked around, looking in every room, getting familiar with the layout. The den was her favorite next to the kitchen. She was itching to cook a meal for him in it. Speaking of which, her stomach rumbled, and Glory shoved her face into Ripley's bicep. When his arm shook, she looked up at him, scowling.

"Not funny."

His face shone with happiness as he grinned at her. "You're right. I'm being a terrible host allowing you to get hungry."

They had watched the first three movies, and Glory thoroughly enjoyed them. She didn't think they were crappy as Ripley put it, but they were the first movies she'd been able to watch, and that made them wonderful to her. "Want me to cook something?" she offered.

"Do you not trust me in the kitchen?" Ripley huffed.

"I don't know. Can you cook?" she teased.

"I'll have you know I'm an excellent cook. Come on, and I'll show you." Ripley stood, holding his hand out. Glory placed hers in his larger one, and instead of turning loose once she was on her feet, he kept them clasped as he led her out of the den. In the kitchen, he lifted her up and placed her on a stool at the island as though she weighed nothing. To someone like him with his bulging muscles, she probably didn't. "Is there anything you don't like?" he asked as he opened the refrigerator door.

"Deer and rabbit. I've had enough of both to last a lifetime." Glory placed her elbow on the island and cradled her chin on her palm. "At Haven, we had a lot of rice and beans. And oatmeal. Please never offer me oatmeal for breakfast. Not that we'll be having breakfast together that often." She was rambling, but instead of laughing at her, Ripley's face was serious.

"I don't blame you for not wanting the things you were made to eat all the time. When I was younger, my mother got on an Italian kick. She and my father visited the country, and when she returned, she tried her hand at every dish with noodles and red sauce she could think of. Don't get me wrong. I love Italian food, but when that's all you have, you long for something different. It took me years to get over it."

"You mentioned your parents are still in Florida. Do you see them often?"

"Not as much as I should, but I spoke to my mom last night, and she suggested we come for a visit soon. How about stir-fry? It's quick and easy." As Ripley pulled various items out of the fridge, it dawned on Glory what he said.

"Wait. We? As in you and me we?"

Ripley continued working on dinner and rocking her world at the same time. "Yes. I told her about rescuing you from Haven. I also mentioned that I'm interested in you, and she suggested a visit once we get to know one another well enough for a trip out of town."

"You're serious." Glory couldn't believe it. Why her?

Ripley placed the container of chicken on the counter, then turned and leaned over the island, grasping both her hands. "I am. I know this is fast, and if I need to slow down at any point, all you have to do is say so. But the moment I laid eyes on you at the market, something about you called to me."

Glory laughed. She couldn't help it. "Right. The thick girl in the too big, frumpy dress and a shiner on her face."

Ripley reached out and ran a finger gently down

her cheek. He assumed Rhi healed it since it was no longer bruised. "The dress and shiner were out of your control. As for being thick, I prefer that over skinny. I like it that you weren't afraid to eat pastries this morning. Or try a little of everything at Martina's. I don't want to hug you and feel your bones sticking out. That's not sexy in my book. I love the way you look, my nightingale." Ripley placed a kiss on the back of her hand before refocusing on the chicken.

Glory wanted to believe him. Chad had loved that she wasn't skinny, so maybe Ripley was one of those guys too. Ripley was dicing the chicken breasts when he paused, looking over his shoulder. "Your phone's ringing."

Glory strained her ears to hear her phone as she climbed off the stool and went back to the game room where she'd left it. When she saw it was Lynette, Glory hurried to answer it. "Hello?"

"Hey, Glory. Nothing's wrong, but I wanted to see how your day was going with Ripley."

"I'm sorry I didn't check in."

"Honey, it's fine. You aren't a prisoner here, but you're fresh out of Haven, and I tend to worry about all the residents."

"I'm good. We went to the bike shop, then we stopped by Martina's for lunch. Ripley brought me to his house to watch movies, and now he's cooking stir-fry. Is that okay?"

"Ripley is one of the best males I know, and I trust him with you as long as you're comfortable alone with him."

"I am. He's been a gentleman, but he's fun and

113

attentive." Glory walked to the farthest corner of the room and lowered her voice. "He said he was interested in me. Do you think he really is? Or is he just being nice? Helen said he welcomed her to Providence House too, and I don't want to make a fool of myself."

"Hang on a second." The sound of a door closing came through the line, then Lynette continued, "He's telling the truth. Rip told Branson so when they went out to the car to get the helmets for you to try on. As for Helen, I don't want to speak ill of her because she's been through a lot, but I think she mistook Rip's kindness for interest. He didn't bring her pastries the morning after she moved in. He didn't personally buy her clothes or a helmet, and he didn't take her to his house and cook for her."

"You don't think this is all too quick though?"

Lynette laughed. "Honey, remember what I told you about meeting Branson? When you know, you know, but if Ripley's moving too fast, just tell him so. He'll slow down."

"He said the same thing. I just... I can't believe someone like him could be interested in someone like me."

"Someone like you? You mean a gorgeous, insanely talented woman?"

"No, a plump woman with no clue as to what she's doing with her life."

"Do you think Branson shouldn't love me because I'm dyslexic and can't read well? It took me forever to learn how to cook because I couldn't read recipes. Instead of that turning him off, he was patient and read the recipes to me, and we learned to cook together. We all have our strengths and weaknesses. As for your weight, I happen to know Ripley prefers women your size over someone smaller."

"Yeah, he told me that too. I guess it's just hard to believe since the only men at Haven who were interested in me were older and not nearly as handsome as Ripley."

"Then the men at Haven were fools. You don't know me well, but I would never lie to you. Neither would Ripley. If you don't believe his words, trust his actions. He wouldn't have spent money on you if he wasn't interested. He definitely wouldn't have bought you a helmet within twenty-four hours of knowing you. If he wants you to ride with him, he's serious about getting to know you."

Glory blew her bangs off her face. "Okay. I'll give him the benefit of the doubt. I mean, he did watch the first three *Star Wars* movies with me even though he thinks they're crappy."

"Oh, he's not wrong there. They could have found a much better actor to play the older Anakin." Glory snorted, then covered her mouth even though Lynette couldn't see her. "Yeah, yeah. My geek is showing," Lynette said, laughing. "Since Ripley's cooking, I'll let you go. If I'm already in bed when you get back tonight, I'll talk to you more in the morning. Enjoy your evening."

"Thanks, Lynette."

"You're welcome, Honey." With that, Lynette disconnected.

When Glory got back to the kitchen, Ripley was leaning against the counter with a beer in his hand.

"Everything okay?"

"Yep. All good. Lynette was just checking in." Glory rounded the island and peered into the funny looking skillet.

"I hope you like it. I used teriyaki sauce. I normally serve it over rice, but you mentioned having lots of it at Haven, so I left that out." Ripley pushed off from the counter, set his bottle down, and scooped some food into a bowl. She waited until he had his own bowl. "We can eat in here, at the dining room table, or we can go back to the game room. Up to you."

"Let's sit in here." Glory rounded the island and climbed one of the stools. "As for the rice, it would have been fine since it was mixed in with everything else."

"I'll remember that for next time." Ripley placed his bowl down beside hers, then poured her a different soda from one of the many varieties. He then got them both forks and napkins before joining her.

Glory took a tentative bite, and nodded. "This is delicious." She bit into something crunchy that didn't have much taste. She dug around until she found another one and pointed to it with her fork. "What's the crunchy thing that looks like a sliced potato?"

"Water chestnuts. They don't have a lot of flavor, but I like the crunch, plus they're good for you."

"They don't look like a nut."

"They aren't despite their name. They're considered a tuber like potatoes, so you weren't far off. I usually put crunchy chow mein noodles on top, but I was out of those. I have a habit of eating them straight out of the can when I want a snack."

"I'll have to try them." Glory stuck her fork in the bowl and froze. "That looks like a little baby corn cob."

"That's because it is, but with it being a baby, you can eat the whole thing in one bite."

Glory had never seen such adorable food. She speared one with her fork and held it in front of her, studying it. "So cute." She shoved it in her mouth and chewed. Definitely something to add to her list of new foods she liked. When she caught Ripley staring at her, Glory ducked her eyes. How stupid she must sound.

"I'll be honest. I'm not a fan of regular corn on the cob. I hate the way it gets stuck in my teeth. But these baby corns? I like that I can eat them whole, plus, like you said, they're cute. Kind of like mini ice cream sandwiches." Either Ripley was being nice so Glory didn't feel like an idiot, or she'd found her soul mate.

After both their bowls were empty, Glory insisted on cleaning the kitchen. Instead of agreeing, Ripley helped. When the last dish was put away, he placed the drying towel over the handle on the stove, then turned to her. "I've thoroughly enjoyed our time together today. Did you have fun?"

Glory shoved her hands in her back pockets so she wouldn't do something stupid like grab Ripley and kiss him. "So much. Thank you for everything."

Ripley reached out, but before he touched her, his hand dropped to his side. "Let's get you back to Providence." He rounded the island and lifted her jacket from the back of the chair where she'd placed it upon entering the house. After Glory slid her arms in the sleeves, Ripley squeezed her shoulders briefly. They exited the house through a side door that led to the garage, which Glory found odd since Ripley had parked outside. A sharp motorcycle was parked on the far side, and Glory couldn't help but walk over and examine it.

"Now that you have a helmet, we can ride soon."

"I can't wait," she admitted. Glory had thought about sitting on the back of the Harley with her arms wrapped tightly around Ripley's waist, her chest snug against his back. She had thought a lot of other things too, but she wasn't going to throw herself at the man and look like a slut.

"I can't either. The weather is supposed to be nice the next few days, so we'll pick one and make a day of it." Ripley gestured toward the door leading outside, and once through, he led her down a stone path to where the Camaro sat. Once in the car, Ripley asked what Glory wanted to listen to. When she said she didn't care, he left it on the rock station. They made the ride back to Providence House without talking, but it wasn't awkward. Ripley took Glory's hand in his as soon as he was through the gate and didn't release it until they arrived. Instead of getting out right away, he shut the engine off and angled toward her.

"Thank you for today. I know you'll be finding your feet over the next few weeks, but I would like to spend as much time with you as you'll allow. I was serious when I said I want to get to know you, but it has to be at whatever speed you're ready for. You have my number, so whenever you'd like to get together again, whether it's to ride or watch movies, just give me a call or text. Tomorrow isn't too soon as far as I'm concerned, but if you need a day or two, I'll

118

understand."

Glory wanted to believe him. Lynette said he wouldn't lie to her, so until he gave her a reason to doubt him, she was going to trust his words. "I want to spend time with you too. Let me talk to Lynette and see if she needs anything from me tomorrow. I don't want to shirk my duties."

"You have no duties here, Sunshine. That's not how Providence is run. Sure, you need to keep your room clean and wash your clothes, things like that, but you staying here isn't dependent on how much you do. It's meant to be a safe place to land while you become acclimated to life outside the cult and figure out your next steps."

"I get that, but I don't want to sit on my ass and do nothing to repay the kindness everyone is showing me either."

"You are something else, you know that?" Glory lowered her gaze, but Ripley placed a finger under her chin. "Don't forget we gave Ryker and Rhi a raincheck, plus you need to call Natalia. I can't wait to hear you play for the twins."

"You'll be with me?" Glory wanted Ripley with her wherever she went, especially as she got to know the other women. Natalia was nice but also a little scary.

"If you'll have me. I was serious about spending as much time with you as possible."

Glory leaned over the console, and Ripley met her halfway. She reached up and placed a hand on his whiskered cheek as he slanted their lips together. He kept it chaste until Glory touched her tongue to his mouth, then Ripley opened for her, and when their tongues swirled, Glory's body came alive. It had been six years since she'd been kissed. Touched. Wanted. If Ripley could cause a fire in her core from kissing, she couldn't wait to see what he could do with his hands or his cock. Ripley broke the kiss but pressed his forehead to hers.

"I need to walk you to the door now." Ripley didn't hide adjusting himself in his jeans, and Glory appreciated it. It was nice to know the effect she had on him. She waited for him to come around and open her door. As they headed toward the steps, he kept her hand in his. Just as they reached the top step, the door opened, and Julia stuck her head out. She glanced at their joined hands, then closed the door without saying anything.

Glory forgot about the other woman's weirdness when Ripley turned her to face him. He lifted both her hands and pressed his lips to her knuckles. "I'll be waiting for your call."

"You won't have to wait long, I promise. Thanks again for a wonderful day."

"You're welcome. I'll see you soon." Ripley didn't move off the porch, so Glory let herself in, waving before she closed the door. After locking the knob as well as the deadbolt, Glory turned and leaned against the wood. She would have remained there, reliving her day with Ripley, but Julia was peeking around the corner from the hall.

"Hey there. Were you waiting up for me?" Glory pushed off the door and walked across the room.

"Uh, no. Not really. My room is at the front of the

house, and Ripley's car is loud. I heard you pull up." Julia turned and ran up the stairs without further explanation. Voices from the kitchen had Glory heading that way. Lynette and Branson were sitting at the island eating ice cream, and Helen was standing across from them with an apple in her hand.

"Welcome back," Lynette said. "Did you have a good day?"

Glory wanted to gush over how wonderful it had been, but she didn't want to do so in front of Helen. "I got to meet Martina. Patrick is a doll, and I'm a big fan of Mexican food. You know, other than fast-food tacos. And did you know you can cook popcorn on the stove instead of microwaving it? One minute there's all these kernels, then you shake it, and soon, there's fluffy white stuff popping all over the place."

Lynette grinned around a bit of ice cream. "What else did you get to eat?"

Glory tugged off her leather jacket, hugging it to her chest. "Stir-fry but without rice. I mentioned having a lot of it at Haven, so Ripley didn't add it to our supper."

"You ate all that after having pastries for breakfast?" Helen asked. Someone – Glory thought it was Branson – growled, and Helen's eyes widened. "I didn't mean that in a bad way. I just don't want Glory's stomach to get upset. If Haven is anything like Sanctuary, she's not used to eating foods that are sweet, rich, or spicy. I've been away from Sanctuary for months, and I'm still getting used to eating things that aren't bland."

Glory didn't know if the other woman was telling

121

the truth or covering her ass, so Glory gave her a pass. "I appreciate your concern, Helen. And you're right. I'll probably pay for indulging tomorrow, but I was too excited to pass any of it up. Being able to try new things, food I wasn't allowed to have even before I was taken to Haven, was a treat."

"Nothing wrong with that," Branson said. "Before I forget, Sutton called earlier. Since you were spending the day with Ripper, he and Rory will come by tomorrow to talk to you about Haven."

"Crap. I totally forgot. Is he mad at me?"

"Not at all. He was glad you were out having fun already."

"That's good. Speaking of fun, I need to go call Natalia. It seems the twins want me to sing for them."

Lynette squealed. "Yes! Make sure you do that here so I can see the little buggers."

"Twins?" Helen asked.

"Yes. You haven't met them, but one of Rory and Sutton's sons has twin boys, Major and Marshall. Natalia is their mom."

"Gah, they are so flipping cute with their goggles and little helmets," Glory added.

"Wow. You've been out of Haven a day and are already making new friends. That's great," Helen said, sounding sincere.

Again, Glory didn't want to rub it in, so she played it off. "I just got lucky they were there when Natalia rescued me." Glory wanted another soda, but she'd already had several that day, so she opted for a glass of water. After helping herself, she said, "If you'll excuse me, I'm going to go call her." Helen was right about

122

Glory making friends, and it had her smiling as she walked upstairs to her bedroom. Closing the door, she walked to her closet and hung up her jacket, making sure to face it the same way her clothes were. Then she untied her boots and toed them off, placing them neatly beside her sneakers. Her hoodie smelled like Ripley, so she kept it on. Plopping down on the bed, Glory stacked the pillows against the headboard and leaned against them before pulling up Natalia's number. The petite woman scared Glory, but still, she found herself wanting to be more like Natalia. Spunky. Fearless.

"Lolly's phone," a cute little voice answered.

"Hello. Is this Major or Marshall?" she asked.

"Major. Who is this?"

"This is Glory. Do you remember me?"

"Yep. You're Ripper's mate. Uh oh." There were muffled sounds of the phone hitting something, then shouting, both from Natalia yelling at her son and him yelling back. Glory couldn't make out the words Major said, but Natalia was laughing when she picked up the phone.

"Glory?"

"Hey, did I catch you at a bad time?"

"No. That's just Major being Major. How are you? Did you have a good day with Ripley?"

"I'm good, and yes I did." Glory told Natalia of all they had done that day, only leaving out the kiss. That was something Glory wanted to keep for herself.

"I'm glad to hear the two of you are getting along. Ripley's a good man."

"So I hear. What did Major mean when he called

me Ripley's mate?"

Natalia covered the phone with her hand and said something to someone else in the room that Glory couldn't make out. "Oh, that you're his girlfriend. He's five, so he doesn't understand these things take time. Unless you've already decided to give him a chance?"

"Isn't it a little soon for that? I just met the man." What was it with everyone trying to get them together so quickly? Glory wasn't opposed to dating Ripley, but as he spent time with her, he would probably figure out she wasn't nearly good enough for him.

"Not really. Sometimes the spark is there from the moment you see someone, whether at a stall at a market or on a crowded sidewalk. Rip took one look at you and was moving. Ace had to hold him back from stalking to the booth and giving William an ass-kicking or throwing you over his shoulder and stealing away with you."

Glory giggled at the thought of both. "Now that I'd like to see. Him kicking William's ass, not him throwing me over his shoulder. That'd throw his back out."

"Okay, Missy. For one thing, Ripley's strong. Like super strong. And two, you are perfect the way you are, so none of that nonsense."

"Says the woman who probably weighs a hundred pounds soaking wet," Glory scoffed.

"Yeah, and you know what? I would give anything to not look like a boy. What is the saying about green grass and a fence?" Natalia asked, her accent getting heavier.

Glory sighed and rubbed her eyes. "The grass is

always greener on the other side of the fence, and I guess it is. I'm sorry, Natalia. Society has tried to make women think if they carry extra pounds, they aren't desirable."

"And that's bullshit. Just look at all the pin-ups from the mid-1900s. They had curves. Anyway, let us talk about something more pleasant like your voice. Rhi said you can sing like those pop stars on the radio. Can you play kids' songs?"

"I can after I learn them. I just need to know what kind of movies or TV shows the twins like so I can find appropriate songs."

Natalia rattled off several names, and when Glory started getting overwhelmed trying to remember them, Natalia said she would text the list to her. They also spoke about getting together with Natalia's sisters-in-law for a girls' day out. Glory didn't know why they were being so nice, but she also didn't care. It had been years since she had a friend to talk to. To confide in. She'd had her cabin mates, but Glory hadn't trusted them enough to speak her mind. She would love to reunite with Sheri, but until then, she would gladly accept Natalia, Rhi, Lynette, and whoever else decided they wanted Glory to be part of their circle.

# CHAPTER TEN

## Ripley

TAKING GLORY BACK to Providence and leaving her was one of the hardest things Ripley had done in many years. Kissing her had been both wonderful and torturous. Ripley wanted to take her back home and spend all night burying his dick in her softness. Hearing she had given herself to her boyfriend was difficult to listen to, but it would be hypocritical to get mad about it. Not only did he want to make love to her, he also wanted to hold her. Spend hours talking. Waking up together. Making breakfast together. Watching more movies. After spending the day in her presence, he was just as convinced as his Gryphon she belonged to them. Then again, he'd thought the same thing about Sara Beth. No. He needed to spend more time with Glory before planning their future. Instead of driving home, he made his way to Ace's house. His buddy arched a brow when he opened the door.

"You okay?"

"Yeah. Sorry for just showing up."

Ace tugged Ripley inside, closing the door behind him. "Come on. Let's grab a drink, and you can tell me what's on your mind." Ace led the way to the den at the back of his house. The French doors were open, allowing the cool night air to blow inside. Ace grabbed a bottle of tequila for himself, and Ripley opted for whiskey. He poured his own drink in a rocks glass, forgoing ice. Ace didn't bother with a glass. He took the clear liquor to the sofa and sank down, tipping the bottle back and swallowing a hefty drink. When Ripley was seated in one of the oversized armchairs, he took a sip of the expensive whiskey.

"Is this about Glory?" Ace asked when Ripley didn't say anything.

"Yes. We spent all day together."

"And? Brother, don't make me pull it out of you."

Ripley leaned his forearms on his thighs, letting the glass dangle between them. "We had a great time. Glory's sweet. You should have seen her with Patrick. He latched onto her and wouldn't even go to Tank when he reached for his son. She's funny, and she's talented as fuck." Ripley told Ace about Glory playing piano and singing that morning. Then he filled Ace in on the rest of their day watching movies and eating supper together. "My Gryphon is convinced she's our mate."

"But you're letting what happened with Sara Beth throw doubt, right?"

"How can I not?"

"I get it, but it's been twenty years. Maybe this is why it didn't work out between the two of you because Zeus knew there was someone else out there who would be better suited for you."

"Maybe."

"You know what I would do? I would show her your Gryphon sooner than later. Don't wait for three years to pass like you did before. Don't get your heart any more involved than it already is. You can always wipe her memory afterward, but at least you'll know if she's going to accept you for what you really are."

Ripley had already thought of that, but fear kept him from letting his beast loose. "You're right."

"But you're scared. Have you thought of letting Rhi talk to her? Maybe have Ryker show his Gryphon with his mate there as a buffer. Or Sutton and Rory. Hell, any of the mated Hounds would be willing to help."

Ripley raised the glass to his lips and tossed back the liquor. "That's not a bad idea, except I'd have to tell them what happened with Sara Beth."

"And you don't want to share that, but Brother, no one is going to think less of you for what happened."

"I told Ryker about Sara Beth while we were waiting on Glory at the salon. Then earlier today, I told Branson. He could tell I was interested in Glory, and he followed me outside so we could talk. They both took it well, so you're probably right."

"Say that again," Ace joked.

Ripley rolled his eyes as he stood and walked over to the bar, pouring more whiskey in his glass. He studied the amber liquid, thinking about asking for help.

Ace waited until Ripley looked up and said, "Playing devil's advocate here. She's been locked in that hell hole for how long?"

"Six years."

"Six years of living in a cult. And how old was she when she went in?"

"Eighteen."

"Are you sure Glory wants to spend time with you personally, or is she latching on because she's got her first taste of freedom, and you're the one who followed her around the mall, buying her nice things? What if I had been the one to see her first? Would it be me she wanted to spend her time with?"

Ripley's Lion pushed forward, his fangs dropping and his bushy mane circling his head. Ace's eyes widened, and he held his hand up.

Ripley shook his head and tamped down his animal. "Sorry."

"That lets me know how serious your beast is. But the question still stands."

"I know you make a valid point, but am I supposed to step back and allow her to date other men? See if she wants someone else who won't be worthy of her? Find the guy she was in love with in high school and put them in each other's path to see if there's still a spark? I don't think I can do that."

Ace took a swig of tequila, then wiped his mouth with the back of his hand. "She already told you about her past?"

"Yes. I asked if she wanted to find her old boyfriend, and she said no. She wasn't in love with him any longer. I also told her about Sara Beth. I didn't want her to find out from someone else I also had a first love."

"At least that's out of the way. Maybe give her time to become acclimated to living outside the cult.

129

Figure out what she wants to do with her life, but don't wait too long to show her the real you."

"I already told her we'd go at her pace, but I want to be the one to help her get acclimated. To figure out what she wants. Fuck." Ripley closed his eyes and scrubbed at his beard. That didn't help because all he could envision was Glory as she laughed at little Patrick, or her smile as she watched a movie for the first time, or the way her face lit up in glee upon seeing baby corn.

"You're picturing her, aren't you?" Ace asked.

Ripley's eyes popped open. Ace had his head tilted, studying Rip. "Yeah, I was. She's just..."

"I think I get it now. You're acting like Spyder did when he found Charlotte."

"Like a maniac?" Rip grinned remembering how Jude "Spyder" Sterling took one look at his pretty florist and it was game over. Rip and Ace hadn't been at the BDSM club when the couple met, but Jude recounted their meeting when he asked Rip and Ace to watch over Charlotte's floral shop after it had been broken into.

"If you think she's your mate, you should do everything in your power to win her over." Ace tossed back another shot of Casamigos Blanco. "I know it's what I'd do if I were in your situation."

For as long as Ripley had known Ace, they'd never discussed his past. Ace didn't date. He didn't have hookups as far as Rip knew. He also never mentioned wanting to find a mate. "You know, you and I have been friends a long time, yet you never talk about mates or even dating." Ace blanched, and Ripley found himself backtracking. "Not that I'm asking. It's none of my business."

Ace sighed, staring at Ripley. There was so much sadness behind his normally bright eyes. "It's not that I don't trust you because I do. Fuck, Rip, you're my best friend. I just..." Ace sighed again and leaned his head back. Ripley gave his fellow Hound time to decide whether or not he wanted to talk about it. Whatever *it* was. Keeping his gaze averted, Ace said, "When I was younger, I thought there was something wrong with me. Something broken. While everyone else my age was figuring out their sexuality, you know, if they were drawn to girls or other guys, I felt nothing for either sex. This went on for years, and I resigned myself to being alone. It wasn't until I was in my twenties that I met someone, but we were only friends. The more time I spent with them, the deeper my feelings became. That was the first time in my life I felt like I wasn't broken. When I mentioned this to them, they said I was more than likely demisexual. I went home that night and did a little research on the term. It fit me to a tee. I need to feel a deep emotional bond before my libido kicks in. The short of it is they didn't feel anything but friendship, so nothing came of it. They took a job out of state, but we kept in touch over the years. I was grateful to them for helping me figure my shit out, and even if they didn't return my romantic feelings, they were a good friend."

Rip didn't miss the fact that Ace was using they instead of him or her. Not that he cared. Ripley felt love was love. He wanted his friend to find happiness with whomever he could. "And you haven't felt that with anyone since then?"

"Several times. But it always ends the same. While I'm taking my time getting to know them, they're looking for someone with that instant spark. Someone who doesn't need weeks or even months to want to have sex."

"I'm sorry, Brother. That can't be easy."

"It's not, but it is what it is." Ace stood and walked to the bar, recapping the tequila. Ripley felt that was his cue to let his friend have some space. He downed the rest of his whiskey and took the glass to the small sink at the bar, washing it, then putting it away.

Rip pulled Ace into his chest for a hug. "Thanks for listening."

"You too. I didn't mean to get all maudlin on you."

Ripley leaned back, leaving his hands on Ace's shoulders. "That's what friends are for. To listen to the good and the bad." Rip squeezed his friend before stepping back. "Wings and beer soon?"

"Sounds good."

Ripley left Ace standing in his den and made his way outside to his car. His heart was heavy for his friend but lighter having told him about his day with Glory. What Ace said about Glory latching onto him was in the back of his mind as he drove home, but his beast wasn't having it. More than once it roared inside his head, making it hard to concentrate on the road.

*I'm not giving up, so you can stop with the theatrics.*

**Good because she is ours.**

Ripley hoped so. Instead of staying up and giving into his wayward thoughts, he got ready for bed. The sooner he went to sleep, the sooner the next day would be there, and hopefully Glory would call or text.

## Glory

USED TO GETTING up early, Glory rolled out of bed before the sun was up. She opened her bedroom door but didn't hear anyone else stirring, so she decided to go ahead and shower. Wiping the steam from the mirror while she dried off, she studied her appearance. After speaking with Natalia, Glory had called Rhi to apologize for not getting together the night before. Rhi said there was nothing to be sorry about. She mentioned getting together soon with some of the others, and that's when Glory asked if Rhi would help her shop for makeup. Rhi told her about the place the others had taken her for a makeover. The lady who helped Rhi would show her the best colors for her skin tone. Glory brushed her teeth, thinking back on their conversation.

"Oh, that's too much. If you'll take me to the drugstore, that'll be good enough."

"Nonsense. If this is about money, don't worry about it. It'll be my birthday gift to you," Rhi said.

"You don't even know when my birthday is," Glory countered.

Rhi laughed. "You're right, I don't. When is it?"

"February tenth, so you'll need to wait a while before

*using that excuse."* Glory didn't mention Ripley had used the same excuse.

*"Or I can say it's a belated gift. Seriously, though. I get it. I felt the same way when the others took me out and showered me with gifts. Let us do this for you, Glory."*

*"Okay, thank you."*

Glory needed to get through the morning with Sutton, then she could focus on spending the afternoon with Rhiannon. Sutton already knew a lot about Haven from Rhi, and Glory had added to it when she first met Ryker's parents, but he felt Glory might know something else to help in their search for Josiah. Choosing one of the T-shirts Ripley bought her, she tugged it on with a new pair of jeans and thick socks. No matter the time of year, her feet were always cold. When she reached the kitchen, Julia was there pouring a cup of coffee.

"Good morning." Julia jumped, coffee sloshing over the side of her mug. "Sorry, didn't mean to startle you." Glory snagged some paper towels to sop up the mess on the counter.

"You don't need to clean up after me." Julia took the napkins and tossed them in the garbage.

"I do if it's my fault you spilled your coffee." Glory found a mug and poured her own drink. As she got the milk out of the refrigerator, she asked, "How was church?" Glory had loved coffee the few times she tried it before Haven, and having it again was a treat.

"Oh, uh, it was fine. Different," Julia said softly.

"I'm sure, if Sanctuary was anything like Haven with all the doom and gloom. It was a shock even for me."

"You went to church before?" Julia sat at the island, cradling her cup between her hands, staring out the back window.

"All the time. My parents are super religious. I remember the church we attended when I was younger was more about Jesus's love and light than the wrath of God, then when I was about twelve or thirteen, my father moved us to a different congregation that was more the Hellfire and brimstone type with a little Jesus thrown in. Haven was all about the Old Testament. I got tossed in solitary more than once for questioning why they didn't focus on the New Testament since that's supposedly where we find our way into Heaven. Now that I know they're more about world domination than saving souls, it made sense."

"What do you mean?"

"Men like Josiah and his brother Gideon don't lead by example. Not when they're kidnapping women and raising armies," Lynette said as she entered the room. "Sorry to interrupt your conversation."

"How do you know that since you were never there?" Julia asked.

"I've helped enough people who've escaped The Ministry. I've heard their stories. Learned what really goes on behind those walls. Became friends with women who were kidnapped and treated less than."

Julia narrowed her eyes at Lynette. "Are you talking about Rhiannon?"

"And Kerrigan and McKenzie among others."

Glory studied the other woman. It felt as though she wasn't happy to be at Providence for some reason. When Julia met her gaze, Glory looked away. With a rumbling stomach, she decided to focus on breakfast instead of whatever was going on with her housemate. "Pancakes, anyone?"

"I could go for some pancakes," Branson called from somewhere in the house. That was the second time he'd answered without being in the room.

"Ignore him," Lynette said, laughing.

A menacing growl startled Glory as Branson rushed across the kitchen. "Don't listen to her." Branson scooped his wife up, blowing raspberries on her neck.

Lynette smacked at the big man, but there was no force behind it. "Put me down, you big oaf." Branson set his wife on her feet, but he kissed her soundly before turning her loose. Julia slid off the stool, taking her coffee with her.

"Was it something I said?" Branson whispered, and this time, Lynette hit him hard on the stomach.

"Behave. You know she isn't used to PDA."

"She should be after all this time. Besides, we aren't in public, and there is nothing wrong with me showing my mate affection in our own home." Branson crossed his arms, pouting. It shouldn't look adorable on such a big man, but it did, and Glory couldn't help but laugh.

When he scowled at her, she rolled her eyes. "So, pancakes?"

Branson unfolded himself, his pout all gone. "Yes, please." He poured a cup of coffee and handed it to Lynette before fixing his own. "I'm going to wait out front for Sutton."

Glory gathered the items she needed for pancakes

and bacon. When she had the meat in the skillet, she asked, "How long have Julia and Helen been here?"

Lynette leaned against the counter, cradling her cup. "It's been a little over a year now."

Glory cracked an egg into the mix. "Is that normal?"

"Each person is different. A lot of it depends on when they joined the cult or were taken there. Those like you, who know what life is like in the real world, have an easier time adjusting to being on the outside. We've had several who came in at the same time as Julia and Helen and have already moved on. Some had family they returned to, and some decided to move in together once they were ready to branch out. Then you have those like Julia, where life inside the cult is all they've known, and it takes them longer to adjust. Not only does she have no life skills, but her education is lacking. You had the advantage of getting most of your education out of the way. You can easily take your test and receive a diploma."

"Ripley mentioned that, and I do want to take the test after I study a bit. Didn't Helen say she was in college before going to Sanctuary?" Glory finished stirring the mix, then plugged the griddle in. "If it's none of my business, just say so."

Lynette lowered her voice. "She did, and now she's taking a few classes while she figures out what area she wants to focus on. She also has a part-time job as an administrative assistant, so she is moving forward. We've been working with her on the life skills her parents failed to teach her so she doesn't fall into the same trap as before. Until she's ready, Helen has a place here as long as she needs it. Same as you, though I doubt you'll be with us too long."

Glory flipped the bacon, then tested the griddle to see if it was hot enough. "Right because I have my shi– uh, stuff together."

"You do have your shit together. It takes most residents weeks if not months before they're ready to leave the house with someone who isn't Rory or myself." A booming laugh interrupted their conversation as Branson returned with Sutton and Rory in tow.

"Good morning," Rory said, coming around to stand by Glory. "How was your first day?"

"It was fine." Glory concentrated on the pancakes so Rory couldn't see her face.

"Just fine? I'll have to talk to Ripley about that."

"What? N-no, you don't need to do that," she stammered.

Rory leaned close. "So it was better than fine?"

Glory looked at the other woman, but the fact that she didn't look that much older than everyone else was still mind-boggling. "So much better," Glory whispered. When Rory raised her eyebrows, Glory shook her head. "Not *that* much better, just, you know, better." Glory looked at the ceiling. "God, take me now."

Rory hugged Glory's shoulder, laughing softly. "I'm sorry. I shouldn't have put you on the spot like that. Ripley's one of the good ones, and I'm sure he treated you well."

Glory didn't want to elaborate on how well he treated her, so she asked, "Pancakes?"

# CHAPTER ELEVEN

## Glory

RORY AND SUTTON waved off breakfast, having already eaten before they arrived, though they did have a cup of coffee while everyone else ate. Helen had to work that morning, so she declined, stating she didn't have time. It surprised Glory when Julia joined them. She didn't say anything unless asked a direct question, but Glory chalked that up to her shyness. Talk was kept to mundane things for which Glory was glad. She didn't want to discuss Ripley in front of the men. After everyone finished eating, Sutton suggested taking things to Branson's office to speak to Glory, and Lynette offered to clean the kitchen.

Glory drew the layout of Haven for Sutton and elaborated on the things Rhi had told them. Even though the other woman had been at Haven longer than Glory, she didn't have as much knowledge of the compound's layout. Then again, Rhi hadn't been allowed outside much. Now that Glory knew about Rhi's gift and affinity for nature, she couldn't imagine how hard that must have been. After sketching a rough drawing, Glory shared things like how many men secured the perimeter as well as how many went hunting and when.

Sutton pulled the drawing closer. "What about—" He snapped his head to the side, looking toward the door. Branson and Rory also stiffened, and Rory held up a hand as she rose, then padded on silent feet toward the door. She turned the knob and pulled the door open enough to stick her head out. She shook her head as she shut it, returning to her seat without saying if there was someone in the hallway. Glory studied everyone in the room. How had the three of them heard someone when she hadn't? It was like when Branson called out from other rooms in the house. Lynette joked about his exceptional hearing. Maybe that explained his ability, but Sutton and Rory too? Something was strange about the situation, and—

"Thank you for your time, Glory. This is helpful," Sutton said.

"Glad to help." And she meant it. She wanted those responsible for hurting Rhiannon to be caught.

"What are your plans the rest of the day?" Rory asked after Sutton and Branson left them alone.

"Rhi is taking me shopping for makeup. I also need to figure out a job so I'll have my own money."

"I promise you don't need to worry about that right now. Have you given any thought to taking the education equivalency? Or if you want to go to college after you have it?"

"I do want to take the test, and Ripley said he would help me study for it. I haven't thought further than that. I would like to do something pertaining to music, but I have no idea what. Ryker mentioned me going on the road, but I'm sure he was joking."

140

Rory hooked her arm through Glory's and led her from the office to what Glory now thought of as the music room. "Would you do me the honor of playing a song? I'd like to hear your talent for myself."

"I'd love to." As before, when Glory began singing, everyone else joined them. It was a good thing Glory didn't get nervous playing for others. She never had. It was the one area where she shined, and it made her feel special to share her talent.

"Do you know 'Kiss From a Rose'?" Sutton asked.

"No, but I'll learn it for you." Glory pulled her phone from her pocket. She opened the search engine and hit play on the first version she found. "This one?"

"Yes. But you —"

"Sutton, hang on a second," Lynette said. Glory was grateful, because she needed to listen. Musical arrangements were tricky because often the melody of the lyrics was different than the background notes. This one was easier than most. She replayed the tune three times, and on the third, she played along with it.

"Okay, I think I have it." Glory searched for the lyrics, and when she had them in front of her, she sang the "ba-da-das" acapella, then played the song to the best of her ability only stumbling over the lyrics a few times as Lynette scrolled the screen up for her.

When she was finished, Sutton said, "Holy Zeus." Turning to Branson, he said, "You told me she was good, but that's beyond incredible." He faced Glory again. "You have a gift, young lady. One that needs to be shared with the world."

"*If* that's what you want," Rory added.

"Yes, if it's what you want. But if you do? We'll

help to make that happen," Sutton said.

"Thank you both. It would be a dream come true, but I have no idea how to begin." Glory's stomach was jittery thinking about making music for a living. She wasn't kidding about it being a dream come true because before now, it had been just that – a dream. Before Haven, her only goal had been to get away from home with Chad. They had talked about moving to Nashville after he'd saved enough money from his construction job. "Ripley mentioned getting in touch with some rock star he knows of and asking how to get started."

"He was probably talking about Desi," Rory said. "If anyone knows about the music industry, it's the lead singer for one of the biggest bands in the world."

"Why would he help someone like me?"

Rory brushed Glory's hair away from her forehead. "Lucy and her husband, Tamian, are friends with Desi and his family. Like the Hounds, Tamian's family is large and close-knit. Lucy is one of them, just like you're one of us."

Glory's eyes filled with tears. "That doesn't make sense. You just met me," she whispered.

Rory cupped Glory's cheek. "That is true, but Ripley has claimed you. Even if he hadn't, everyone in this room already considers you one of our own. We're your family now."

Glory threw her arms around Rory, and Rory hugged her tightly. It was too good to be true. All she had ever wanted was to be part of a normal family. One where love was freely given. Where kind words were spoken and hugs were offered just because. Soon, she was bracketed from all sides in the best group hug ever. The only way it would have been better was if Ripley was part of it. Thinking of the man, she had promised to call or text him.

"I need to call Ripley," she blurted.

Everyone except Rory stepped away. "I expect an invite when you play for the twins."

"And I expect a front row seat to your first concert," Sutton said, adding a wink.

Glory bounced on her toes. "Deal."

## *Ripley*

THE FARTHER FROM New Troy Rip got, the more his beast raged. Glory hadn't texted or called that morning, so he decided a little two-wheeled therapy would do him some good. It would have if his Gryphon would calm the fuck down. When he reached out to Ace earlier and asked if he wanted to join Rip, his best friend readily agreed. It wasn't unusual for the pair to head north to the Canadian border, stopping to eat, then returning, making a day of it. If Ripley wasn't afraid Glory would call, he would have been all for it. Since he was, he kept them closer to home. When they stopped for an early lunch across the Massachusetts state line, they'd only been riding an hour.

While they ate, Ace grilled Ripley about Glory's life. He shared the parts he didn't feel were too personal, like how her father caught her with Chad. Ripley didn't want to think about Glory with another male, even if it was six years ago.

Ace stood from the picnic table and gathered their trash. After tossing it in the bin, he suggested Rip text Glory as he retook his seat.

"I left the ball in her court."

"Doesn't mean you can't let her know you're thinking about her."

Ripley didn't want to pressure his female, but sending her a "how are you?" text wouldn't hurt. Before he could pull his phone from his back pocket, it vibrated with an incoming call. When he saw Glory's name, he couldn't help but grin. "It's her."

"Well answer it, dumbass," Ace chided when Ripley let it continue to ring.

"Fuck." He tapped the screen and put the phone to his ear. "Hello, Sunshine."

"Rip. Uh, hi. How are you?"

"I'm better now. How are you?"

"Good. Really good. I met with Sutton and Rory, and we talked more about Haven. Then I played for them. Sutton offered to help with my music."

Ripley's beast growled, and Ace pointed at him and mouthed, "*Be nice.*"

"That was kind of him," Ripley managed to say without too much anger.

"It was, but he mentioned talking to Desi too. Since that was what you suggested, I'd rather you make the call."

144

Ace smirked, and Rip shot his best friend a bird. "Does that mean you've decided to move forward with a music career?"

"Well, I'd like to talk to you about that. Can, uh, we maybe get together?"

Ripley hated how nervous Glory sounded. "I'd love that. Ace and I took the bikes out for a short ride, so I'll be back home in about an hour. How about I pick you up and you can try out your new helmet? It's a gorgeous day for riding."

"Oh, uh, Rhi, Natalia, and Sadie are taking me shopping, but I can call and cancel."

As much as Ripley wanted to tell Glory to do so, she needed time with the other mates too. "No, don't do that. You and I can always ride after you get back or tomorrow if it's too late today. This is probably a stupid question, but is Ryot going with you?"

Glory snickered, and Ripley smiled, imagining her adorable face. "Yes. According to Rhi, he won't let her out of his sight other than to pee, and even then, he's hovering by the door."

"I can't say I blame him. Anyway, why don't you call me when you're done shopping?"

"I can do that."

"Then I'll see you soon." After saying goodbye, he thumbed his phone off and sighed. "What the fuck am I doing?"

Ace stood and gripped Ripley's shoulder. "You're letting yourself be happy for the first time in twenty years, my friend. Instead of you sitting here doubting yourself, let's head back. Maybe take the long way since you have a while before picking Glory up?"

145

Ripley wanted to be happy, but how did he trust his heart not to be shredded again? Then he thought about Ryker and Warryck. Both males had lost females tragically, yet they had opened their hearts again and found their mates. If what Rip's beast felt was solid, they could also have that kind of love with Glory.

*Wouldn't it be better to find out I am right than miss out on the love of our life?*

His Gryphon had a point. If he didn't give Glory a chance, he could be missing out on the greatest gift of all. And if it didn't work out? He had many centuries ahead of him to get over it.

Before he and Ace were loaded up, Rip's phone rang again. "Bishop?"

"Hey, Rip. I wanted to give you a heads up. I've already alerted Sutton, but he told me to call you. Some of Haven's men were caught on camera sniffing around New Troy. One of them was Amos Yearwood, Glory's father."

"Fuck. Send me photos, descriptions, vehicles, everything you have. I need to call Glory and warn her to stay at Providence House for the time being."

"Sutton was there when I called, and he said he'd talk to Glory."

"Ace and I are out for a ride, but once we look at the intel you have, we'll head back that way."

"It's coming through now."

"Excellent. Did you already send off for Glory's birth certificate?"

"Yeah. Rhi mentioned changing her name, but she said for now to order the original."

"Perfect. When she changes her name, I'll put the

paperwork through."

"Sounds good. Ride safe." Bishop disconnected. Ripley didn't have to tell Ace what was said. With his Gryphon senses, he heard both sides of the conversation. They waited the few minutes for Bishop to send what he had before heading back home. The photos showed four men. One of them was that bastard William. Two were dressed in all black, so Ripley assumed they were guards. The fourth was an older man, who had to be Glory's father. He was the one Ripley studied the most, committing every detail to memory so he could get revenge on Glory's behalf for the bruise on her sweet face.

After looking at the photos, Rip and Ace hit the road and headed directly to the area in town the men had been seen. New Troy wasn't a large town, but they still split up to cover the area quicker. After searching for an hour, they hadn't seen any of the men. Rip's phone buzzed, and he figured it was Ace. After pulling over at a convenience store, he pulled his phone out and saw a missed call from Havyk. When he listened to the voicemail, his blood ran cold.

*"We just had a visit from some Haven bastards at the clubhouse. One of them was that William fucker, and one was Glory's father. They demanded Glory be turned over to them, and I told them to get bent after I assured them I had no idea what they were talking about. I couldn't voice them because I had customers in the shop. When they finally left, I had Legend follow to make sure they left town."*

"Fuck." Rip sent Ace a text relaying Havyk's message. While he waited on Ace, Rip called Glory to check on her.

"Hello?"

"Glory, hey. I just wanted to make sure you're okay."

"Yeah, uh. Hang on a second." Glory told someone she was going to her room. Rip waited patiently as she jogged up the steps. Rip could picture the sway of her hips in his mind. "Okay, I'm back. Sorry about that."

"No need to apologize. Are you okay?"

Glory blew out a breath. "I guess? Sutton said my father can't make me go back, but I don't want to cause trouble, you know? Maybe I should agree to meet him and tell him I ran away on my own. That way he and Brother Thomas won't call the authorities and say I was kidnapped."

"They won't call the cops. Haven doesn't want any more scrutiny than they already have with the FBI watching."

"The FBI? What the hell? How did I not know about that?" Glory huffed.

"It's a long story, but when Ryker was protecting Rhi, he managed to alert the FBI there were crates of guns at Haven." Rip couldn't tell Glory the whole story because it involved Ryot using his Gryphon voice on some of Haven's men.

"So that's why the guards stopped patrolling and went back to wearing regular clothes for a while. But if the FBI is watching, why aren't they being more careful?"

"That's a very good question. Maybe Haven has someone on the inside. It wouldn't be the first time an agency has been paid off."

"I don't want to put Providence House in jeopardy.

Maybe I should leave," Glory muttered.

Ripley knew it was too soon to ask, but getting Glory away from New Troy wasn't a bad idea. "I have a proposition for you. Remember I said my mom asked that we visit once we'd spent some time together, but how would you feel about a road trip to the beach until things settle down in New York?"

"Are you serious? I... Uh, I'd love to go to the beach, but I'm not so sure about meeting your parents."

"Glory, I promise they're going to love you. As for the ocean, I want us to spend a day there, swimming and enjoying the sunshine."

"I don't know how to swim, but enjoying the sun would be nice." Glory paused, and Ripley held his breath while she decided. "You know what? Let's do it. If me leaving takes the heat off the Hounds, then why not?"

Ripley hoped she wanted to go so they could spend time together, but at least she'd agreed.

"It's a nineteen-hour drive, but we can take our time and stop anywhere along the way you'd like if there's somewhere new you want to visit."

"When are we leaving? I'll need to pack. Oh, I don't have a suitcase."

"I'm sure Lynette has one you can borrow. If not, I'll loan you one of mine. As for when, I think the sooner the better. I'll go home and pack, then come get you. Send me a text if you need a suitcase."

"Sounds good. I'm going to talk to Lynette now."

"Okay, Sunshine. See you soon." Ripley leaned over his handlebars after disconnecting and blew out a

149

breath. A road trip to see his parents? It was either the best idea he'd had in forever or the worst. Only time would tell. By the time Ace arrived half an hour later, Ripley was ready to pull his hair out.

"Where the fuck have you been?" he blasted his best friend.

Ace scowled. "I ran into Legend, and he motioned for me to follow him. Said he was trailing the Haven crew. Why are you so fucking pissy?"

"Sorry. This shit has me antsy. I'm taking Glory down to Florida until this all blows over. Did they leave town?"

"No. That's what took me so long. They pulled over and went into Martina's place. I called Tank and gave him a heads-up, then left Legend to watch them. Do you want me to come with you to Florida? I could use some of Regina's home cooking."

"You know you're always welcome at my parents' place." Ace had become a second son to Ripley's parents and had visited them by himself more than once since his own parents were no longer living. Ace had been a "late life" baby.

"But? You want a little alone time with your mate?" Ace wiggled his eyebrows like an immature jerk.

"She's not my m—"

"Not yet, but she could be. Take the time to let her get to know you without all this bullshit hanging over your heads. Maybe she'll decide you're too much of a dick and send you packing."

"Asshole," Rip muttered. "I'm headed home to pack. If you hear anything, keep me posted."

Ace held out his hand, and Rip bumped his knuckles against Ace's. When they pulled out of the parking lot, they went their separate ways. As soon as Rip walked into his house, he called his mom while he went upstairs to pack.

"Hello, my gorgeous son. Are you calling to tell me you're bringing your mate home?"

Ripley knew when he told his mom about Glory she would be chomping at the bit to meet her. "I am, but there's more to it than meeting the parents." Ripley filled his mom in on the men from Haven, and by the time he was finished, Regina was ready to come to New York and rip William and Amos a new one.

"We'll see you either late Wednesday or early Thursday. I promised Glory we could stop wherever she wants to see new places."

"Don't rush, just be safe. Your father and I love you."

"Love you too." Ripley disconnected, feeling a little lighter knowing his parents were looking forward to meeting Glory. Now he prayed to Zeus they lo— liked her as much as he did.

# Chapter Twelve

## Glory

GLORY STARED OUT the window after she hung up the phone. Getting to see the ocean would be a dream come true, but spending two days in a car with Ripley? Insanity. Nineteen hours was plenty of time for him to realize she wasn't good enough for him. Plenty of time for her to make a fool of herself. And meeting his parents who were also lawyers? Why hadn't she bought something besides jeans and T-shirts? She needed to ask Lynette about a suitcase anyway, so Glory made her way downstairs. Lynette and Branson were standing by the back door, arms around each other. When she entered the kitchen, they both turned to her.

"Everything okay?" Lynette asked.

"Uh, do you have a suitcase I can borrow? Oh, and maybe some nice clothes? I know you and I aren't the same size, but..."

Lynette strode to Glory and took both her hands. "Slow down, Honey. What's this about?"

"Ripley wants to take me out of town while my father and William are sniffing around. We're going to—" Glory stopped talking when Julia strolled into the room.

"Don't mind me," Julia said as she padded past them to the refrigerator. After snagging a can of soda, she closed the door and leaned against it as she popped the top. Taking a sip, she stared at them. Glory stared back, wondering where the shy woman had gone.

"Come with me, and I'll see what I have." Lynette gently took Glory by the elbow and led her down the hall. When they entered the master bedroom, Lynette closed the door. "Okay, you and Ripley are going…?"

"To see his parents, thus my freak out about clothes. They're both lawyers, and I—"

"Are perfect the way you are," Lynette interjected. "Regina and Conrad might have had high-profile jobs, but they aren't going to judge you for the way you're dressed. The only thing those two will be looking for is how you treat their son." Lynette walked over to her closet, and after some huffing and grunting, returned with a suitcase, which she placed on the bed. "I have a few blouses that'll probably fit that you can pair with your jeans." She held up a few options, and Glory took them from her.

"Do you mind if I try them on? No sense taking them if they're too small."

"Not at all." While Glory did just that, Lynette went to the door and put her ear to it. When she turned back around, she whispered, "Can't be too careful."

Glory chose three of the four shirts, hanging the one that was too small back on the hanger. "About?"

Lynette took the blouse and returned it to the closet. When she exited, she crossed her arms over her

153

chest. "About prying ears. Julia isn't subtle with her nosiness. I honestly don't think she means any harm, but she's been hanging around the kitchen more than she used to."

"Isn't that a good thing?" Glory folded the blouses and placed them in the suitcase.

"It is if it's for the right reason. Before you showed up, she rarely left her room without Helen as a buffer." Lynette uncrossed her arms and picked the hangers up, returning them to the closet. After closing the door, she said, "I think maybe she wants to be around you because you let her sing with you. That was the most interested in anything she's been since arriving."

Glory didn't have as much faith in Julia's intentions, but what if she was wrong? "And now I'm leaving. Maybe I shouldn't go."

"Oh, you definitely should. The farther away from Haven the better. Not that we can't handle your father and the other men, but you should have the opportunity to get your bearings away from that place without having to watch over your shoulder all the time. Think of it as your first vacation with Ripley. His parents are wonderful people, and I promise they're going to love you."

Glory doubted that, but she would do her best to at least not embarrass Rip. "Do you have some makeup I could borrow too? Rhi and I didn't get to go shopping."

"You're welcome to anything you want, but Glory, you don't need makeup. You're beautiful without it. Do you know how many women would give up their life savings to have the kind of complexion you do?

You have naturally long lashes, and your eyes are stunning." Those same eyes filled with tears. Glory tried to blink them back, but it didn't work, and Lynette pulled her in for a hug. "Oh, Honey, don't cry."

"But I also have stick-straight hair, and my hips are too wide."

"Your haircut is cute as hell, and your hips are perfect. Nothing wrong with a little junk in the trunk," Lynette said, smacking her own ass.

"Why couldn't my family see what you do?" Glory muttered while also smiling.

"Probably out of jealousy. There's no other reason for anyone to avoid complimenting you. But let's forget about them and focus on getting you ready for Florida" Lynette motioned toward the bathroom. "I don't have a lot of makeup, but what I have is yours."

Glory thought about what Lynette said, and if another woman could compliment Glory, maybe she didn't need to worry about it. "No, I think I'll go without it for a while. I probably wouldn't apply it right anyway." Glory's father wouldn't allow her to wear it when she was a teen.

Lynette zipped the suitcase and picked it up. "Okay, then, let's get you packed." When she opened the bedroom door, Branson was standing in the hallway. Lynette smacked him playfully in the stomach. "Eavesdropping, Old Man?"

"Something like that."

Glory didn't miss the look he gave Lynette, but instead of asking him what was going on, she exited the room without another word. Branson followed them upstairs and stood outside Glory's room while Lynette helped her decide what to take with her. Since they were going to the beach, Glory would have to give in and wear shorts because wearing jeans, even short ones, would look stupid. She would need to ask Ripley to stop along the way to his parents' place.

"You and Branson are couples' goals," Glory said as she zipped the now full suitcase.

"What do you mean?"

"You can talk without speaking aloud."

Lynette frowned but just as quickly turned her mouth up into a big grin. "When you've been together as long as we have, you tend to know what the other is thinking."

"Ripper's here," Branson said, leaning his head in the doorway.

Glory shook her arms and wiggled her body. "I can do this."

Branson grinned as he retrieved the luggage. "You're gonna be fine, Glory. And if all else fails, just sing."

"Right. If they think I'm weird, then burst into song and dance. That'll teach 'em."

Branson threw his head back, letting out a deep belly laugh. Glory shook her head, but she was grinning as she made her way downstairs. When she reached the bottom step, she paused. Helen had her hand on Rip's arm, whispering to him. By the look on his face, the man wasn't happy. That is until he noticed Glory, then his frown morphed into a gorgeous smile.

"Hey, Sunshine. You ready?" he asked.

"Are you going somewhere, Glory?" Helen asked.

"Super-secret road trip," Julia muttered as she walked into the room from the kitchen.

If Glory hadn't been standing next to Branson, she wouldn't have heard the low growl. He put himself between Glory and Julia. "Not so secret. Ripley has offered to take Glory back to her hometown and reconnect with friends."

Helen clasped her hands in front of her. "Oh, how exciting. And where exactly is home? I don't think you mentioned that when we were talking the night you arrived."

Before she could answer, Ripley said, "A little town in Kentucky." He strode over and took the suitcase from Branson, who nodded at Rip. Something strange was going on because Glory wasn't from the Southern state. She didn't correct him though. "Let's get going." He held out his hand, gesturing toward the door.

Glory didn't get far when Lynette stepped up to hug her. "Please be safe," Glory whispered. She didn't want her father to cause trouble for the woman and her husband.

"Enjoy your trip. I hope it's everything you wish for," Lynette whispered back.

Glory said bye to the others, then she and Ripley headed outside to his Camaro. After stowing her suitcase in the trunk, he opened her door and closed it behind her once she was seated. When he slid into his own seat, she asked, "What was that about?"

"Buckle up, Sunshine." Ripley waited until he had the engine started to answer. "Just a safety precaution. If your father were to get Helen or Julia alone outside

Providence House, they won't be able to give away our destination."

"You think one of them would?"

"I do. Not because they would want to see you go back to Haven, but because it would be easy to break either one of them with the slightest bit of torture."

"I don't understand why my father wants me back so badly. It's not like I was important to the community other than skinning animals, and any of the men can do that."

Ripley took Glory's hand and slotted their fingers. "It's about control. He and William lost it, now they want it back. At least that's what Branson and I think."

"But how did they know I'm with the Hounds? You weren't wearing your vest when you came to the stall, and Natalia is the one who convinced me to go with you."

Ripley rubbed his thumb back and forth across her hand. "That's a good question, one we have also asked ourselves. All we can figure is we're on their radar because of Rhi as well as Gideon's compound. You being with us would be an obvious place to start."

Glory dipped lower in her seat to get comfortable for the long ride, wanting to forget all about her father and William. She tried to revel in the fact that she was safe from her prison, but she couldn't shake the feeling there was more going on than the Haven men getting it right from assuming.

"As much as I'd love to drive the Camaro to Florida, I'm going to switch cars to be on the safe side."

Glory couldn't fault Rip for taking precautions, but how would the men from Haven know what kind of car he drove? Before she could ask, he was pulling into a driveway where the garage door was open. A man she recognized from the mall met them when they got out.

"Glory, this is my best friend, Asher McMurray. Ace, this is Glory."

Asher inclined his head. "It's a pleasure, Glory." Asher was shorter than Ripley with spiked brown hair and green eyes. He had ink covering both hands and arms as well as his neck. When she'd seen him at the mall, Asher had frowned every time he looked her way, but today, he was smiling, and that made him more approachable. Asher popped the trunk on an expensive looking four-door sedan. Being an attorney, it was the type of car Glory could picture Rip driving. She didn't know what Asher did for a living, but his appearance fit better with Ripley's sports car.

Rip moved their luggage over from the Camaro, then the men exchanged keys. "I appreciate the assist, Brother."

Asher grinned. "And I promise to take real good care of Sheila while you're gone."

"Who's Sheila?" Glory asked, blinking fast at Ripley.

Asher stepped closer to the Camaro, running his fingertips along the trunk. "Rip's baby."

"Ah. For a second there I thought she was your girlfriend." Ripley sucked in a breath, and Glory smirked until he pulled her tight against his chest.

With his mouth against her ear, he husked, "That'd be you." It was her turn to gasp and his turn to smirk. Rip pressed his lips to her forehead before stepping

159

back.

Asher moved to his car and opened the door for her. "Your ride awaits, M'lady."

"Hey, she's not your anything," Rip demanded, and Glory giggled.

She patted Rip on his rock-hard abs before stepping up to Asher and curtsying. "Thank you, kind Sir."

As Asher closed her door, she heard him say, "I like her."

Glory couldn't hear Rip's response, but he had claimed her as his girlfriend, so she hoped he responded in kind. As soon as they were back on the road, Glory asked, "Girlfriend, huh?"

"Yes. I'm claiming you now so nobody else gets a shot at you. Like I told you before, we can take this at your pace, but not too slow. I mean, I *am* taking you to meet the parents."

"Don't remind me," Glory muttered.

Ripley snagged her hand again. "I promise they're going to love you, Sunshine. Just be your spunky self."

Spunky? Is that how he saw her, and was that a good thing? "Wouldn't they rather see you with someone, I don't know, more polished? Someone more fitting an attorney?"

Ripley sighed. "I can see we're going to have to work on your self-esteem, Sunshine. Yes, my parents are attorneys, or I should say were, since they're both semi-retired now, but please wait until you meet them before you freak out, okay? They are both laid-back and some of the nicest people you'll ever come across, and I'm not just saying that because they're my folks."

160

Glory traced one of the tattoos on Ripley's arm. "What do they think about all your ink?"

Ripley chuckled. "My father has plenty of tattoos, and my mom got the bug when she went with him one time. While neither have as many as I do, they both have plenty."

"Oh. That's..." Maybe they would be cool with her.

"That's?" Rip prodded.

"That's awesome. I can't imagine having parents like them. Well, I sort of can. My best friend's mom was young when she had Sheri, and she listened to rock music and wore torn jeans and faded band T-shirts. Sheri's stepdad was cool too even though he was older than Monique. As a matter of fact, Monique and Tommy remind me a lot of Branson and Lynette. They were always in tune with the other. Dancing around the kitchen, not caring who was watching. They sat close on the sofa when watching TV. Tommy brought Monique flowers for no reason other than to see her smile, and Monique always had Tommy's coffee fixed for him when he got out of the shower. At least that's what Sheri told me. Since I wasn't allowed over there, I didn't witness it firsthand, but Sheri had no reason to lie about it. My parents didn't speak to each other unless it was my father barking orders."

"I'm sorry you didn't have good parents. Mine are like Branson and Lynette, and by the sounds of it, Sheri's folks. If I could find a genie in a bottle, my three wishes would be for all kids to be loved unconditionally, have food in their bellies, and to be able to live their true lives without repercussions."

If Glory hadn't been smitten with the man already, that statement would have sealed the deal. "You really are a good man."

Ripley glanced over at her, his thick eyebrows dipping low. "You doubted that?"

"No, but you have to remember who I've lived with the last six years and my father for eighteen before that. Other than Tommy, who I didn't really know, I've not been around men who care about women and children. Men who put others before themselves." Glory swallowed hard. "Please be patient with me, Rip. I don't want to screw this up, whatever this is between us. I appreciate the Hounds getting me away from Haven, but I appreciate you more for taking me out of town. For everything you've done in such a short time."

Ripley lifted her hand and kissed the back of it. "You don't have to thank me, Sunshine. It's my pleasure. As for what this is between us, I hope it's the beginning of something special."

"Me too."

Changing the subject, Ripley asked, "Are there any places between here and Florida you'd like to visit?"

Glory chewed the side of her thumb as she thought about it. The only place she knew of along the way was her grandmother's, but Glory didn't even know if her granny was still alive. Surely, if she'd passed away, her mother would have told her. Then again, would her mom have gotten word at Haven? "There is one place…"

# CHAPTER THIRTEEN

## Ripley

WHEN GLORY SAID she wanted to visit her grandmother, Ripley called Bishop.

"Hey, Ripper. What's up?"

"Glory and I are taking a road trip to see my parents, and she would like to visit her grandmother, but first we need to know if she still lives at the same address as the last time Glory visited. Can you help?"

"Of course. What's her name and last known address, Glory?"

"Her name is Leona Fay Perkins, and she lives in a little town called Pickings in South Carolina on Putter Lane. Or she did. That was a long time ago, and to be honest, I don't even know if she's still alive."

"That will be easy enough to find out. Do you want to hang on, or should I call you back?"

"Since we're nowhere close to South Carolina, you can call us back," Rip said.

"You got it."

"Thank you," Glory said when he disconnected. "Granny was the only person in my life besides my sisters who gave a crap about me. She's the one who taught me to cook when I was younger. Hope and I got to spend summers there before Splendor and Majesty came along. They were the best times of my life. Then, for some reason, my father decided we couldn't visit any more. When I asked my mom about it, she said it wasn't in the budget, but I think there was more to it than that. I asked Granny about it one time on the phone, but she wouldn't say anything other than sometimes folks have different opinions about life."

"Sounds like maybe she and your father didn't see eye to eye, and your mother took his side. Hopefully, you'll get to ask her about it."

Ripley prayed Bishop would have good news when he called because Glory needed something positive in her life. He wanted to be the one to put a smile on her face and keep it there. She had been through too much at such a young age, and it reminded him of what a charmed life he'd led. He was going to give both his parents a big hug when he saw them.

It wasn't ten minutes later when Bishop called, and Ripley put him on the Bluetooth. "I have good news. I found your grandmother, Glory, but she's no longer in Pickings. She now lives in New Live Oak, Florida, in a retirement community. I'll send the address and phone number through to your phone, Rip."

"Thank you so much, Bishop," Glory said.

"My pleasure. Let me know if there's anything else you need, and in the meantime, enjoy Florida."

Glory tapped her free fingers against her leg as she stared out the window. Ripley wiggled the hand he was holding. "What's wrong?"

"I think I should call Granny first instead of dropping in on her. I don't know where New Live Oak is or how far it is from where your parents live, but maybe we can save visiting her for the trip back home?"

"I'm not familiar with the town either, but no matter where it is, we'll go there whenever you're ready." Glory's stomach rumbled loud enough for a non-Gryphon to hear it. "Are you hungry?"

"God, that's embarrassing. I didn't eat lunch because I was upset about my father."

"So that's a yes. What are you in the mood for? There are several restaurants at the next few exits, so I'm sure we can find something you'd like."

Glory tensed. "Are you hungry? You and Asher were out to lunch when you and I talked earlier. I can wait if you aren't."

"I can always eat, and I'm not picky," Rip admitted. There were certain foods he didn't care for, but if they stopped at one of the chain restaurants that served a variety of dishes, he'd be set. "What about somewhere like Gordon's? They have everything from steak to pasta to burgers to fish and pizza."

"That sounds good, but only if you're hungry too." Glory remained stiff, and Ripley hated it.

"Sunshine, let me explain something. It wouldn't matter if I wasn't hungry. You are my priority. Your well-being, your safety, and your happiness are all important to me. You will always come first, so please do not hesitate to tell me if there's something you need. I don't care if it's something you find foolish like stopping for a candy bar and soda. Or if you see a

165

stand on the side of the road selling fruit. Or you need feminine products because you ran out. Nothing is off limits. I can only imagine the type of men you're used to, and I can assure you I'm nothing like any of them."

Glory's free hand covered her mouth as she tried to hide a sob. *Fuck.* Rip should have waited until he wasn't doing ninety down the freeway to have such an intimate discussion. He maneuvered into the slow lane so he could take the next exit. Thankfully, it was only a couple miles, and after getting to the bottom of the ramp, he turned right, then pulled into the first parking lot he found. After putting the car in park, he unfastened Glory's seatbelt, then slid his arm around her shoulder and pulled her across the console against his chest.

She shook her head against his neck. "I'm sorry. I'm sorry."

Ripley pressed his lips to her silky hair. "You have nothing to apologize for. I'm the one who's sorry, Sunshine. I didn't mean to make you cry."

She shook her head again, hiccupping as she caught her breath. "You're just too good to be true."

"I can assure you there are more men like me than not. Men who put their females above themselves. Men like Branson, and Ryker, and Sutton. All the Hounds. We might be bikers who look rough around the edges, but we're taught from our fathers how to treat our partners." Rip threaded his fingers through her hair, caressing Glory's scalp. "All I ask is you give me time to prove it."

This time, she nodded. When she sat back, Ripley thumbed the tears off her cheeks. "Probably a good

166

thing you don't wear makeup, or you'd look like a racoon," he joked, grinning.

"I haven't had time to buy any."

"Then we'll add that to our list if it's something you truly want, but don't wear it on my account. I think you're perfect the way you are."

Glory cocked her head to the side. "You mean that, don't you?"

"I do." Ripley stroked a thumb across her cheek. "Your skin is flawless, and your eyelashes are naturally long. It's your decision though. If you want to wear makeup, I won't object."

Glory leaned into his palm. "Okay, I'll think about it." When her stomach growled again, she closed her eyes and huffed. "I guess we do need to find somewhere to eat and tame the beast."

Ripley leaned in and pressed a chaste kiss to her lips. "Let's see what we can find." Glory moved back to her side of the car and buckled up. Fortunately, the exit he'd taken had several options, and he drove them to a well-known chain that had plenty of dishes to choose from. They took their time eating, both opting for steak and baked potatoes. Talk was easy with Ripley telling her more about his parents and life growing up in Florida. When they were back on the road, Ripley said he'd drive a couple more hours, then find them a hotel for the night.

Instead of talking, Ripley turned on the radio and had Glory choose a station. "What kind of music do you like?" she asked.

"Mostly rock, but this isn't about me, Sunshine. I want you to pick something you like." Ripley was seeing a pattern; one he didn't care for. It was evident Glory hadn't been allowed to make her own choices. She once again chewed her thumb on one hand while pressing buttons with the other. When she stopped on a pop channel, she asked if it was okay.

"Perfect," he assured her. Rip took her left hand and settled their entwined fingers on the console. Glory tapped her free hand against her thigh, and by the end of the first song, she was singing along. Her ability to learn a tune quickly was amazing. Ripley was even more determined to purchase a piano for his house sooner than later.

Around the two-hour mark, Glory yawned, and Ripley took the first exit that had hotels. He pulled into the parking lot of one of the nicer chains, and when he put the car in park, he started to ask if he should get two rooms, but he knew she would say whatever he wanted. He wanted to sleep beside her, but was she ready for that? This was one decision Glory would have to make.

"Do you want your own room?"

Glory looked out the windshield, biting her lip. "I should say yes. That would be the right thing to do."

Ripley reached over and pulled her chin toward him. "Right according to who? And right *for* who? Tell me what you want. There is no wrong answer here. It's just you and me." When Glory didn't respond, Ripley admitted, "I would love to sleep wrapped around you all night, but if you aren't ready for that, it's not going to hurt my feelings." *Much.*

"It's not that I don't want to, but..." Glory closed her eyes, and a lone tear rolled down her cheek.

"Sunshine? Talk to me," he gently urged.

Glory looked at Rip, trying to blink back tears. "I'm damaged goods," she whispered. "At Haven, the only men who wanted me were older and desperate. You can have anyone you want. Someone gorgeous like Helen, some—"

"You are *not* damaged goods. I don't know who told you that, but it's a fucking lie." When Glory sucked in a breath, Ripley took a calming one. "Sorry, but it's just not true. Those who have antiquated ideas about purity or keeping oneself a virgin before marriage are insane. Sex is a natural need, and just because you had it with your ex-boyfriend doesn't make you a bad person. Or flawed. In my opinion, everyone should have sex before they get married to see if they're compatible with their partner. Not that sex is all there is to a relationship, but it's a big part of it. What if the two people involved have different needs? Different ideas of what a healthy sex life looks like? I have friends who are part of the BDSM community. Do you know what that is?"

"Like whips and chains?"

Ripley grinned. "Bondage is part of it, including whips and chains, as well as impact implements. So is rope play, like tying someone in intricate knots that doesn't have to be sexual. There are many facets to kink play, some hardcore and some not, but what I'm getting at is those who are into various kinks need a partner who is likeminded. What if one partner is a masochist, someone who needs pain to get off, but their partner can't or won't give them that pain? Shouldn't they find that out before they agree to a life commitment? And before you ask, no, I'm not a masochist. I'm not into any kinks. I'm just a plain 'ol vanilla kind of lover. Not that I'm boring..."

Glory snickered, and Ripley goosed her in the side. "Sorry," she squealed, wiggling as much as she could while belted in.

Ripley brought her hand to his mouth and kissed her wrist before continuing. "My point is sex isn't taboo, no matter what some humans think." When Glory narrowed her eyes, Ripley silently chastised himself. "Not that I expect us to have sex tonight. We can go inside, get a room, and cuddle all night. I happen to be a fan of cuddling."

"I've never cuddled with anyone other than my sisters, but I wouldn't be opposed to trying it with you."

Ripley was relieved. He was also fighting his Gryphon, who wanted to seduce Glory the second they had her alone in the room. "Then let's get one room and commence with all the cuddles." Ripley turned the motor off and got out, coming around to help Glory from her seat. "I should have thought about stopping along the way and having you pack a smaller bag for the night." Considering all her things were in a large suitcase, Ripley hoisted it from the trunk along with his duffel. Being a biker, he'd learned to roll his clothes so they fit in a smaller bag. He looped the straps over his shoulder, and after closing the lid, he grabbed the handle of her luggage with one hand and took her hand with the other.

Being late, it didn't take long to get checked in and upstairs to their suite. Ripley took their bags to the

170

bedroom, giving Glory a moment alone to get acclimated. It might be overkill for one night, but Ripley was all about spoiling her. He also figured having a bigger space wouldn't make things as overwhelming as a regular room.

"Wow." Glory crossed her arms over her chest as she took it all in. "This is almost as big as the house I grew up in," she said when he rejoined her.

"I thought it would be better to have somewhere to sit and watch TV instead of on the bed. I don't want you to feel any pressure about being alone with me."

Glory uncrossed her arms as she closed the distance between them. When she reached Rip, she laid her hand on his chest. "You really are a gentleman." She stood on her toes and pressed a kiss to his cheek.

Ripley placed his hands on her hips, fingertips aching to dig into her soft flesh. "I try my best." He squeezed her hips before backing away. "Are you tired, or do you want to see if we can find a movie?"

Glory walked to the sofa and plopped down, bending over to remove her shoes. "A movie, please. If that's okay with you?"

It was perfect because Ripley didn't know if he'd be able to keep his hands off Glory once they were in bed. His Gryphon was trying to take over, and it was getting harder to hold it back. "Sounds great." He found the remote, and once he had the TV on, he handed it over. "Why don't you scroll through the guide for our options, and I'll see if there's popcorn in the snacks." Ripley silently cheered when he found a bag. He put it in the microwave, and while it was popping, he snagged two sodas out of the fridge.

Having a well-stocked room was one of the reasons he preferred this particular hotel chain. He hated leaving the room to go down to the lobby once he was settled. It might make him sound snobbish, but having the means to afford a nice suite had its benefits.

When Rip took their snacks to the sofa, Glory had the remote in one hand while she chewed on her thumbnail of the other. He was going to break her of that bad habit one day. Until then, he would use it as a clue that she was nervous or undecided.

"What did you find?" He sat down beside her and handed over one of the cans while placing the popcorn on her thigh.

"Well, I was searching for *Star Wars* so we could continue our marathon, but then I saw this one." She pointed to the screen with the remote where the first movie in *The Lord of the Rings* trilogy was cued up.

"Oh, I like those too. The second is my favorite of the trilogy, but they're all good."

Glory looked up at him. "Wouldn't you rather watch something you haven't seen?"

"Nope. I love watching movies over and over and trying to spot things I missed previously. Like in one of the episodes of *Game of Thrones,* there was a Starbucks cup sitting on the table when the time period is the supposed Middle Ages. There's also several in this movie." Ripley gestured toward the TV. "I didn't spot them the first few times I watched, but when I saw them later, it made me smile."

"Will you point them out to me?"

"If you don't notice, I will."

Glory must have believed he was being truthful.

She bumped his shoulder with hers, then pointed the remote at the screen and hit the play button. Sitting with his female watching movies and eating popcorn was easy. Too easy. He had never had this with Sara Beth. Oh, they watched movies together, but they were always genres Ripley had no interest in. Whenever he suggested an action adventure like the one currently playing, she pouted, and he gave in. He thought a relationship was about compromise, but Rip had found himself being the one to always cave. She hadn't liked flavored popcorn or butter on hers. If there was too much salt, she would refuse to eat it. Ripley then made it plain even though he hated it that way. There were other little things that shouldn't have been a big deal, but when those little things added up, he found they became big red flags he should have paid attention to.

When the first scene came on with the blooper, Rip waited to see if Glory caught it. When she didn't, he paused the movie. "Take a look at the screen and see what shouldn't be there."

Glory was leaning against him with her head on his shoulder and her fingers laced with his. She didn't turn loose, but she did sit up and study the TV. "Are those tire tracks?"

"Very good. Most people are too busy looking at the kids to notice."

Glory grinned, then leaned back, putting her head on his shoulder once again. They continued enjoying the film, the salty popcorn, and more bloopers. When the end credits rolled, she sat up, grinning. "I think I have a new favorite movie. I can't wait to see the next two."

"We can watch them whenever you want."

Glory yawned, covering her mouth. "Sorry. I would say let's start the next one now, but I doubt I'll stay awake for much of it."

"We have all the time in the world. Why don't you take the bathroom first and get ready for bed while I clean up our mess?"

"Okay." Glory kissed his cheek before standing, and when she strode toward the bedroom, Ripley touched his face. Such a small gesture had his heart racing. Ripley took the empty cans and popcorn bag to the kitchen, and then he strode to the window and looked out over the town while having a chat with his beast.

*Cuddling only.*

**You're an idiot.**

*I'm merely being a gentleman.*

**Fuck that noise. Weren't you the one who told her sex was a natural, biological need?**

*Yes, and I also told her we'd go at her pace. She's had enough of men telling her what she should and shouldn't do. We'll know when she's ready.*

Ripley was so intent on their inner dialogue he didn't hear Glory return to the living area. Her hand on his arm startled him, and when he turned around, his beast crowed.

**I think that's your sign.**

# CHAPTER FOURTEEN

## Glory

GLORY WAS EITHER the bravest woman in the world or the most foolish. When she approached Ripley in nothing but her underwear, she held her breath. But when he turned to see how she was dressed? His eyes darkened as they scanned her from head to toe.

"Wow. You are stunning." Rip placed his hands on her shoulders and ran his fingertips down her arms. Glory didn't have to look to know there were goosebumps. When he linked their fingers, he pulled her arms out away from her body and drank in all her bare skin. And there was a lot of it. "Before I get the wrong idea, do you normally sleep in your underwear, or is this a hint of what you want to happen?"

"It's a hint. That is, if you want me," Glory whispered.

"Oh, I want." Ripley released her hands, and before she knew what was happening, he lifted her in his arms. She wrapped her arms and legs around his body as he strode to the bedroom, carrying her as though she weighed nothing. When they reached the bed, he lowered her onto her back, then pulled his shirt off and tossed it aside. Glory scooted back against the pillows and kept her eyes on his inked hands as he simultaneously kicked off his boots while undoing his jeans. When he pushed them down his muscled legs, Glory couldn't help but notice the bulge behind his boxer briefs. Instead of removing them, he lay down on top of her, his erection nestled between her legs. Keeping himself aloft on his forearms, Rip pressed his lips to hers in a gentle caress.

"You are something else." Rip peppered her face with soft kisses before nuzzling her neck with his nose. Inhaling deeply, he muttered, "Holy Zeus, you smell divine."

*Zeus?* Glory couldn't think about why Ripley was mentioning the Greek god longer than a second because he nipped at her neck at the same time he rubbed his hardness against her mound. She let out a breathy "oh," and he did it again.

"You sure about this, Sunshine? Because if you don't stop me now, there's no going back."

"I'm sure. I need you, Rip." And she did. More than she'd needed anything in a long time. Sex with Chad had been quick and a little painful, but she knew in her heart it would be different with Rip.

Ripley angled off her, standing so he could remove his briefs. Glory slid her panties down her legs, then took off her bra while he pulled a condom out of his wallet. Thank goodness one of them had their wits about them. She wasn't on birth control, and the last thing she needed was to get pregnant. Not that she would be opposed to having Rip's baby, but not this soon after meeting.

Once he was suited up, he returned to the bed, kissing his way down her body. Glory wanted to hide her extra pounds, but with Rip on top of her she couldn't. He latched onto one of her nipples with his mouth, tonguing the bud into a hard peak. He blew across it, then gave the other one the same attention. Then he nipped his way down her stomach, easing his body down the bed until his face was between her legs. "Gonna get you ready for me," he husked before licking her clit. Glory arched off the bed, and Rip pushed her hips down as he set about taking her apart. She didn't want to think about why he was so good at licking, but she was glad for his experience. Ripley slid a finger inside while sucking on her nub, and when she began writhing, he added another digit. If he kept that up, she was going to come before he got his dick inside her. By the way he was focused, that seemed to be his plan.

"I'm close," she admitted.

"Good," he said before going back to licking and fingering.

Well, okay then. If that was his goal, she wasn't going to fight it. Instead, she enjoyed the new sensations. She and Chad had been intent on getting the deed done quickly, which meant he orgasmed, but she didn't. She really liked Ripley's way of doing things better. Having given herself orgasms in the shower at Haven, Glory recognized the tingle, and she grabbed his hair to keep his head where she needed it. Ripley growled as she tightened her hold, the rumble adding to the excitement. Her release hit her soon after, and she squirmed against his face, praying she wasn't smothering the man.

Ripley pressed a kiss against her clit, then crawled up her body, pushing her legs back, and inserting his cock into her wet channel. "Fuck, Sunshine. You're so damn tight, but god do you feel good." Glory had expected slow and sensual, but what she got was a hard pounding. Not that she was complaining, because with each thrust, Ripley's dick was lighting another fire deep inside. Holy Zeus was right. Her core tightened and tingled again, surprising the heck out of Glory.

"Rip, I'm almost there," she told him.

"Good, because I can't hold off much longer. Come for me, Sunshine." Ripley doubled his efforts, hitting a spot deep inside that detonated Glory's release. That must have set off his, because Rip threw his head back and groaned as he remained buried in her slickness. Muscles twitched and convulsed, and Glory sank back against the pillows. When Ripley finally looked at her, his smile was a mixture of wild and tender, but it was his eyes that had her bewildered. They were gold. Then he blinked, and they were once again blue. It had to be a trick of the light.

Ripley kissed the inside of her knee. "You are fucking perfect." He released her legs and bent down, slanting their mouths together. When his tongue met hers, Glory tasted herself. It should have been weird, but she liked it because of what it represented.

When Ripley broke the kiss, he pressed his forehead to hers. "You are mine, Glory Yearwood. Mine to keep. Mine to cherish. Mine to walk through this crazy life with." Glory couldn't believe he wouldn't eventually change his mind, so instead of contradicting him, she ran her fingers through his dark hair. He must have wanted a response of some kind because he raised up, his brow furrowed. "Sorry if that scares you."

Glory continued massaging his scalp. "It doesn't scare me. I just find it hard to believe."

Ripley goosed her side. "You calling me a liar?"

Glory squealed, squirming against his strong hands. Ripley grabbed her wrists and held them above her head, bringing his face inches from hers. "You don't believe me now, but I vow on all that is holy, I will spend every day proving myself." He kissed her again, slowly and with so much emotion; Glory wanted to cry. Okay, she didn't want to, but Rip was good at showing his feelings with both words and actions. She wriggled her hands, and when he loosened his grip, she hugged him to her, loving the feel of his chest hair against her bare breasts. When his cock began plumping, Glory widened her legs, wrapping one around his thigh.

"You hinting again, Sunshine?" he asked against her mouth.

"Yes." Glory initiated the next kiss. After a beat, she asked, "But maybe we can slow things down this time?"

Ripley raised up. "Was I too rough? Zeus, I was. I'm so sorry." He pushed up on his hands as though he were going to leave the bed, but Glory tightened her grip around his neck.

"No. I promise you weren't. Our first time was perfect. I just thought we might change it up." Glory kissed him again, doing her best to show him her

179

sincerity. When his body relaxed, she rolled her hips.

Ripley said, "Hold that thought." He reached down and grabbed hold of the condom as he pulled out. Rip tossed the used rubber into the garbage before getting another and sliding it on. Then he did as she asked and made love to her, working her body over, his eyes never leaving hers. The orgasm that followed was no less intense than the first two. If anything, it was more powerful. More meaningful. He kissed her again before removing the condom and dumping it over the side of the bed. He rolled to his back, taking Glory with him so she was resting against his side with her cheek on his chest.

"Thank you," she said, tracing the tattoos on his chest.

Ripley brushed his lips across her hair, inhaling deeply. "You never have to thank me for that, Sunshine. It was truly my pleasure."

She turned her head to ask, "Why do you smell my hair?"

Ripley brushed her hair back from her face. "Because I crave your scent. Sorry if you find that odd."

Glory did think it strange, but instead of telling him so, she said, "I noticed Branson does the same thing to Lynette."

Ripley rubbed his hand down her back, stroking his fingers along her spine. "Do you want to shower? Or are you ready to sleep?"

"I don't want to move from this spot if that's okay with you."

Ripley leaned over and turned off the lamp. There

was a bit of light coming from the living area, so they weren't in complete darkness. When he reached down and pulled the covers up over their naked bodies, Glory had her answer. She wanted to say something. Anything that would let Rip know how she felt about what they'd done, but she didn't want to sound like a fool, so she snuggled against his side and closed her eyes. Just as sleep pulled her under, she could have sworn Ripley muttered, "Thank you, Zeus, for my mate."

When Glory woke, she was alone. Her body was deliciously sore from sex, but it was a wonderful kind of ache. She sat and stretched, but seeing she was naked, she pulled the sheet up to cover her breasts.

"Don't ever hide your body from me," Ripley said, standing in the doorway. He strode across the room and took the cover from her hands, lowering it to the foot of the bed. Rip's eyes darkened as he drank in her naked form. Glory was sure he had been kidding when he said he liked what he saw, but the pure desire on his face told the truth. Maybe instead of shrinking away, she should embrace the fact he had been truthful about not wanting a skinny woman. Glory held her arms out to the side, and Rip took advantage, lowering his face to her chest. He kissed his way from her breasts, down her stomach, until he was between her legs. It didn't take long for him to bring her to orgasm with his talented tongue and fingers.

Rip once again place a gentle kiss to her clit before standing beside the bed. "I fully intended to wake you for breakfast, but I'll never complain about that type of distraction, and you, my beautiful female, are all kinds of distracting. I'm going to go back in there" — he hitched a thumb over his shoulder — "and order room service. I'll leave you to shower because if I don't, we'll never get to eat." Ripley licked his lips, then turned and walked out.

Glory was disappointed that she didn't get to reciprocate, but they did have a long drive ahead of them, so she showered and dressed. When she joined him in the living area, Rip was standing by the window, looking out. He turned and held his arms open. "Come here." Glory padded across the carpet straight into his waiting embrace. "Good morning," he said against her hair after inhaling. Yes. It certainly was a good morning.

After eating their fill of pancakes, eggs, and bacon, they packed and got back on the road. The drive was filled with small talk and singing to whatever Glory chose on the radio. She liked the fact that Ripley let her choose the music. She loved the fact that he was easy to be with. He held her hand and kissed her knuckles whenever the mood struck. He didn't fuss when she said she needed to pee. He anticipated when she was hungry, stopping before she asked. Rip let her choose the restaurant, which was sweet if daunting. So many types of food were available. Some she had never tried and wasn't sure she wanted to. Instead of asking to get Thai food, then not liking it, Glory picked somewhere she knew would have something familiar. One day, she would gather the courage to try something different.

It was late when they stopped for supper. Instead of taking a direct route to his parents' house, he opted for going out of the way so they could eat at a restaurant on the beach. When Glory first caught sight of the Atlantic ocean, she stood in awe of the magic spread out before her. The full moon cast a long light across the dark water, and the waves rolled in, one after the other. Never had she witnessed anything so spectacular. She had thought a sky full of stars was something to behold, but seeing the ocean for the first time brought tears to her eyes.

Ripley wrapped his arms around her from behind, letting her have a moment to enjoy the scene playing out in front of them. Glory turned and pulled his face down for a kiss. "Thank you."

He brushed the tears off her face. "Come on. Let's get something to eat, then we'll walk on the beach."

Glory wanted to take off running across the sand until she could put her toes in the foam left by each wave, but she took his offered hand and let Rip lead her into the restaurant. Growing up, she had eaten catfish, so she opted for a plate of it with slaw and cornbread. She had grown tired of pintos at Haven, but when she noticed red beans and rice on the menu, she decided to try it. When Glory took the first bite, she was glad she had chosen it. After they finished their meal, Glory turned down dessert because she was itching to get back outside.

Ripley took Glory's hand and led her down the wooden staircase to the sand. The breeze coming off the water was brisk, but she didn't care. "Can I take my shoes off?" she asked.

"Of course. I'll join you." They both removed their footwear and socks, and Ripley set them beside the steps.

"Won't someone steal them?"

"Nah. It's kind of an unwritten agreement to not pilfer someone else's shoes at the beach," he replied, grinning.

Hand-in-hand, they crossed the thick sand. Glory had never walked on a beach, so it was awkward at first. She twisted her feet as she went, enjoying the softness peppered with little bits of sharpness she figured were broken shells. At least she hoped that's what it was. When they reached the shoreline, the softness gave way to damp hard-packed sand. Glory was amazed. She had on a pair of capris, but she still bent over and rolled them up before walking closer to the water. When it splashed gently onto her feet, she squealed. It was cold but exhilarating.

"I can't imagine growing up with this in your backyard."

Ripley had rolled his own jeans up and joined her. "Like I told you before, having it at your disposal takes away some of the glamour, but I admit I miss it. Usually when New York gets several feet of snow."

"Do you ever think about moving back?" she asked, looking out over the vast darkness.

"Not really. I have a good life up North, and the Hounds are my family. I can visit my folks whenever I want if I feel the need to get my fix. Or I can take a vacation anywhere there's a beach. I'm not limited to Florida. In fact, how would you feel about taking a trip with me somewhere tropical? The Atlantic is nice, but there's nothing quite like the crystal blue waters of the Mediterranean."

"Can you just take off whenever you want?" Glory

didn't know enough about Ripley's life, so she asked, "I know you help rescue people from cults, and you work as an attorney, but what's your day-to-day life like?"

Ripley stepped behind Glory so her back was to his chest. She appreciated the warmth of his arms wrapped around her. "My days are mostly my own. I help Sutton when he needs me, I take cases for those who can't afford a good lawyer whenever someone recommends me, and I ride with the other Hounds whenever we feel like it. Our MC isn't like most. We have a clubhouse, and Ryker is our president, but it's not like where all the members hang out at a clubhouse with booze and naked women everywhere. Don't get me wrong. Some of the single males do hang out and drink, but Sutton made sure things stayed PG-13 with some of the members having wives and kids who tagged along, and Ryker has kept to the status quo. The Hounds are more like a big family than a group of one-percenters."

"What's a one-percenter?"

"They're the type of bikers who sell drugs and guns, do the drugs they sell, and swap women back and forth, treating them like property. We don't call our females 'old lady'. I'm not saying all motorcycle clubs are like that because they aren't. Some form a brother or sisterhood and ride together because they share a love of all things two-wheeled. They host charity rides and collect money and toys for kids. They have poker runs and donate the proceeds to a good cause. It's like-minded people hanging out; they just do it on bikes."

"What if I want to be your old lady?" Glory joked.

"Oh, you're definitely mine, but I'll never treat you like property. You aren't something to be owned but rather cherished and treated with respect." Ripley pressed a kiss to Glory's temple, and she did feel cherished. She shivered when another breeze came off the water, and Ripley hugged her tighter. "As nice as this is, we need to get back on the road. We can either find another hotel, or you can nap in the car while I take us the rest of the way."

Glory didn't want Rip spending more money on her than he already had, but she also wasn't ready to meet his parents. "How about a cheap hotel? I don't need a suite like we had last night. As long as there's a clean bed, I'll be happy."

"Hotel it is, but there's something you should learn about me." Ripley turned her around and cupped her cheek. "I try not to flaunt the fact that I have money, but you deserve the best of everything life has to offer, and that means no cheap hotels." He kissed her nose. "Ever." He kissed her lips briefly. "If this is your way of putting off seeing my parents, they'll be asleep when we arrive."

"I am nervous, but once we get to their house, we won't get to sleep together."

"Says who? Their place is large, and we'll have our own room on the opposite side of the house. If you think for one second we aren't sleeping in the same bed, you'd be wrong. I've had a sample of what being with you is like, and you've ruined me, Sunshine." Ripley slanted his head and kissed her like he'd never get the chance again. It was hot and sensual, and it took her breath. It also made her panties damp. Who knew you could get so turned on from making out? She sure didn't. Being with Chad had never been like it was with Ripley. When he came up for air, he said, "Never mind. I need you in a bed now. Hotel it is."

And that's how, less than half an hour later, Glory found herself being taken apart and put back together for the second night in a row.

# Chapter Fifteen

## Ripley

RIPLEY WASN'T UPSET that they were arriving at his parents' house later than planned because he'd spent two glorious nights with his mate. Sex with Glory had been beyond anything he'd ever experienced, even with Sara Beth. His beast had pushed to the forefront, and Rip barely kept it at bay. He knew Glory had witnessed the change in his eyes, but she didn't mention it. For that, he thanked Zeus since he wasn't ready for that conversation. Rip also witnessed Glory's amazement at the ocean. The Florida weather was warm enough to enjoy the beach, and he convinced her to buy a swimsuit and a pair of shorts in the hotel gift shop, with her declaring them another birthday gift. She refused to take her T-shirt off as they played in the water or relaxed under an umbrella. Rip made sure she was slathered in sunscreen, but her nose was a little pink, adding to her cuteness. If Ripley didn't love New York so much, he would sell his house and buy Glory one close to a beach. If Ripley didn't love New York so much, he would sell his house and buy Glory one close to a beach. When they dressed for the ride to his parents' Glory was back in capris instead of wearing the shorts he bought her, and that bothered Ripley. He was going to work on her self-esteem.

Glory was quiet as Rip stopped at the guard shack leading into the private lake community. She didn't say anything until he turned into the driveway leading to the massive house.

"Holy shit," she muttered. "This is unbelievable." Glory unbuckled and leaned forward when the house came into view. The scenery along the paved drive was something to behold, but the house itself was a massive two-story structure situated on six acres with lake access, although the water wasn't visible from the driveway. "Rip, I can't go in there."

"Yes, you can, Sunshine. My parents are the most down-to-earth people you'll ever meet." When his parents rushed out the front door, Ripley didn't pull into the garage as planned. Instead, he parked in the circular driveway or else he'd have run over the two crazies rushing down toward them. "Get ready to be crushed in mom hugs," he warned her.

Regina had her long blonde hair braided and was dressed down in cutoff denim shorts, a vintage band T-shirt with the sleeves cut off to show the ink on her upper arms, and was barefooted. She bypassed the driver's side and rushed to Glory's door, pulling it open. "Glory! It's so good to meet you." Glory glanced over at Ripley, her eyes wide.

"You might as well get used to it, Sunshine."

Glory put on a smile before getting out. She was engulfed in Regina's arms as his mother said how lovely Glory was and how Regina couldn't wait to get to know her. Then, before he could get out of the vehicle and stop her, his mother voiced Glory, convincing her Regina and Conrad looked like an older couple. Ripley exited the vehicle, where his father waited with open arms. They were a touchy-feely couple, and Rip wouldn't have them any other way. Usually. He went to bypass his father, but Conrad grabbed Rip's bicep and pulled him into a hug.

"It needed to be done. For now," his dad whispered. Ripley knew his dad was right. Glory had already questioned how Sutton and Rory appeared as young as their son. If Regina hadn't voiced Glory, they would have to come up with some other explanation.

"Gina, let the poor girl come up for air," Conrad chided.

"Oh, hush, you." Regina did turn Glory loose only to wrap an arm around her shoulder and escort her into the house.

"I'll get the luggage if you want to save your mate," his dad offered.

Ripley didn't hesitate to hand over the keys and rush into the house. As he strode through the foyer, he stopped short when he noticed the baby grand piano in the front corner of the living room that hadn't been there the last time Rip visited. Shaking his head, he followed his mother's voice to the kitchen, where she was already pouring Glory a glass of tea. Only after Glory took a sip did Regina come around the island to give Rip his own bone-crushing hug. "Hi, Son. I'm so glad you both are here. I just wish the circumstances were better. Glory, you can hide out here for as long as you need. And if the Hounds don't take care of your father, I'll fly up to New York and stomp a mudhole in his ass."

Glory choked on the tea she'd just sipped, and Regina crossed the room to pat her back.

"So, Sunshine, this is my mother, Regina. She has no filter."

"Bah. Filters aren't needed with family!"

Glory wiped her mouth on the back of her hand, then mumbled, "Sorry. I promise I have better manners."

Regina brushed Glory's hair back from her face, then left her palm on Glory's cheek. "Oh, Darling, don't you worry about that. We don't stand on ceremony in this house. I'll tell you the same thing I told Rip when he was younger; this is a safe space. Manners, once taught, have their place, but home is somewhere you can relax and be yourself unless you're hosting a lavish party. While you are here, please consider this your home."

Glory's smile was stunning when she said, "Thank you."

"You're welcome. Now, are you two hungry? Or do you want to unpack your bags?"

Ripley poured himself a glass of tea. "I'm sure you have something ready for lunch, but let us unpack first. I want to show Glory the house, and by the time we're finished with the tour, we'll be ready to eat."

"Sounds good."

Ripley held out his free hand for Glory. "Bring your tea."

Glory grabbed her glass, then took Ripley's hand. Ripley didn't rush her as Glory took in her

191

surroundings. He showed her every room on the ground floor as they headed to their wing. He bypassed the living area, wanting to save it for last. He wasn't surprised at the grand gesture his parents had made. Like his mom said, they wanted Glory to feel at home.

"Oh, my god." Glory stopped just inside the doorway to Ripley's part of the house. His suite consisted of a large bedroom with an en suite bathroom as well as a living room adorned with a fireplace on one wall and sliding glass doors opposite, which led outside to a covered patio. The patio extended across the back of the house, where it ended in another covered area outside his parents' room. Where Rip's patio was open to a view of the lake, the other end was a party area with a fireplace, large-screen TV, and outdoor kitchen.

"No wonder you thought nothing of the hotel suite we stayed in. This is unreal."

Ripley was used to the opulence of his parents' home. Their previous home had been just as lavish, only not as large. Why two people needed so much space was beyond him, but it was their money. They had worked hard for many years, so if they wanted to spend their retirement in over five thousand square feet on six acres, that was their business.

"Let's unpack, and then I'll show you the rest of the house." Ripley led Glory into the bedroom, which like the rest of the interior was painted white with light blue accents. Conrad had placed their luggage on the bed, and Ripley unzipped Glory's suitcase before doing the same to his duffel. "There are plenty of hangers in the closet if any of your things need to be hung up. The left side of the dresser is empty for your other items."

"Do you always leave the left side empty?" Glory asked as she pulled clothing from the suitcase.

"Yes. I travel light, and anything I leave here fits in a couple drawers." Ripley removed his T-shirts first, unrolling them before folding them in tidy squares.

"Do you think we can run to the thrift store later? I'm gonna need more shorts," Glory asked as she hung a couple blouses in the closet.

"I'm not sure New Boca has a thrift store, Sunshine. Please don't worry about money. If you need new clothes, I'm more than happy to provide for you."

"Okay, but when I become an international pop star, I'm paying you back."

Ripley closed the dresser drawer, then turned and leaned against it. "Is that what you want?"

"When I was younger, that was my dream. Now? I have no idea. I don't think I'm ready to go from living in a prison to jetting off across the world where my life isn't my own. Not that I believe that'll ever happen. I love music, and I love to sing, but..." Glory sat down on the edge of the bed, her hands folded in her lap.

Rip took the few steps between them and sat next to his mate. "You have all the time in the world to figure out what you want to do, if anything. If you want to play and sing because it makes you happy, you can do that. I have more than enough money for both of us to live on for the rest of our lives without either one of us having to work a day. Why don't you enjoy your freedom for a while? Then, if you decide later you want to pursue a career, you can."

"Your mom worked."

"My mom loves to argue, and she turned that love into a career. If she hadn't been an attorney, she'd have found something else to fill her days, like cooking. She doesn't do well sitting still. Instead of relaxing with a book, she listens to one on audio while walking on a treadmill."

"Don't you want something like this?" Glory waved her hand, indicating the house.

"No, I don't. I don't begrudge my parents their home, but this isn't my style. You've seen where I live, Sunshine. That's plenty big enough for me. Unless *you* want something this large."

"Oh, heck no. I don't mind cleaning, but that's all I'd have time to do if we lived somewhere this size."

Ripley grinned. "You're so cute. Like I'd allow you to spend your days cleaning bathrooms." He picked up Glory's hand and turned her palm up. Tracing her fingertips, he said, "These hands are intended to make music, not scrub six toilets."

"Do you really want someone who doesn't cook or clean for you?"

"I didn't say that, Sunshine." Ripley tapped her cute nose. "I've lived on my own a long time, and I have no problem with chores. Granted, I do have a housekeeper who comes in once a week to deep clean, but if the floor needs sweeping or mopping, I can do that. I do my own laundry. As for cooking, I enjoy it. If you do too, it's something we can do together or take turns. What I'm trying to say is I want you to find joy in life with me by your side."

Glory launched herself at Ripley. He placed his hands under her ass and lifted her so she was straddling his legs. His mate kissed him passionately, and as much as he wanted to take things further, he knew his mom was waiting with lunch. When Glory broke the kiss, she leaned back. "How did I get so lucky?"

"I'm the lucky one. Let's finish the tour so I can show you your surprise, and then we'll eat lunch."

Glory crawled off Rip's lap and held out her hand. Knowing his mom would want to eat on the patio, he didn't bother showing Glory the outside of the house. He took her the long way until they ended up in the living room.

"Do your parents play piano?" Glory asked as she admired the new instrument.

"Nope. This is all for you."

Glory gasped. "What? But it's too much. This is a Steinway."

"I take it that's a good one?"

"Good? It's one of the best." Glory ran her fingers along the keys. "I know they have money, but we're only here for a few days."

"We're here until it's safe to return home, and we'll be back to visit in the future. Do you want to test it out?" Ripley really wanted to hear her play again. Glory plus a piano equaled pure magic.

Glory wiped her hands on her jeans. "Not right now. Do you mind if we eat first?"

Ah, his female was nervous. That didn't make sense considering how she played for Lynette and Branson without really knowing them. But if she needed time, he'd give it to her.

"Don't mind at all. Let's go see what the wild woman has prepared for us." Ripley placed his hand on Glory's back and led her to the kitchen. His mom was nowhere to be seen, so Rip opened his shifter senses and heard his mom's voice on the back patio. He normally would have called out to her, but with Glory not knowing about Gryphons, he had to go outside to speak with her.

"Are you ready to eat?" Regina asked, standing when she saw them.

"Yes, ma'am." Ripley pulled out a chair for Glory so she was sitting between him and his mother.

"Is there anything I can do to help?" Glory asked.

"That's my job," Conrad said, rising to help his mate. He patted Glory on the shoulder as he passed by.

"They're really nice," Glory said once they were both seated. Her words were complimentary, but her tone was off.

"What's wrong, Sunshine?"

Glory's eyes were misty when she asked, "Why can't all parents be like yours? I'm not talking about the tattoos because those are cool. I mean they'd never met me, yet they bought me an expensive gift. And it's not about the price tag but the fact that they were thoughtful enough to get me something that means so much."

Ripley scooted his chair close enough he could put his arm around Glory's shoulder. "I can't answer that because I don't understand it either. I think some people just have a skewed idea of what being a good parent is. And not just good parents but good people in general. My folks didn't always have the kind of money they do now, but they still had good hearts. If I had grown up in a trailer park instead of the kind of house we had, I know I would have turned out okay because I still would have been loved and cared for."

"Do your parents throw many parties?" Glory's change of subject was unexpected yet not. He couldn't imagine the hurt she felt with having shitty parents.

"Not as many as they used to. Why do you ask?"

"Your mom mentioned them when she was talking about manners."

"I'll answer that," Regina said as she returned from the kitchen with a platter of sandwiches and a bowl of pasta salad. His mother's mini sandwiches were piled high with different meats and cheeses. "Back when we worked full time as attorneys, we often held gatherings to network with others in our field, but now that we're mostly retired, we don't host many of those anymore. Con and I like our peace and quiet after so many years spent arguing in a courtroom. We also held parties for our family members whenever they would visit. Mine and Con's siblings are scattered across the country, so we don't see them as often as we used to."

Conrad set down potato salad and baked beans in the middle of the table. "We realize our house is quite large for two people, but we're looking forward to the day when our grandchildren will come stay with us."

"Dad," Ripley warned.

"What? You want me to lie to Glory and say your mom and I are pretentious snobs who can't imagine living somewhere smaller? We looked at a house half this size when we relocated, but this one is on the lake with plenty of privacy. That more than the square footage was what sold us on this one."

"Your home is beautiful, and I like that you want to fill it with grandchildren," Glory stated.

"You do?" They hadn't discussed kids at all, but that little tidbit had Ripley crowing inside.

"Yes. You're an amazing man, and I would venture that has everything to do with how you were raised. I've only known your parents like, a minute, and I can already tell they are wonderful too." Glory turned to his parents. "I cannot thank you enough for the Steinway. I know it's not technically mine since it's in your house, but you bought it for me to play. Your generosity is…" Glory choked up, and Regina rushed around the table.

Kneeling at Glory's side, she said, "You have amazing talent, and we were hoping you would share your gift with us. Besides that, you deserve the world, Glory, and Con and I have the means to give you a small part of it." Glory threw her arms around Regina's neck.

After hugging it out, Glory leaned back. "You haven't heard me play, so I might suck."

Con chuckled. "Oh, we've heard you all right. Branson sent a video of you playing and singing. Be right back." He disappeared into the house with a smirk on his face.

Glory winked at Ripley, then waited until his dad returned with a tray of condiments to comment. "Lynette mentioned knowing you. I didn't realize she and Branson knew you well enough to share things like *private* concerts." His mate had a twinkle in her eye although she was scowling at Conrad.

"Now don't go shooting the messenger, young lady. I was the recipient, not the sender."

"So is that like drugs? It's okay to purchase them but not okay to sell them? Was that your defense in court?" Glory sassed.

Conrad turned to Regina for help, until Glory giggled. Rip's dad huffed at Glory, but he was smiling. "I like you. You're sassy."

They each filled a plate, and his parents kept Glory smiling with stories from when Rip was a little kid while she tried different meat and cheese combos. She admitted only having ham and American cheese, and not the good kind. "What even is cheese food?" she asked. Rip did his best not to stare as she took a bite, then declared it her new favorite. "I've never heard of Asiago, but I love it." When she polished off the last of her sandwich, Glory asked, "Can we get some of this when we get home?"

"You can have all the cheeses, Sunshine." Her smile warmed his heart, even though it was hurting for all she'd missed out on so far in her life. When most of the food had been devoured, Glory insisted on helping clean up.

"I have a better idea," Regina said. "Rip mentioned you needed more shorts. How about I take you shopping while the men clean up?"

Glory asked Rip, "Is that okay with you?"

"I think it's an excellent idea. Mom knows where the stores are around here better than I do."

"Okay, then. Yes, please. I need to grab my shoes." Glory kissed Rip on the cheek before heading to their room.

"I really like her," Regina said.

"I do too, but it scares the shit out of me that she'll turn out like Sara Beth," he admitted.

Con gripped his shoulder and squeezed. "She won't. If you don't trust your Gryphon, at least trust your mother. You know she can read people like no one else."

"I wish you'd have *read* Sara Beth and saved me the heartache."

"I did," his mom stated, crossing her arms. Shit. Regina didn't get mad at him often, but when she put on what he called her court face, he knew he was in for it.

"No, you're right, and I'm sorry."

Regina's face softened, and she walked over to where he was still seated and ran her fingers through his hair. "We were all young and stupid once."

"Speak for yourself," Con muttered.

"*All* of us at one point in our lives think we know best when maybe we don't. You couldn't wait to find your mate. You wanted it so badly you weren't willing to believe she wasn't the one. I'm sorry you had to go through such pain, but you did have to endure it since you wouldn't believe what we were telling you. I was right then, and I'm telling you I'm right this time too. That young lady is made of steel, and when the time comes for you to admit your truth, she's going to roll with it."

Ripley prayed his mother was right. Again.

# CHAPTER SIXTEEN

## Glory

GLORY EXPECTED REGINA to change clothes before they went shopping, but she didn't. Rip's mom slid her feet into a cute pair of slip-ons and grabbed her purse. "Let's do this." She then led Glory through a side door to one of the garages. Glory had never seen a house with garages on both sides. Then again, she'd never seen a home as large as the Davidson's. She was surprised once again when Regina asked, "You mind getting a little windblown?" as she indicated a Jeep with the top off.

"No, ma'am." Glory climbed into the passenger seat and buckled up. Once Regina was also seated, she cranked the motor and pulled out of the garage as soon as the door rolled up. The woman shifted the manual gears like a pro, and Glory was awed more than she already had been.

"Do you need anything other than shorts while we're out?" Regina asked.

"Maybe some shoes like you're wearing. I got flip-flops at the hotel gift shop when Rip convinced me to buy a swimsuit. I was going to get some makeup, but

201

Rip said I don't need it."

"He's right. Your skin is flawless, and you're beautiful without it."

"Thank you. I know I said it before, but I really appreciate the piano."

Regina slowed at the end of the driveway to check for oncoming traffic, then turned left. "You're welcome. We could have bought an upright, but when Con and I discussed it, we decided if you had something a little flashier, it might entice you to come visit more often," Regina admitted with a grin.

"Bribery. I like it." Glory couldn't help but return Regina's infectious smile. Ripley was built like his dad and had his same dark hair, but he had Regina's blue eyes. The older woman was stunning. More than that, she was kind. Glory wished her own mother... No. Glory had to stop pining for impossibilities. Her mother would never change, and Glory doubted she'd ever see her again. That didn't hurt as bad as not seeing her sisters though. Having practically raised Splendor and Majesty, their loss hit her the hardest. Glory prayed they found good men to marry and didn't get saddled with someone like William.

Shopping with Regina was fun. She didn't go to the high-dollar stores like Glory expected. When Glory mentioned thrift shops, Regina frowned, then said she knew of a boutique where they sold nice, yet previously owned clothes. The items were name brands yet cheaper than Glory expected. She guessed it was New Boca's version of a thrift store. By the time they walked out, she had ten pairs of shorts, several tops, and even a silver ankle bracelet Regina insisted

Glory needed. She then drove Glory to a shoe store because in Regina's words, "Used shoes are gross." Glory grinned at the sentiment.

Having changed into a new-to-her outfit, Glory felt a little self-conscious when they returned to the house. Her legs hadn't seen the sun in six years except for the previous day at the beach, and then she was covered in sunscreen. Regina helped carry the shopping bags, and as they walked through the garage, a monstrous roar came from inside the house.

"Oh, no." Regina dropped the bags and grabbed Glory's arms. "Let's wait out here."

"What the hell was that?"

"Ripley Anders Davidson, calm your ass down now!" Conrad yelled. Damn, the man's voice carried. Glory broke away from Regina's hold.

"Glory, wait!"

She didn't. Glory burst through the door and skidded to a halt, landing on her ass. There was a lion pacing the area between the kitchen and dining room. "What the hell?" she asked again, and the massive animal turned her way. She may have squeaked. When the beast shook its fluffy mane and huffed at her, she most definitely squeaked. "Uh, Conrad? Am I crazy or is there a lion in the house? And where's Rip? I heard you yelling at him to calm down."

"You're not crazy. That's—" Before he could finish explaining, the lion shifted, and in its place stood Ripley. A very naked Ripley.

"Rip, you're naked. And a lion."

Glory started giggling, and Ripley frowned. "And that's cause for giggles?" he asked, narrowing his eyes.

"Oh, no. The laughter is because you just changed from a lion to a man." She looked over her shoulder where Conrad was hugging Regina. "Did you guys see that?"

"We saw," Regina muttered.

Okay. If his parents weren't freaking out, she wouldn't either. Yet. "Wait! That's why you growl all the time. Right? Oh, my god. You're a... a... What exactly are you?"

"A Gryphon, which is half Eagle, half Lion. I'm too big to show you in the house, but I can also shift into my Eagle form."

"Really? Like right now, if I asked you to show me, you would?"

Within seconds, a massive eagle with fiery red wings stood mere feet away from Glory. "Wow. You're beautiful. And huge. I've never seen an eagle with wings that color."

"That's because he's a fire Gryphon. Our Eagle's wings represent the color of our element. I am also a fire Gryphon, but Gina is an air Gryphon, so her wings are solid white."

"Shut the front door. You're all shifters?"

Ripley returned to human. "We are. All the Hounds are. Hounds of Zeus is more than a motorcycle club. Zeus called his shifters Hounds even though we're Gryphons. You're taking this surprisingly well."

"Right? I should be freaking out because my boyfriend, who is still naked in front of his parents, can turn into a large cat. Is it wrong that I want to cuddle you in that form? Do you like belly rubs? Oh, crap. I'm not being politically correct, am I? But you're my

204

boyfriend, so I should be granted at least a little leniency. Right? *Right*?"

Ripley strode across the room, his manhood swinging between his legs, and lifted Glory off the floor. She wrapped her legs around his waist, because one, he was still naked with his parents in the room, and two, her legs dangling was all kinds of awkward even if she was being held tightly. Rip kissed her as though he'd not seen her in days.

Conrad cleared his throat. "We'll just let you two…" Glory assumed he and Regina left the room. She wasn't going to stop kissing Rip long enough to look. He carried her across the room and set her on the island.

"Are you really okay with this?" Ripley's eyes weren't on hers, so Glory lifted his chin.

"So okay. But what the hell? Shifters are real? I mean, yeah, they obviously are. I just saw one with my own eyes. Holy crap. Wait, you said all the Hounds are, so that means Ryker and Sutton and Branson and Ace too? And Rhiannon knows this? Lynnette knows about Branson?"

Ripley grinned. "Yes, all the men you named are Gryphons. Rhiannon knows, as does Lynette. Rory is also a Gryphon. It's the reason she and Sutton don't look their age. They're over a hundred. My parents are in their seventies."

"Yeah, but they look it."

"Not really. My mom voiced you when she first hugged you. Gryphons have the ability to skew human minds to make them forget things or see things not exactly as they are. I apologize on her behalf, but I wasn't ready to have that conversation, so she made you think they appeared older than they actually do."

"Why would she do that though?"

Ripley sighed. "I told you about Sara Beth. What I couldn't tell you was before I proposed to her, I needed her to know my true nature, so I shifted. She freaked out. Like inconsolable, crying, and refusing to come near me. I could have voiced her to forget what she saw and continue with the proposal. Some Gryphons do that. They are mated to humans who have no idea what their partner is. But I didn't want that. I refused to live having to hide my true nature from the person who was supposed to be my other half. I did voice Sara Beth, but I made her forget what she saw. Then I convinced her she was no longer in love with me."

"Oh, Rip." Glory took a deep breath. "I'm sorry you went through that. Truly. But why were you upset just now? Why did your dad tell you to calm down?"

Ripley leaned his head back and blew out a breath. "Because someone burned my house down."

"What? No! Oh, god. This is all my fault. I knew I should have talked to my father." Glory pushed against his chest. When he stepped back, Glory jumped down from the island and took off for the bedroom.

"Where are you going?" Ripley was right behind her. When he grabbed her bicep, she tried to jerk away, but he was too strong. "Sunshine, talk to me."

"I'm going back to New York and… And stomp a mudhole in my father's ass."

Ripley grinned, but Glory didn't get why. Someone burned his house down. He should be crying or turning into a freaking lion. No wonder he'd let the beast loose.

"So fucking sweet," Ripley whispered before kissing her again.

When they came up for air, Glory pushed him back. "Okay. You really need to put your clothes on. This" — Glory motioned down his body — "is distracting."

"Good." Rip picked Glory up and tossed her over his shoulder.

"Ripley!" Glory grabbed onto his hips, then she got a good look at his muscled rear as he strode down the hallway. She couldn't help but grab a handful of one glorious cheek. Then she slapped it, and he growled. "Eek! Is that you growling or your lion? Now that I know why you do that, I don't want to piss it – him – off. Is he separate from you? Like when you shift, is it still you in there? I have so many questions."

Ripley gently placed her on the bed, then stretched out on top of her. Holding himself aloft on his forearms, he grinned again. "My Gryphon has a mind of his own, although we are one being. The first time we laid eyes on you at the market, he assured me you were our mate."

"What does that mean? Like girlfriend or something else?" And that's why Major had called her Ripley's mate on the phone.

"Something so much more. For a shifter, a mate is the one being designed especially for them. He never once claimed Sara Beth, so that should have been my first clue she wasn't meant to be mine. But he took one look at you and that was it. It was all I could do to keep him from coming out and dragging you away from that booth."

"So being a mate is serious business."

"It is. Mating is for life."

"You said he thinks I'm your mate. What do *you* think?"

"I agree. I must be honest though. After what happened with Sara Beth, with her freaking out, I was hesitant to trust him. I didn't want to go through the heartache again, but now I don't have to."

"I don't get why you would be stuck with someone like me." Ripley's chest rumbled, and his eyes changed from blue to gold. She sucked in a breath, carded her fingers through his hair, and said, "Easy, big guy. Please don't eat me."

Ripley pressed his face to her neck, and his body shook. It took a few seconds to realize he was laughing. "So fucking cute," he muttered. Rip then kissed her neck and nibbled her earlobe. Glory spread her legs farther to accommodate his lower body. She had this fabulously naked man on top of her, so who could blame her for wanting him again? Then she remembered where they were.

"Ugh. We can't have sex in your parents' house."

Ripley raised his head. His eyes were back to their normal color. "Why not? You think they're going to refrain just because we're here?"

"Uh…" Glory hadn't thought about that, but now that he'd put it out there, nope. She didn't want to imagine his parents together. "Wait up. If your mom voiced me, or whatever you called it, what do your parents actually look like?"

"Let me get dressed, and you can see for yourself. I

need to call Ace back and find out more about what's going on with my house."

"I really think I should go back to New York and talk to my father." Glory didn't want to, but if it would take the heat off Ripley, she'd do it.

"Not going to happen, Sunshine. We don't have proof it was him, but if we find evidence it was? Let's just say you might not have a father to worry about for long."

Glory thought about that for a second, then said, "Yeah, that should probably bother me, but it doesn't. Amos Yearwood is not a good man and hasn't been as long as I can remember. Maybe then my mother could get away from Haven." Then again, her mom would have no way of taking care of Glory's sisters. She'd never worked outside the home, and there was no home to return to. Maybe Granny would be willing to take them in. "I think I need to talk to my grandmother sooner rather than later."

Ripley rose from the bed. Glory couldn't help but admire his body as he asked, "Yeah? Why's that?"

"If my father is going to meet his end soon, my mother has nowhere to go."

"And you think your grandmother would help with that? It's not like you can tell her your father is going to die soon, Sunshine. And we don't know that he is. I'm not a killer. Not unless I or someone I love is in mortal danger."

"I still want to call her and find out what happened in the past. Let her know I'm okay."

"We can do that." Ripley, now dressed in shorts and a T-shirt, held out his hand. He pulled Glory to her feet and wrapped his arms around her waist. When Glory looked up, Rip bent his head and kissed her softly. "Thank you."

Glory placed her hands on his chest. "For?"

"Not freaking out. It was my biggest fear."

"Fear not, my handsome Gryphon. I think it's cool as hell you can shift into different forms. And you never answered my question about belly rubs."

"Oh, we love belly rubs. I'll shift for you later, and you can snuggle with my Lion."

Glory couldn't wait. As they walked to the main part of the house, she asked, "How big is your Gryphon?"

"About that big," Ripley said, pointing out the back door.

Glory squeaked, tugging on Rip's hand to stop walking. "Holy moly. Is that...?"

"My dad. Come and meet my parents properly." Ripley's voice was weird, and something washed over Glory as he led her outside. She hung back, keeping him between her and the big mythical animal, though she guessed it wasn't mythical since it was real. Conrad – and it was weird to think of the Gryphon as Ripley's dad – sat on his lion's butt with his eagle's wings spread out behind him. Glory didn't want to get anywhere close to the pointed beak or sharp talons. Regina, who no longer resembled an older woman, walked over and wrapped her arm around the feathered neck of her husband. Mate. She was holding a robe in the other hand, and when the Gryphon shifted into a man, Regina covered him from behind, and he slipped his arms into the robe, tying it around his waist.

"I thought you might want to see our Gryphon form, so ta-da," Conrad said when he turned to face her. Conrad now looked the same age as his son. With their dark hair and tanned skin, they looked more like brothers than father and son. Regina had long blonde hair pulled back in a braid, and she was dressed like a gorgeous band groupie.

"That was amazing." Glory turned to Ripley. "Does your Gryphon look like your dad's?"

"Pretty much. I think his wings are a deeper red since he's older, but we're the same size. Mom's is not quite as large."

"This is so surreal. And I'm glad I get to see your real faces, not those older versions."

Regina crossed her arms over her chest and glared at Rip. "I'm glad too, Glory, but Ripley, what are you going to do about your house?"

"Ace and some of the other Hounds are handling it. I'm not taking Glory back to New York while there's a threat, and I'm not leaving her here without me, so what other choice do I have?" When Glory opened her mouth, Ripley pressed his fingers to her lips. "No, Sunshine. You are not going to confront your father."

"Fine. I'm going to put away my new clothes, and then I'm going to call my granny." Glory left Ripley outside with his parents and headed to the garage where she and Regina had left the packages. It didn't sit well with her that all this was her fault and there was nothing she could do about it. She couldn't sneak out and return to New York on her own since she had no money. And that was another thing she didn't like.

Sure, Rip had enough money for them both, but in cases like this, it would be nice to have her own. Was this how things were going to be if they continued in a relationship? Him calling all the shots and her going along with it, just like her parents? She didn't think so.

When she got to the suite, she closed the door, then dumped the bags on the bed and proceeded to pull the price tags off each garment. They probably needed washing, but Glory didn't want to use the laundry room without asking, so she piled them together on the bed. She had left her phone on the charger, and when she tapped the screen, it beeped with several notifications. Glory ignored them all except one. Pressing the last missed call, she walked over to look out the window while it rang.

"Glory, are you okay?"

"No, I'm not okay. I need your help."

# CHAPTER SEVENTEEN

## Ripley

RIPLEY RUBBED THE back of his neck as his mate walked away. "I think I screwed up."

"You're doing the right thing, Son. It's too dangerous for Glory back in New York, especially if her father and those other Haven fuckers know she's with you."

"I agree, Dad, but she thinks this is her fault, and she wants to confront her father."

Regina lifted her chin. "Think about this from her perspective. Glory is a strong woman, but she's lived with a dad who ruled with an iron fist, and her mother had no say in anything. Then Glory was taken to that cult where men ruled, and women were expected to obey without question. Her life has never been her own, and with you saying she *can't* go back, well, I think she's feeling as though she still has no say in her life. Glory has no identification, no money, no job, or any means of taking care of herself. You have plenty of money, but you've only known her a few days, and she doesn't see the two of you as partners. Not yet. And of course she feels as though this is her fault since her escaping Haven is the reason you're being targeted. I know you want to protect her, Rip, but think about this from her point of view."

Rip blew out a breath. "You're right, and I'm going to talk to her." He didn't wait for either of them to argue about giving her time or space. Rip let himself in the back door and opened his shifter senses. Glory said she was going to unpack her new things, and when he heard her voice, he assumed she was talking to her grandmother. What he heard chilled his blood.

*"No, I'm not okay. I need your help."*

Rip rushed through the house to his suite. When he pushed open the door, Glory's eyes widened. "Let me call you back." When she hung up, she tossed the phone on the bed and gestured to her clothes. "I need to borrow the washing machine."

"Sunshine, I'm sorry." Ripley crossed the room and pulled his mate close, kissing the top of her head. Glory was stiff, her arms remaining at her side. "I wasn't trying to control your life. I only want to keep you safe. If you feel confronting your father is the best course of action, we'll head home in the morning."

Raising her head, she asked, "Really?"

"Really. *But* I will be going with you to confront him. That part is non-negotiable. We don't know if he's directly responsible for the fire or if he was only part of the plan. We also don't know if they were aware that the house was empty. If they weren't, that means they didn't care that we could have been hurt or worse."

"I just don't understand why they want me back so badly. It isn't as though I was important to Haven. All I did was skin animals. Anyone can do that. And I'm

214

sorry to say it, but William can find another woman to marry. There are plenty of prospects for him to choose from. Not that I wish that on any of the single women, but still. It also shouldn't be about me telling their secrets. I don't know anything, and Rhiannon was there longer than I was."

"Psychopaths don't need a good reason. They —" Ripley's phone rang. He kissed her hair again, then reached into his back pocket for his phone, keeping one arm banded around Glory. "Ace?"

"I have good news and bad news."

"Hit me with the bad first."

"Is Glory around?"

Ripley's arm tightened around Glory's waist. "She's right here. Do you want me to put it on speaker?"

Ace sighed. "Only if you feel she's strong enough to hear we've captured her father."

Before his mother read him the riot act, Ripley would have wanted to shield Glory. Hell, he still did, but he had to trust that his female was strong. He also had to show her he was willing to treat her as an equal. He put the phone on speaker, and told Ace as much. "Go ahead."

"An arson investigator was brought in. They found evidence of an accelerant, so they've opened an investigation. I'll text you the number of the male in charge because he wants to speak with you. Bishop was able to download your security feed from last night, and it clearly shows two males setting the fire. One of those men is Amos Yearwood. The other is William O'Day. That's the bad news. The good news is

Sultan and I caught up with the two men on their way back to Haven."

"Are they alive?" Glory asked.

"For now. We can either handle them in house or turn them and the security feed over to the authorities."

Glory wiggled away from Ripley and sat on the bed, biting her thumbnail. "I want to talk to him first."

"To what end?" Ace asked.

"To find out why he's hellbent on getting me back, and to ask if he knew that there was no one in the house," Glory said, a tear rolling down her cheek.

Ripley closed the distance, sat down next to her, and pulled her against his chest.

Ace cleared his throat. "I can answer that. We questioned them, and your father said he had promised you to William. They didn't intend to kill you, only flush you out of hiding."

"But how did they know about Ripley? Something doesn't add up."

When Ace didn't answer, Ripley prodded, "Ace? I don't have to ask if you voiced them, so what aren't you saying?"

"That someone told them you two are together. Rather, someone told Brother Thomas, and he informed Amos. We don't know who that someone is. Yet."

"The only ones who knew were in Providence House. We know it wasn't one of the Hounds or their mate, so that leaves Julia and Helen," Glory said.

"She knows about mates?" Ace asked.

Rip chuckled. "She found out the hard way. I

216

might have lost my shit when you told me about the fire, and my Lion was pacing the house when she and Mom returned from shopping."

"That's one way to let the big cat out of the bag. So you've claimed her?"

Rip inwardly cringed when Glory looked at him with raised eyebrows. "Not yet. We're working up to that. But back to who knew about us. Helen does have a part-time job, and Julia sometimes leaves Providence, but only if she's with Helen. They both go to church on Sundays. Have Branson question them both."

"On it. Are you coming home now?"

Glory responded before Ripley could. "I still want to confront my father and let him and William know I have a man, so they can both kick rocks."

Ripley grinned. "We'll leave first thing in the morning. We have a pit stop to make on the way, so we should be back day after tomorrow. Since I don't currently have a home to return to, we'll check into a hotel."

"Or you can stay with me. Glory too, unless she wants to return to Providence."

"Nope. I stay where Rip does."

"Then I'll see you both Friday," Ace said.

After saying their goodbyes, Glory asked, "Why are we waiting until tomorrow?"

"Your father and William aren't going anywhere, and I want to hear you play your new piano. Plus, I thought you wanted to call your grandmother?"

"I do. I'm not sure when I'll get back down this way. Besides, if my father is going to jail, my mother will need help if she decides to leave Haven."

Ripley pulled Glory onto his lap, wrapping his arms around her. "I can't promise not to screw up where you're concerned, but I vow on all that is holy, I will do my best to treat you with respect and not dictate your actions."

"I appreciate that. Now tell me about this claiming Ace mentioned."

"After you saw my Lion, we were talking about mates. Claiming is making that official."

Glory threaded their fingers together. "And what does that entail? Do we say words in front of someone, or is it a crazy shifter ritual that involves a blood sacrifice?"

"Your mind is a wonderful, scary thing, Sunshine. All that's needed is intent from both parties, and the Gryphon, me in this scenario, bites you. So just a teensy bit of blood is involved, but I promise it doesn't hurt."

"You bite me? Or your Gryphon does? Because there's a big difference in your blunt human teeth and... Wait. Your Gryphon has a beak." Her eyes widened. "Are you talking about your humongous cat fangs?" she whispered.

Ripley nuzzled Glory's neck. Letting his Lion's canines extend, he scraped them across her skin. "I've heard it's euphoric for the receiving party." Glory shivered at his words. Or maybe it was the anticipation of being bitten.

"Oh, my. Is... Is that something you want with me? To claim me?"

"More than anything I've ever wanted in my life."

Glory tilted her head, exposing more of her skin. "Do it."

"I could, or I could wait until tonight when we're naked and having sex. Euphoric, remember?" Ripley's teeth ached to plunge into her shoulder, and his beast was pushing him to claim Glory, but he wanted her to have more than a minute to think about it.

"I still don't want to have sex with your parents in the house, and when we get back to New York, we'll be staying with Ace. How about we get a hotel tomorrow night and do it then?"

"That sounds perfect. Now, let's get your clothes in the washer and then tell my parents we're leaving in the morning."

"And I still need to play for them." Glory slid off his lap. "Let's do this thing."

After dropping her new clothes in the wash, Glory went to the piano to warm up, and Ripley stepped outside, finding his parents where he left them. He sat down and poured himself a glass of Sangria. He wasn't a big wine drinker, but he loved the fruity concoction his mother had most afternoons.

"How did it go?" Conrad asked.

Ripley filled them in on their talk with Ace, the fact that they were leaving the next morning, and that Glory was going to sing for them.

"Why didn't you lead with that?" Regina was out of her chair and in the house before Ripley could respond.

"I guess that's our cue to follow," Conrad said, grabbing the pitcher of Sangria and his glass. Ripley followed with his own drink. Once inside, he nearly ran into his dad, who had stopped a few feet into the kitchen. "Holy, Zeus," Con muttered as Glory's voice

219

rang out strong through the house. "That young lady needs to share her gift with the world."

"I agree, but I promised to give her all the time she needs to acclimate to her new life outside of Haven."

Conrad inclined his head, then found his feet. They headed to the living room where Regina was poised on the edge of a sofa with her wine glass cradled between her hands and her eyes closed. Ripley understood. Glory's ability with the piano was amazing, but her voice was indescribable. If he believed in angels, he would swear Glory was one.

When the song ended, Glory let her fingers rest on the keys. "So, any requests? I probably won't know them, but I can learn them given a few minutes."

"What do you mean?" Regina asked.

"I wasn't allowed to listen to secular music, but my friend, Sheri, would loan me her MP3 player, and when my parents were out of the house, I would teach myself the songs. That's the easy part. I have to look at the lyrics because I can't remember them that quickly." Glory proved her point when Regina requested a P!nk song called "Glitter in the Air." Even Ripley knew that artist although he didn't listen to pop music. After running through it several times, Ripley held his mom's tablet in front of Glory. He'd asked to borrow it so the lyrics would be larger than on a phone. Glory played flawlessly, and her voice was as good as the original artist's. It was better in Rip's opinion, but he might be a little biased.

"Bravo!" Conrad cheered, clapping loudly.

Regina stood and walked over to the piano, leaning her hip against it. "I saw P!nk in concert about forty years ago. I was blown away by this song, but you… Zeus, Glory. I have no words. The fact that you can listen to a song a few times, then play it without sheet music? You have an extraordinary gift in that, but your voice?" Regina touched her chest above her heart and shook her head. "Unbelievable."

"Thank you so much." Glory reverently ran her fingertips over the white keys. "For the longest time, I was afraid I would never be able to play and sing this way. In high school, it was my dream to become a pop star. Now…" Glory huffed and looked over her shoulder at Ripley. "Now I want to get past this craziness with Haven, be there for Rip as he rebuilds his house, and just enjoy my freedom for a while. Your son has promised to take care of me while I figure the rest of it out, and I'm going to trust him to do that."

Turning to Rip, his mom asked, "Speaking of the Haven craziness, do you want us to come to New York? We can get a hotel suite."

"I'll never say no to you visiting. Glory still needs to call her grandmother, and if things go well, we'll be stopping on the way home to see her. That'll put us in New Troy on Friday. I already agreed to stay with Ace, but having you both close for moral support would be nice. Glory can always use another female in her life."

"Then it's settled. We'll book a flight for the day after tomorrow. If you feel cramped staying with Asher, we can get you a suite as well," his mom offered.

"I might take you up on that. Being newly mated might get to be too much for Ace to listen to."

"Rip!" Glory hissed.

221

"What? They remember what it was like when they first claimed one another."

Conrad stepped next to Regina and grabbed her, dipped her low, and kissed her passionately before returning her upright. "We sure do."

Glory turned her head, but she was smiling. Placing her hands on the keys, she began playing the song Sutton requested. Ripley found the lyrics on the tablet in case she needed them, and set it in front of her. She sang and played until dinnertime, and Ripley wasn't the only one falling in love with his little songbird.

After dinner, which Glory helped Regina prepare, they retreated to their suite to call Leona. Ripley pulled up the number from Bishop's text message and held out the phone. Earlier, when he heard her asking someone for help, Rip thought it might have been her grandmother she was speaking to, but while Glory was busy in the kitchen, he and his father retreated to the patio, where Con told him Lynette phoned earlier to see what was going on. Glory had said she'd call her back but never did, and Lynette got worried. Conrad explained Glory's frustrations and Rip's apology. Once Glory spoke with her grandmother, Rip planned to have her call Lynette as well.

"Okay, here goes nothing." Glory tapped out the number, and the phone rang several times before going to voicemail. "Granny? It's me, Glory. You might not have answered because this is a strange number, but it's really me. I'm in Florida, and I want to come visit you, but I don't know if you're home, or if you even want to see me. In case you don't see the number on your screen it's… What's the number?" she asked Rip. He slowly stated the digits into the speaker, then Glory continued. "Uh, that was my boyfriend, Ripley, by the way. Anyway, please call me back. We're leaving his parents' house tomorrow morning headed north, and I'd really love to stop and see you if you're home. Okay, well, I love you." Glory cradled the phone in her hands. "Her voice is the same. Is it weird I thought she would sound different because she's older?"

"No, Sunshine. You haven't spoken to her in a long time, so that makes sense."

The phone rang, and Glory fumbled it. Ripley reached out and steadied her hand. "Oh, god, it's her."

"Well answer it, Baby."

Glory did, her eyes wide at either the anticipation or him calling her baby. "Hello?"

"Glory? Is that really you?"

"It really is me. It's so good to hear your voice."

"Oh, my precious girl! I can't believe it. I never thought I'd hear from you again. After a few years of silence, I gave up."

"I'd honestly given up too, but then a miracle happened." Glory launched into the tale of her dad hauling them to Haven, then her being rescued at the market. Leona asked a million and one questions, and Glory answered them all honestly.

"I should have shot that bastard when I had the chance," Leona muttered.

"Granny!"

"What? Amos is a snake. I never liked him, but when he got caught up with that Josiah Talbert fella, I knew no good would come of it. I was right. Dammit, I

223

wish we could go get your sisters. I'd take you all in."

"Now that Father has been captured, you might get your wish. I'm not sure Mother will be able to stay at Haven or even want to without him there."

"My place isn't very big, but we can make do if she wants to get away. Glory, I know you were planning on stopping by here, but will you do me a favor?"

"Of course, Granny. Anything."

"Go on back to New York and get that boyfriend of yours and his biker brothers to help rescue your momma. I'm going on the assumption she'll want to get out of Haven, and until you tell me different, I'm gonna get my house ready for her and your sisters."

"Granny, I don't want you to get your hopes up."

"Sugar, you got your miracle in escaping. I'm going to pray I get my own miracle and Marjorie agrees."

"Okay, Granny. I love you so much."

"I love you too, Sugar Pie. I'll be waiting for your call."

Glory was crying when she hung up. "I really wanted to see her."

Rip took the phone and placed it on the bed. He then cradled her face in his hands, swiping the tears with his thumbs. "I know, but I have something that I hope will make you feel better about not seeing her."

"Yeah?"

"Since we're not cutting north through the state, how about we head up the coast and find another hotel on the beach? We can leave as soon as we get packed so we have two nights of privacy." Ripley was ready to claim his mate.

"I'd really like that."

"Excellent." Ripley helped Glory to her feet. "I'm going to start packing, but you might want to call Lynette. She's worried about you."

"I can see why. I called her panicking, and then you barged in all apologetic, and I forgot to call her back."

Ripley tapped Glory on the nose. "It probably won't be the last time I have to apologize." He left her to her call and retrieved his duffel from the closet. The sooner they hit the road, the sooner he could claim his mate.

# CHAPTER EIGHTEEN

## Glory

GLORY WAS THRILLED about seeing the ocean again, but she was more excited about Rip claiming her. Glory didn't understand how he could be certain she was the one after such a short time. Maybe it was a shifter thing. Or maybe she'd fallen and hit her head, and this was all a dream because, come on, shifters?

How crazy was it that she had known this man less than a week, yet she was considering pledging her life to him? Before she spoke to Lynette, Glory had been second-guessing herself. During their call, Lynette assured her being mated was everything Glory could ever want and more. Lynette suggested Glory talk to Rhiannon and Natalia for further confirmation since both were also humans mated to Gryphons. She then reminded Glory that Martina was also mated to Tank. Glory had seen all four women with their mates, and there was no doubt how much each was adored and protected. She wanted that for herself. There was so much she still didn't know about Ripley or Gryphons, and she planned on asking all her questions on the drive to the beach.

Saying goodbye to Rip's parents wasn't hard since they were also traveling to New York. After hugs all around, she and Ripley were loaded in Ace's car and headed north. Ripley held Glory's hand as she asked her questions, and he answered every one of them. The only thing that troubled her was the fact that she would continue aging. "Will that not bother you?" she asked.

"It'll wreck me if you die before I do, but Gryphons aren't like some other shifters, who are practically immortal. There's nothing to say I won't die before you, but know this, Sunshine. I'd rather spend every day loving you for as long as I can than not know what having you in my life is like."

"So fucking sweet," Glory whispered, borrowing one of Rip's sayings. She had already asked if there were other types of shifters out there, and Ripley admitted to knowing Gargoyles and wolf shifters. He told her about Ryker's sister-in-law and her daughter being dire wolves, and Glory would meet them eventually. Glory still wasn't sure she was awake and not in some elaborate dream.

Rip stopped for the night sooner than she expected. There was a sense of urgency surrounding them, and Glory assumed it was due to what they would be doing once they were alone in the room. This time when she packed, Regina loaned Glory a smaller bag so she didn't have to haul the larger suitcase inside. It was big enough for a couple changes of clothes and her toiletries. Ripley grabbed it and his own bag out of the trunk, then they headed directly to the room he must have reserved before they left New Boca. He used his phone to access entry, and Glory wasn't surprised to find another well-appointed suite.

Ripley placed their bags by the bedroom door and turned to Glory. She kicked off her flip-flops and padded across the room, snuggling against his hard body. "Any more questions?" he asked, pressing his cheek to her temple.

"Just one." She leaned back and looked up. "Are you sure about this?"

"I should be asking you that, Sunshine."

Glory cupped his jaw, rubbing his whiskers with her thumb. "If you're certain you can see yourself with me the rest of your life, then of course I'm going to say yes. In case you haven't noticed, you're quite the catch, Mr. Davidson. Oh, I do have one question; do Gryphons get married, or is claiming me as your mate the same thing?"

"It's basically the same thing, but to make it legal in the eyes of humans, we can get married so the paperwork doesn't have to be forged. I try to stay on the right side of the law. Anything else?"

Glory pulled his head down for a kiss. Ripley picked her up, keeping their lips locked as he walked to the bedroom. Instead of putting her on the bed, Rip placed Glory on her feet. "There's no rule that says I have to claim you this soon." Rip's mouth said one thing, but his eyes told a different story. There was so much hope there, and Glory wouldn't deny how much that thrilled her. *Her.* The woman only gross, old men at Haven wanted.

"Rip, unless you have some dark side you haven't shown me, I want you. I want this with you. To be your mate." And his wife, but that would come with time. Once bitten, Glory would be his in all ways that mattered.

"No dark side. I might look like a roughneck with my ink and bike, but I vow on all that's holy, I'm a good male."

"Then claim me." Glory pulled her T-shirt over her head, letting it fall to the floor. She undid her shorts, pushing them down her legs, kicking them off to the side. "Is this going to be done with only one of us getting naked?" she sassed.

Ripley got with the program and was standing bare before her while she still wore her underwear. He arched a dark brow. "You were saying?"

Glory quickly lost her bra and panties, the urge to cover herself great, until Rip's eyes smoldered as he took in her skin. "Absolutely stunning," he husked as he pulled her body to his and slanted their mouths together. His dick hardened against her stomach, and Glory wanted it inside her. She reached between them, but as her fingers wrapped around his shaft, Rip grabbed her wrist. "No. I'm too close already, and I want to be inside you when I come. Let me grab a condom."

Ripley released her, but when he dug into his wallet, he stared at it a few seconds before throwing it down, growling.

"What's wrong?"

"I don't have protection. Shit."

"Do you not want kids?"

"I do, but I thought we'd have more time with each other before we added to our family."

"There's no guarantee I'll get pregnant tonight. I'm okay with not using them if you are." Glory had imagined her belly being round with Ripley's baby more than once, but she didn't tell him that.

"Good because my Gryphon is about two seconds away from shifting." Ripley tugged the covers down, and Glory climbed on the bed, flipping onto her back. Rip didn't hesitate to join her. "I need to claim you. I promise I'll make it good for you after, but like I said, I'm barely holding my beast in check." Glory didn't understand why he thought sex wouldn't be good for her. Having all this man's attention, having his thick erection stroking her core, it was so much more than good. Rip grabbed hold of his length and stroked the tip against her clit, down through her folds, and back again. Glory squirmed, needing him inside. She widened her legs, wrapping her ankles around his thighs, pulling on his butt to give him one of her hints.

He didn't make her wait. Ripley thrust inside to the hilt, not pausing before pulling out almost all the way and sliding back inside her slickness. He set up a quick rhythm, his eyes never leaving hers. "I'm close, Baby. I gotta ask once more, are you sure?"

"Yes. Claim me, Rip." Glory angled her head to the side, and when his fangs elongated, she bit the inside of her cheek so she wouldn't gasp. She had seen the sharp teeth. Had felt them scraping against her neck but anticipating the pain— Ripley struck before she could ask him to wait. There was no time to register the initial sting as ecstasy coursed through her body. Ripley sucked at her skin, and Glory writhed beneath him. Sex with Ripley before the bite had been wonderful. But this? This went beyond anything she could have ever imagined. If Gryphons could bottle this euphoria, they would have the newest, best-selling drug on the market. Glory gripped his biceps and held on as he pounded into her. The roughness should have scared her, but instead, it had her screaming for more. Or maybe it was the orgasm he pulled from her. Glory's vision faltered as her release pulsed around his cock.

Ripley removed his fangs from her neck, swiped at the area with his tongue, then threw his head back. The roar that came with his own orgasm shook the windows. Glory was mesmerized as a single drop of blood fell from the tip of one sharp canine. His golden eyes locked on hers, and his chest rumbled. In that moment, Glory was seeing man and beast sharing one body. Ripley retracted his fangs before lowering his head. As frantic as their claiming had been, Rip was now gentle. He cradled her head in his large hands as harsh breaths fanned across her face. "Thank you," he whispered.

"You're welcome. Thank you for wanting me."

Ripley kissed her with so much tenderness Glory thought she might cry. Never did she imagine having something like she did with this man. Strong yet gentle. Fierce yet tender. Ripley's release leaked down her ass crack, but instead of pulling out, he began moving again, this time slowly. His dick was getting hard again, and Glory was more than ready for round two.

Ripley made love to her, his eyes never leaving hers as he murmured sweet adorations. He angled his erection so it rubbed against her clit, and once again, Rip brought her to orgasm without his mouth. It was magnificent. This time when he came, his eyes remained their vibrant blue. Ripley eased out and rolled to his side, pulling Glory half on top of him. She rested her cheek against his chest, the steady thump of his heartbeat loud against her ear. The afterglow was serene with her stroking the hair on his chest and Rip ghosting his fingertips along her spine. Their peacefulness was interrupted by a loud knock at the hotel door.

"What the fuck?" Ripley kissed her hair before sliding off the bed. He didn't bother with underwear before pulling on his shorts. "Stay here," he ordered. Glory didn't follow Ripley, but she did climb out of bed and retreat to the bathroom to clean up. She turned the faucet on so she could wet a washcloth, and while the water heated, Glory took notice of her appearance, mainly her neck. There was no puncture wound. No blood. The only evidence of his claiming was the liquid running down her thighs, her disheveled hair, and the blush on her cheeks. Glory patted her face, grinning at the woman in the mirror.

Glory stuck the washcloth under the water, and when it was saturated, she turned the faucet off, then wrung the excess out of the cloth. She was wiping her thighs when Ripley appeared in the doorway.

"Damnit, I wanted to clean that up." Ripley licked his lips, and Glory tossed the washcloth in the sink and leaned against the counter.

"Have at it." Her brazenness surprised her, but then again, having his mouth on her body was like nothing else except having his dick inside her. Oh, and his kisses. The man knew how to kiss.

Instead of dropping to his knees like she expected, Rip shook his head. "Later, Sunshine. I need you to get dressed and show the manager you're okay. Someone called the front desk when my Lion roared." Ripley's grin said he wasn't at all sorry for disturbing the other guests. "I told him it was from a movie we were watching," he whispered.

Glory giggled as she brushed past him. Pulling on her clothes, sans underwear, Ripley growled. "Your bra, if you would." Glory thought he was joking, but he stood holding the garment toward her, his face dead serious. Glory removed her tee, slipped on her bra, then pulled the shirt back on. "Thank you," he said, gesturing for her to walk in front of him.

When she reached the living room, an older man was waiting with his arms crossed. He studied Glory from head to toe, glancing from her to Ripley and back. "Miss, are you okay?"

Glory held out her arms and twirled around. "Perfect. My husband and I were watching *The Lion, The Witch, and The Wardrobe*. It was the battle scene where Aslan is pissed off and roars at the White Witch. Have you seen it?"

"I can't say I have, but if you would, please keep the volume down."

"Of course. Please give the other guests our apologies." Glory smiled at the man, and he blushed before checking out her legs. When Ripley took a step toward the manager, he made a hasty retreat from their suite.

Ripley picked her up, put her over his shoulder, and stomped back to the bedroom where he tossed her playfully onto the bed. "Is that really a scene from the movie?" Glory nodded, biting her lip as she watched him undress. "Brilliant." His claws came out, and before Glory could protest, her shorts were sliced open. Glory gasped as Ripley gripped her ankles and pulled her butt to the edge of the bed. He removed the ruined bottoms as he dropped to his knees. Pushing her thighs toward her chest, Rip pressed his mouth against her clit, sucking and biting. It didn't take long before she was coming, and afterward, Ripley licked her clean.

A couple hours later, after more orgasms, Glory was nestled against his chest. It was her favorite place in the world. "Why aren't you more upset about your house?"

"Oh, I'm pissed as fuck, but those responsible are being held until I return. My house, even though it was mine, wasn't anything special. You and I can either find one we both like to buy, or I can have one built especially for us."

Glory's fingers paused their circuitous path across his skin. "You want me to live with you?"

Ripley eased Glory off his chest and sat up against the headboard. "Sunshine, we're mated now. That's as good as married. What part of that says I don't want to make a home with you?"

"Well, when you put it that way…" Glory climbed to her knees and straddled his lap. "How is this my life?"

Rip placed his hands on her hips. "Karma, Baby. Good things come to those who do good. Just like bad is going to be rained upon those who have harmed you."

Glory tilted her head, studying his serious face. "But doesn't that bring bad to those offering retribution?"

"I don't believe so. I think there are injustices in the world that when dealt with as your father and William will be, then that helps balance the scales of justice."

Glory sighed. "I don't want you risking your soul for me."

"Not sure I have a soul, Sunshine. I don't believe in your God. I like to think that since the Hounds were created by Zeus, he or whatever god took over his reign weighs our deeds while we're on Earth, then when we die, we either hang out in some form of a good afterlife, or we cease to exist. Either way, I'm not worried about it. It's the same reason I have no problem with evil humans being tortured before death. I would rather they feel some type of pain for their crime than merely getting off easy with a bullet to the head."

Glory leaned over and rested her head on Rip's shoulder. His arms came around her, and they stayed that way for several minutes. She hated her father. Hated William. Glory knew hatred was toxic, but she couldn't help it. Both men had made her life hell, but now they were coming after Rip, and that she couldn't abide. If turning a blind eye to whatever he and Ace had planned for the two men put a stain on her own soul, Glory would be okay with that. Maybe they'd let her be part of the torture. She'd love to kick William in the nuts.

"Let's take a shower, then get some shuteye. I'd like to hang out at the beach in the morning before we take off," Ripley said against Glory's hair. She pushed off his strong chest and crawled from the bed, holding her hand out for him. There was no sexy time under the water other than a few stolen kisses. Ripley stripped the sheets, and together, they replaced them with fresh bedding he found in the closet. Glory didn't bother with pajamas since she was hoping Rip would wake her with either his mouth or his cock. Her libido had woken, and Glory didn't think she would ever get enough.

# CHAPTER NINETEEN

## Ripley

IT WAS AFTER midnight Thursday when they rolled into New Troy. Instead of rushing home, Ripley had convinced Glory to enjoy the beach. Once he assured her she was sexy in a swimsuit, she let go of her insecurities and had fun. They splashed in the waves, lounged under an umbrella, took selfies on their phones, and spent the day talking about the future. They scrolled through listings of houses for sale, but Glory was hesitant to speak her mind on any of them. Ripley could tell when one caught her eye she liked because she lingered over the pictures, often going back and looking at them more than once. If nothing else, it told him the type of home she wanted. Since he was ready to get their new life together started, Rip decided to purchase a home already built, then they could always build something different later.

During the drive, Rip called the fire inspector and lied, stating he had no idea who would want to burn down his home. While he did his best to be a decent Gryphon and obey rules, this was one time Rip had no remorse in being on the opposite side of things. Amos and William deserved the fresh hell coming to them instead of rotting away in a prison cell for a few years. Voicing the inspector wouldn't help with Rip's insurance company, so he didn't stop the man from continuing his investigation. If he happened to figure out who was responsible, Rip would cross that bridge when he came to it, but he asked Bishop to erase the security feed, making the investigator's job harder.

Rip called Ace and his parents, letting them know he and Glory were close. Considering the amount of sex he and his mate were having, Rip opted to stay at the same hotel his parents were instead of torturing Ace. Conrad secured a suite on the same floor but on opposite ends of the hallway after Rip admitted he had claimed Glory. When Glory agreed to not using condoms, Ripley wanted to shout the hotel down. His mate wasn't worried about getting pregnant, and that had his Gryphon preening like a fucking peacock. It also had Ripley overjoyed.

After getting a few hours of sleep, they joined his parents in their suite for breakfast. Regina presented Glory with her birth certificate. It had arrived at his parents' the day he and Glory left. She stared at it with tears in her eyes, but he and his parents let her have a moment. Ripley understood what the piece of paper meant to her – another part of her newfound freedom.

Conrad and Regina insisted on accompanying Glory and Rip when they went to confront Amos and William, and Rip couldn't find a good reason for them not to. After eating, the four of them piled into his parents' rental SUV and headed east. When Ace informed Rip where the two Haven men were being kept, Rip wasn't surprised. Lucy's house was previously owned by her adoptive father, a scientist who experimented with Gargoyle DNA. As far as Ripley knew, Lucy, who was also a brilliant scientist as well as computer specialist, no longer used the downstairs laboratory. With Lucy and her Gargoyle mate, Tamian, in New Atlanta, the house was empty and the perfect place to hide Amos and William.

What did surprise Ripley was the number of cars and bikes in the driveway once they passed the gate. It seemed the Lazlo brothers were there for support. He parked the SUV, then walked around to open Glory's door and help her down. He kept hold of her hand as he explained which bike belonged to which brother. There was one bike he didn't recognize, but that could be one Havyk was working on. The family shared the big, black SUV, and Ripley assumed Ryker was driving it since he didn't ride with Rhiannon so close to giving birth. He led his family to the front door, and it opened as they started up the steps.

Havyk greeted them. "Hey, Rip. I hope you don't mind that we all crashed your little party. When Ace told us what was going on, the mates thought Glory might want some female bonding time after."

"Are Rhiannon and Natalia here?" Glory asked.

"They sure are. So are Kerrigan, Quinn, and my Sadie. Nikita is with Mom watching the boys. Come on in."

Ripley followed Hayden into the game room where everyone was gathered. "Thank you all for being here. For those who haven't met them, this is my mate, Glory Yearwood, and these are my parents,

239

Conrad and Regina." As Rip went around the room introducing Hounds and their mates, Rhi waddled over to stand with Glory.

"I'm so happy you're officially one of us," Rhi whispered, giving her a side hug. She looked like she was ready to give birth at any second. Ripley figured that explained Rev's presence since he was a doctor.

"Me too," Glory said, her smile tenuous as she gave a little wave to the other females in attendance. Kerrigan, Quinn, and Sadie were seated together, but Natalia was standing with Mayhem, and the former assassin glared as though she were ready to whip out her firearms. Rip hadn't seen the Russian in action, but he'd heard what she was capable of, and he never wanted to get on her bad side.

Branson stepped forward. "Before we get to the bloodletting, I spoke to both Helen and Julia. Neither one spoke to Amos or William. I asked about that Brother Thomas fucker, and they both denied having talked to him either."

"Then how the fuck did they know?" Ripley growled.

Ryker stepped up beside Branson. "I've got Bishop scrolling through various CCTV camera feeds to see if anyone has been lurking around town. We were already on their radar with Rhi escaping and us searching for Talbert." He clapped Rip on the shoulder. "I'm sorry about your house, Brother, and we will find whoever alerted them." Ryker glanced at Glory, then back to Rip. "What is the plan for the two downstairs?"

Ripley held out his hand to Glory. "My mate wants to confront them, then I'm going to use them both as punching bags. After, I'll voice them."

"They deserve worse than that. I say we end them," Regina snarled.

"Mom, we're not killers."

"Speak for yourself," Kyllian muttered.

"In normal circumstances, we aren't, but they burned your house down, Rip. You could have been killed." Regina tugged Glory to her side. "They don't get to come after my kids without feeling this momma Gryphon's wrath. Amos may have wanted to flush Glory out, but his intentions were to take Glory back to that hellhole. He hit her, Rip. His own daughter who he should protect, not put bruises on! I want my pound of flesh." Her Lion eyes flashed, and Ripley sighed.

He turned to his dad. Maybe he would try to stop her. Instead, Conrad nodded. "Let us do this, Son." His parents had fought for justice in a courtroom. Not once had he known them to break the smallest of laws, yet they were willing to commit murder for him and Glory. He took in the faces of his fellow Hounds, most of whom were mercenaries. Ripley never judged them for killing, so how was this any different? Amos and William didn't deserve to breathe.

"And what should we do with them afterward?" Ryker asked.

"I say we drop them off in the middle of the Haven compound during the night. Show those fuckers what happens when you mess with the Hounds," Ace growled.

"Sounds good, except I don't want to traumatize the women and children." Ripley replied.

"How about the surrounding woods? The men

who hunt for food can 'stumble' upon them," Glory suggested.

Rip pulled Glory away from his mother. "That's not a bad idea, but Sunshine, are you sure you're okay with what's about to happen?"

"It's like your mom said; Amos planned to take me back and force me to marry William against my will, and if that happened, we all know what William would have done without my consent. So basically, my dad was condoning rape. Yes, I'm okay with this plan."

Natalia clapped her hands once. "Then let's do this." When she took a step forward, Maveryck grabbed her by the waist and pulled her back.

"Where do you think you're going?"

Natalia turned and put a finger in Mav's face. "We discussed this. They tried to hurt my friend. I hurt them. Simple as that." Her accent deepened the madder she became.

"Come on, Lolly. This is a family affair," Mav said, gesturing to Rip, Glory, and his parents.

Natalia narrowed her eyes. "I know this. Glory is my family. My sister. I adopted her, so deal with it." Glory's breath caught, and Natalia looked her way and winked. "These females here" — she waved at the other women — "they are also my sisters. Now you are too."

Glory pressed a hand to her chest. "Thank you. And I'd appreciate you being downstairs with me."

"See!" Natalia smacked Mav's chest. "She wants me with her. Let's go." This time, Maveryck didn't try to stop his female. Ace stood by the door leading downstairs and opened it when Natalia strode forward. Ripley took Glory's hand, and they followed the spitfire down the stairs into the former laboratory. Sultan stood sentry behind Amos and William, who were strapped to metal chairs, their mouths gagged. Both men glared at Natalia, who said something to them in Russian. Rip didn't speak the language, but by her tone, he assumed she wasn't calling them saints. Natalia moved to the side, and Amos caught sight of Glory, his eyes widening as he shouted against the rag.

"Hello, Amos," Glory said. His eyes narrowed, probably because she hadn't referred to him as Father. Ignoring William, Glory strode up to Amos and removed his gag.

"You release me this instant."

"Release you? After what you've done?" Glory's hands were fisted at her side. Ripley wanted to go to her. Protect her from her father, but he had to let her say her piece.

"I've done nothing wrong, while you are out here living with these sinners," Amos spat at Glory's feet. "I never should have given such an insolent child *His* name. You're nothing but a whore."

Glory slapped him. He jerked his head back, eyes lit with fire. When Glory struggled with the gag, Sultan stepped forward and shoved it into Amos's mouth. "All I ever wanted was a normal childhood. To be loved. To have the kind of family my friends had. I have that now." Glory took a step back and grabbed Ripley's hand. "I have a mate who wants what's best for me." She gestured at Conrad and Regina. "Parents who have shown me more love in a few days than you did in twenty-four years. They accept me exactly as I am."

"Damn right we do," Conrad interjected.

Glory took a deep breath. "They bought me a piano before they ever met me because they knew it brought me joy. Did you even know I can play a song just by listening to it a few times? No. You didn't care about things like that. Only that I was useful as a babysitter." Glory then indicated Natalia, who was shifting from one foot to the other, her fists balled at her sides. "I now have friends who have my back for no other reason than they consider me one of them. Me!" Glory pounded her chest, her voice rising. "The one you call whore, they call family. I was your daughter, and you should have loved and protected me instead of trying to pawn me off on that piece of shit," she yelled, pointing at William. "You uprooted our lives all because I had sex one time with my boyfriend. The boy who cared enough about me that he was willing to take me out of New York to Nashville where I could pursue my dream of music. You didn't care about my dreams. You didn't care about me, or Hope, or Splendor, or Majesty. Hell, I doubt you even love my mother."

Amos rocked the chair, yelling behind the gag. Glory ignored his outburst and continued. "I was willing to come talk to you. Convince you I was where I belong and let you go back to Haven where *you* belong, with all those other crazy bastards." Glory tightened her grip on Rip's hand. "You came after me and Ripley and burned our house down. Whether you intended to kill us or not no longer matters. What does matter is that you could have. You said you wanted to flush me out, well here I am. It worked. But this story doesn't end the way you thought it would. I'm rewriting the script. I told you I'd rather die than marry William, but now..." Glory leaned over, grinning. "Now I'm ready to live. I'm ready to ride off into the sunset on the back of a bike with an amazing man. You thought I didn't deserve someone special, that I deserved a nobody like William. But this man right here?" Glory held up their joined hands. "Ripley is as special as they come. He's an attorney. His parents are also attorneys. They're smart. And kind. And they. Love. Me." Glory pounded her chest with each heartfelt word.

Glory took a deep breath. "You fucked up, and now you're going to find out what Rip and I mean to those in this room. Oh, and don't worry about Mother. I'm going to rescue her and the girls from Haven. Hope might want to stay, but if not, I have plenty of help getting her and Scott out of there. Goodbye, Amos." Glory turned her back on the man, waving her free hand in the air. "Have at him." She caressed Ripley's jaw before striding across the lab and up the stairs. He watched her until he could no longer see her feet. He listened until he was certain she was back with the other mates, and then he spun around to exact retribution for his mate, but Natalia and Regina were moving in. Natalia held a long hunting knife in one hand, and Regina shifted to her Lion.

Amos rocked his chair so hard, he fell backwards, his head bouncing off the floor. Regina's Lion stalked across the room until she stood over the man with her sharp teeth inches from his face. Ripley didn't want

245

blood on his mother's hands – fangs – so he took a step forward, but a strong hand on his shoulder stopped him.

"Let her have this," Conrad said. Ripley nodded, but with the low rumble coming from the Lion's chest, he was afraid Regina was going to take more than a pound of flesh, as she put it. With Amos tied to the chair, there was nothing he could do except scream against his gag as Regina's teeth tore into his neck. Ripley watched in both horror and fascination as the woman who brought him into this world ripped Amos Yearwood's throat out.

Regina didn't shift back to human. Instead, she stalked over to where William was whimpering. He pissed himself when Natalia stood before him with the knife pointed at his eyeball.

"Pissing your pants? Not so tough, are you? Hmm, what should I do to you? Make it quick?" She pretended to swipe across his neck. "Or make it slow and painful?" The knife tip dug into his pants where his dick was most likely shriveled up like a raisin. "Trying to force Glory to marry you? I guess that's the only way someone would agree to being stuck with a loser such as yourself." Natalia struck, stabbing the knife between the man's legs. William screamed as much as he could being gagged, struggling against his bindings, but it was no use. The man wasn't going anywhere except possibly his version of Hell. Natalia ran the blade down William's face, cutting a line from his hairline to his chin. Blood dripped off the blade as Natalia pointed it once again at his eye. Regina's Lion bumped Natalia's hip, and the Russian turned to look at her. "You want me to take his eye? Or did you want to finish him off?"

Regina nudged Natalia out of the way, and the female stepped back. "Looks like you pissed off the wrong momma," Natalia said, smirking at William.

"Gina," Conrad said. "Save some for me, will ya?" Her Lion chuffed, but she backed off, prowling over to stand next to Ripley, leaning against his leg. Rip placed his hand on her large head and scratched behind her ear. His dad requested, "Everyone move back please." To William, he snarled, "Not only did you piss off the wrong momma but the wrong papa too." Conrad stripped down to his boxer briefs, then looked behind him to make sure everyone was out of the way before transforming into his Gryphon.

Natalia grinned. "That never gets old."

Tears and snot were leaking from William at the sight of the eagle/lion hybrid, who had his sights on the man. Conrad squawked once, the only warning William got before sharp talons sliced deep gashes into his face, removing an eye the way Natalia had threatened. With his other talons, his dad swiped across William's chest, crimson blood blending with Conrad's red feathers. Then, with a quickness the human couldn't process, the Eagle's deadly beak broke through William's chest, and when it emerged, it was grasping his heart. Conrad dropped the organ onto the floor and stepped back. He shifted to his Lion and padded over to stand on the other side of Ripley. Sandwiched between his parents, Rip took in the carnage. He gripped both Lions tightly and whispered, "Thank you."

"I'll go grab you some clothes, Regina," Natalia offered, then took off up the stairs. Conrad shifted to his human form and got dressed while the female was out of the room.

While they waited on Natalia to return, Ace gestured to the dead men. "Sultan and I will take care of the bodies. Maybe don't let Glory come back down here until we're gone."

"Thank you. Just be careful taking them to Haven."

Natalia jogged down the stairs. "These are Lucy's. You two are about the same size, so they'll do until you can get back to your hotel." Natalia twirled a finger in the air. "Turn around and give the lady some privacy." Everyone did as she instructed except Conrad. His eyes were on his mate as she shifted back.

Ripley nudged his dad's shoulder. "Thank you for that. I sometimes forget how protective you both are."

"No thanks necessary, Son. Your mom had it right when she said nobody messes with our kids, and we do consider Glory ours. Is she really going to try to get her mother away from Haven?"

"Yes. We'll have to wait for the dust to settle once the bodies are dumped. We don't know how long it'll take for them to be discovered, and until they are, Marjorie won't have a reason to leave. Let's get upstairs. I want to make sure Glory's okay."

When Rip topped the steps, he found his mate more than okay. She was surrounded by females who were teaching her to shoot pool. Someone had mixed a pitcher of drinks, and Glory's clear cup was half empty. As though she felt his presence, Glory's eyes turned Ripley's way, and they were a little glassy. She

248

held her cup out in front of her and sashayed across the room. Oh, his girl was tipsy.

"I'm learnin' to poot shool. Poot pool. Shoot shool. Shit." Glory giggled. "I am learning the art of bill-i-ards," she exaggerated.

"Bill-ee-yards, huh?" Rip took the cup and sniffed. It smelled as though someone mixed a batch of margaritas but forgot to add much triple sec. Or lime juice.

Glory retook the drink from him and downed the remaining liquid, smacking her lips. "This is good stuff."

Kerrigan approached, and when she reached for the cup, Glory protested. "Hey. I wasn't done with that."

Kerrigan rocked the cup back and forth. "It's empty. You want a refill?"

"Yep. It's 'licious." Glory leaned into Ripley as the redhead walked away. "They thought I needed distractin'." Not only was his girl cute when she was getting sloshed, but she spoke with a Southern accent. "Is it over?" Glory whispered.

"Yeah, Sunshine. It's done."

"Did you—?" Glory pressed her forehead to Rip's chest. He wrapped his arms around her and kissed the top of her head.

"No, but let's save the details for later. You want to hang out with your new friends, or would you rather go back to the hotel?"

"They're not my friends," Glory mumbled.

Ripley tightened his hold. He knew these females, and they would have done their best to make Glory

249

feel welcome in their circle. "They're not?"

"Nope," she answered, popping the p. "They're my sisters."

# CHAPTER TWENTY

## Glory

WHILE GLORY RECOVERED from her hangover, she and Ripley lounged in their hotel suite and talked about houses. They looked at more listings, and when Ripley convinced Glory to be honest about what she did and didn't want in a home, they narrowed the search down to three. He contacted a realtor and scheduled the showings for the next day. Luckily, the houses they chose weren't under contract, so they wouldn't have to get in a bidding war with other potential buyers. Rip's words, not Glory's, since she knew nothing about buying a house. In fact, she didn't know much about anything, and that bothered her. Ripley never made her feel stupid, but Glory's lack of education and real-world experience kept her from feeling like an equal. She wanted to change that, so she planned to focus on a music career. If she could make money by singing, she could bring something into their relationship other than sex.

On Sunday, Glory was excited as they drove around New Troy, looking at the three empty houses. Ripley promised if Glory didn't like them, they could continue looking. All three properties had at least five acres, unlike the house Rip had been living in. Currently, they were on the deck of the third house. She stood with her back against Ripley's chest, and she knew they didn't have to look further. Glory could envision herself and her mate hosting get-togethers in the big yard that was surrounded by tall shade trees. The house had four bedrooms, which Rip had said was important to him. He didn't have to say why. There was a massive stone fireplace in the den that had plenty of room for furniture and a piano. The kitchen was like something out of a magazine, and Glory could see them cooking together.

"What do you think about this one?" Rip asked.

Glory turned and smiled up at the sweetest man she'd ever met. "I love it."

"Good because it's my favorite of the three. Can you see yourself here? Or do we need to keep looking?"

Glory scratched his beard before tugging it gently. "It's perfect, just like you."

Ripley kissed the hell out of Glory, then pressed his forehead to hers. "Shall I go let the realtor know we'll take it?"

"Yes, please."

Rip kissed her temple before heading back inside. Glory leaned against the railing, imagining having her new friends over. She would have to keep Kerrigan away from the bar because the redhead was heavy-handed when mixing margaritas. Glory's stomach churned remembering the hangover. When she woke the previous morning, Glory was sure she had a brain tumor. Her skull pounded, and she just knew her scalp was going to split open from the pressure. It hadn't, but it had been close.

Ripley took great care of Glory while she recovered, making sure she had pain medicine, plenty of water, and lots of greasy food to soak up the alcohol. They lounged in bed most of the day watching movies and looking at house listings. She appreciated him and told him so.

His response? "Anything for you, Sunshine." Glory believed her mate *would* do anything for her. So would his parents. Glory had a moment of guilt over what happened to her father, especially after learning it was Conrad and Regina who dealt the final blows, but it didn't last long. When talking with the other mates, Glory learned their stories of how they came to be with their Gryphons. She and Rhi weren't the only ones who escaped The Ministry. Kerrigan had as well. Hayden rescued Sadie from a drug lord but only after he'd been sent to kill both her and her husband. As it turned out, some of the Hounds were mercenaries, so taking out the trash, as they called it, was part and parcel for their group. Then there was Quinn, who escaped her late mother's dire wolf pack and found her daughter in the process. Natalia had been freed from a mafia family. It turned out that the lavender-haired pixie was also a former assassin, so her willingness to confront Amos and William made sense. Each mate had endured heartache and pain along the way to finding their mates. They had also been claimed as quickly as Glory once safe from their tormentors, so the one-week timeline didn't seem as ridiculous now.

Instead of fearing Natalia, Glory was intrigued and in awe. The woman was fierce and a badass yet so loving when it came to the twins. When she called Saturday to check on Glory, Major yelled in the background that he was ready for his concert. Now that she and Rip had chosen a house, Glory intended to make Major happy as soon as possible. Ripley returned with the realtor, who congratulated Glory on finding her future home.

"I'll head back to the office and get the paperwork started. I'll also email you a list of inspectors as soon as I get back to my computer."

"Thank you. We're paying cash, so barring any unforeseen issues an inspector finds, this should be a quick process." Ripley took Glory's hand, and they followed the realtor out to where their cars were parked in the driveway.

"You have now reached the end of the birthday gift tally," Glory said as soon as the realtor drove off.

"The house is for me too, Sunshine. So that's a big fat nope." Ripley tapped her nose with one hand and opened the door with the other. Glory rolled her eyes but didn't argue. "What would you like to do to celebrate?" Ripley asked when they were seated in his Camaro. The car had been at Ace's house, so it was safe from the fire. Rip's Harley hadn't been as lucky.

Glory hesitated telling him the truth. Ripley was probably expecting to go back to the hotel and have sex the rest of the day, but she needed something different. Glory needed her music. Sex was wonderful, but now that she'd started playing again, it was like part of her soul had been returned after a six-year absence.

"I can hear you thinking, Sunshine. What is it you want to do?"

"I promised Major a concert, so I'd like to head to Providence and practice. Not only that, but Lynette and Branson want to put eyes on me to make sure I'm okay after what happened with Amos and William. That's probably not the celebration you were expecting."

"Maybe not, but that doesn't mean it isn't a perfect way to spend the afternoon. Listening to you sing is like a cold drink on a scorching day. It's soothing for me, and I suspect it's therapeutic for you. I should have taken you there yesterday."

"I was exactly where I wanted to be yesterday. Do you think your parents would want to join us?"

"I know they would. My parents adore Lynette and Branson, and they love you."

The fact that his parents loved Glory helped heal some of the heartache from her own parents' lack of affection, but it wouldn't be completely stitched back together until Ripley loved her. Glory had fallen hard for her Gryphon, but she wasn't going to say the words. Not yet. She wanted them to be on the same page. Maybe they never would be. Maybe being mated was enough for Rip.

"Hey." Rip tipped her chin up. "What's with the frown?"

"Just thinking how your parents have shown more love for me in a few days than my own parents ever did."

"Your parents were idiots because you are easy to love." Ripley leaned across the console and kissed

255

Glory gently. Her heart stuttered. Did he mean...? "Now, let's go to Providence. I'm ready for some of my nightingale's songs." Ripley called his parents during the drive across town, and they readily agreed to meet them at Providence.

Lynette was waiting out front when they pulled up to the house. She jogged to the car and practically dragged Glory out. "Let me look at you." Her hands cupped Glory's cheeks as Lynette studied her face. She then pulled Glory into a fierce embrace. "I'm so happy for you," she whispered.

"I told you she was fine," Branson said from the porch.

"I really am," Glory assured her friend. And she did count Lynette as a friend, much like the other mates. When Lynette released her, Glory said, "I promised Major I'd play for him, so I thought I'd come by and use the piano to learn some kid-friendly songs."

"Yes!" Lynette pumped a fist in the air. "One day, I'll be able to claim I knew you before you were famous."

Glory laughed and shook her head. "I don't know about that. I haven't decided if I want to go that route. Especially now."

"Why? What's changed?" Lynette asked.

Glory glanced over at Ripley. "Him. I have a ma—"

"Hey, Glory. Glad to see you're in one piece," Julia called from the open door.

"Why wouldn't she be?" Ripley snapped.

Julia took a step back. "Because of her dad sniffing around. Jeeze. Are you back for good?" she asked

Glory.

"Just coming by to borrow the piano."

"Oh? Can I listen?"

"You can do more than that. You can sing with me." Glory grasped Ripley's hand when he held it out. The two couples made their way inside where Julia lingered.

"Speaking of singing together, I want to talk to you about something."

"I'll go grab drinks," Lynette offered.

"Nothing with tequila," Glory called after her as she walked toward the kitchen.

Lynette turned with a grin. "Yeah, I heard all about you learning to poot pool."

Glory groaned. "Ugh. Who told?"

"Natalia. She and the twins stopped by with Rory yesterday. Major insisted he see where your 'concert' was going to take place."

"That kid," Glory muttered, grinning. When Lynette walked off, Glory turned to Julia. "So what did you want to talk about?"

"When Helen and I were at church this morning, the preacher's wife mentioned their soloist had moved away, and Helen told her I could sing." Julia rolled her eyes. "I didn't want to lie and tell her I can't, but I don't think I'm ready for that, you know? So I was thinking, what if you come with me? We could sing together until I feel confident enough to do it on my own. We could practice a couple of songs this week, then you can go with me next Sunday."

"Oh, well…" Glory hated to hold Julia back from something she was interested in, but Glory hadn't planned on going back to church. Ever. "I guess I could do that."

"Thank you. This means a lot to me." Glory was stunned when Julia launched herself at Glory, hugging her tightly. Glory returned the embrace, her eyes wide at Ripley. She didn't know how he would feel about Glory going to church. Since he didn't worship the human God, would he want to go anyway? Or would he expect her to go without him. Just because Amos and William were no longer in the picture, was Glory safe from the others at Haven? Ripley was glaring at Julia, but Glory would have to wait to find out why he was upset. When Julia stepped back, she grabbed Glory's hand. "Come on. Let's get started."

Glory was happy the other woman was finding her place outside the cult, but she was also shocked at the difference in her attitude. It had only been a few days since she'd last seen Julia. Maybe instead of the shy awkwardness, this was who Julia really was.

Ripley followed Glory to the piano. "How different is it to play this instrument than the one my parents bought you?"

Glory sat on the bench and caressed the keys. "This is a nice piano, and if it was the only one I ever got to play for the rest of my life, I would be appreciative." Glory didn't want to hurt anyone's feelings, especially Lynette and Branson. "But let's say this is like a high-end sedan, and the Steinway is like a Ferrari."

Julia asked, "They bought you a Steinway?" at the same time Helen asked, "You met his parents?"

Glory hadn't noticed Helen enter the den, but now that she had, she wanted to grab Ripley and run. The

258

woman was wearing a form-fitting dress that hugged her curves in just the right places.

Before she could answer either one of them, a booming voice came from behind Glory. "Yes, we did, and yes she has." Glory turned on the bench and grinned at Conrad.

"You're Ripley's father?" Helen looked between the two men, her eyebrows dipping as she took in Conrad's youthful appearance.

"And I'm his mother," Regina announced as she took her place beside her mate. Conrad gripped her nape and kissed her. With tongue. Glory giggled as Julia and Helen both gaped.

Glory tugged on Ripley's shirt sleeve. When he leaned over, she whispered, "Why didn't your parents do that voice thing?"

Ripley pressed a kiss to her lips, sadly without tongue. "They can later if it becomes an issue. Now, what are you going to play?"

Natalia had texted Glory a few songs she thought the twins would enjoy, and Glory had already found them on her phone. She knew the tunes in her head, but she still needed to look at the lyrics. When she held her phone out for Ripley to hold in front of her, he frowned. "This is what they want you to play?"

"I guess they like pop music too. And I already checked the lyrics. There's nothing about them the boys shouldn't hear." Glory ran through the notes a few times before adding in the words. She played all the songs Natalia suggested, then Glory took requests including a few hymns Julia wanted to practice. After a couple hours, they took a break for lunch, which

Lynette and Regina had prepared at some point. Since there were so many of them, they gathered in the dining room. Glory leaned against Rip's arm, enjoying the camaraderie between his parents, Branson, and Lynette.

When everyone finished their meal, Lynette brought out a decadent chocolate cake covered in cherries as well as a couple bottles of champagne. While she sliced the cake, Branson popped the corks and poured flutes of bubbly for everyone. Glory didn't miss Helen's frown as he passed a glass to her. Julia sniffed hers, then took a tentative sip. Her eyes widened before she set the flute down in front of her. Lynette, being the wonderful person she was, went to the kitchen and retrieved a bottle of sparkling cider to replace the alcohol so the two women could enjoy a drink too.

Conrad stood, holding his champagne in front of him. "I'd like to propose a toast. Gina and I are thrilled to welcome Glory to our family. We adore you, and we wish you and Ripley as much love as the two of us have shared over the years. Cheers."

Glory raised her glass, tapping it against Conrad's, then Regina's. Lynette and Branson leaned over the table to also get in on the festivities. When she turned to Ripley, his smile was blinding. "Welcome to the family, Sunshine." He tapped her glass, and they took a sip of their drink, staring into each other's eyes. It was the most romantic moment of her life. It was almost as exciting as when he claimed her, but that hadn't been romantic. It had been erotic and life changing. Something only the two of them shared. This was special in that they were among friends and family. Oh, and two females who were staring at them with their mouths open. Glory ignored Julia and Helen. She figured Helen was jealous, and Julia? Glory didn't know what to think about her.

Ripley fed Glory bites of cake from his plate, then moved to hers when his was empty. He ignored the stunning woman sitting across from him and gave Glory all his attention. She was finally believing that he only had eyes for her. That is until the back door opened and a little voice yelled, "Where's the cake?"

Ripley's smile morphed from sensual to ecstatic when the twins ran into the room. "Hey, little dudes. What's shaking?"

Both boys froze, turned around, and wiggled their butts. "Our asses," one of them yelled, giggling.

"Major Lazlo, your ass is going to be hurting if you don't watch your language," Natalia said.

"Sorry, Lolly." Major grinned up at his mom, clearly not afraid of getting in trouble. Natalia rolled her eyes and ruffled his hair. The boy turned and walked up to Glory. "Are you Glory hallelujah?"

Glory laughed, and nodded. "That'd be me."

"Lolly says you have the voice of an angel, and I really want to hear you sing, but I was promised cake."

"I promised cake if you behave. You haven't started off well, have you?" Natalia asked with a straight face.

"But, Lolly! Grammy Rose—"

"Don't you throw me under the bus," Rory said as she entered the dining room with Sutton behind her. "Sorry to show up without calling, but this one" —

Rory tossed a thumb Sutton's direction — "heard Glory was singing and wouldn't stay home."

"And miss a concert? Never." Sutton swatted Rory on the butt as he maneuvered around her into the dining room. "Or cake. Boys, let's go wash our hands." The twins followed their grandfather into the kitchen, and Rory went with them. When they returned, Rory had found more cake plates and silverware.

"Where's Maveryck?" Ripley asked.

"He's talking to Uncle Right about ledges," Marshall said softly.

Rory laughed and explained, "He's talking Ryot off the ledge. Rhiannon has been having contractions, and Ryker wants to take her to the hospital so they'll be there when she goes into labor. Mav is there as a buffer so Rhi can relax."

"Are the contractions close together?" Regina asked.

"Not close enough to be worried. We have plenty of time for cake and music." Rory served Sutton while Natalia plated small pieces of cake for the twins. She poured sparkling cider into cups with lids and straws she pulled out of a messenger bag. While this was happening, Julia stared at Natalia, watching every move she made. Glory understood the fascination. The lavender-haired woman was so freaking cool except when she was spilling Glory's secrets.

"Thanks for telling Lynette about my pool shooting incident."

Natalia winked at her. "You're welcome. You were just too cute not to share." Glory stuck her tongue out at her new friend, laughing.

Helen pushed back from the table and took her untouched cake and glass of cider to the kitchen. When she didn't rejoin them, Glory assumed she'd gone to her room. She almost felt bad for the woman. This was Helen's home for however long it took her to acclimate to being away from the cult, and Glory's presence was making her uncomfortable, even if it wasn't her fault Ripley chose her over Helen.

As it turned out, Rory was partially correct regarding Rhiannon going into labor. Glory managed to play for half an hour with the twins dancing and singing along when Maveryck called to inform them Rhi's water broke, and they were on their way to the hospital. The party broke up with Sutton driving Rory to be with them, and Natalia took the boys home. Glory helped Regina and Lynette clean up the dishes from lunch and their impromptu celebration before Ripley took her back to the hotel, where they celebrated buying a home in private.

# Chapter Twenty-One

## Ripley

THE NEXT WEEK passed in a blur. The inspection on their new house came back with a few minor repairs needed, but Ripley signed off on the sale anyway. He and his dad could make those updates after he and Glory moved in. What hadn't been destroyed by fire in his old house had been water damaged beyond salvaging, so Ripley had to replace all his furniture, dishes, linens, everything for cooking and eating, clothes, and a new bike. He was basically starting over, and Glory was starting at the beginning. This was her first home away from her parents, and Rip wanted her to have everything her heart desired.

His parents took them furniture shopping, insisting they make the purchases even though Ripley had more than enough money in the bank. Ripley wanted everything bought and ready to put in the house when they had the keys in hand, so the four of them spent that week getting everything he and Glory needed. It took a bit of nudging from Regina to convince Glory it was her home too, and she should decorate however she wanted. When he sensed his mate getting overwhelmed, Ripley would kiss Glory, resetting her mood.

In between shopping excursions, they dropped by Ryker's to meet the newest Lazlo. Daisy, named after Rhiannon's late mother, was the tiniest baby Ripley had ever seen. Little Patrick, Tank's son, hadn't been this small, and Rip was afraid he'd hurt her. Glory had no problem cradling the infant, cooing at her, then singing to her when she got fussy. Daisy wasn't the only one mesmerized by Glory's voice. The twins, along with Mateo, were there every time Rip and Glory visited, and the three boys gathered around Glory's chair, singing along if they knew the words. If they didn't, they clapped and shook their butts.

"You should record an album of lullabies," Ryker told Glory. She got a faraway look in her eyes, so maybe Ryker had planted a seed. Rip didn't care what his mate did for a living as long as it made her happy. If she wanted to stay home and raise little Glorys and miniature Ripleys, that would be fine too.

On Friday, Glory visited Providence House so she and Julia could practice. Ripley sensed it wasn't something Glory was looking forward to, but when he asked her about it, Glory said she wanted to help Julia find her place in the world, and if that was singing in church, Glory was happy to help. Ripley still didn't like it, but he trusted his mate to know her own mind.

While they were singing, Branson said, "Let's grab a beer and go outside." Once they were seated on the patio, Branson leaned forward, his arms resting on his thighs with the bottle dangling between his legs. Letting out a sigh, he glanced at Ripley. "You ever have one of those feelings, but you can't figure out what it is?"

"I take it this is a bad feeling?"

"Yeah. I keep waiting on those Haven fuckers to come after us now that they've found the bodies, but they haven't." Ace and Sutton had patrolled the sky in their Eagles. It took a few days, but a couple of Haven's hunters found them, then sounded the alarm.

"Amos and William appeared to be mauled by animals, so how could they pin that on the Hounds without knowing what we are?" Ripley wasn't discounting Branson's bad feeling because they still didn't know how Amos found out Glory was with Ripley.

"They can't, but my Gryphon is still twitchy." Branson leaned back and took a long pull of his beer. "Are you going to church with Glory Sunday?"

"No. Mom's going with her so Dad and I can start working on the house. The seller agreed to give us the keys before closing when I offered half the cash up front as earnest money. The hotel suite is nice enough, but I'm ready for Glory to get settled in her new home. Since tomorrow is the fourth, I paid to have everything delivered Sunday." If it weren't for Regina going with Glory, he would be there to watch over her himself, but his mother was a badass, and she wouldn't let anything happen to Ripley's mate.

"Do you need help moving furniture?"

"I paid extra so the delivery drivers will unload it all, but if you want to help install the washer and dryer, I'd appreciate it. They're being delivered first so we can wash all the linens while the bed is being set

266

up."

"I can do that. If you tell me who all is helping, I'll pick up breakfast on the way."

"That sounds perfect. It'll be you, Dad, Ace, Sutton, and me. Are you and Lynette coming to the party tomorrow?" Every year, some of the Hounds rented a pavilion at a local park. They set up inflatables for the kids, and the adults played volleyball, horseshoes, and cornhole. Ripley rarely attended because it was a day for families. This year he had Glory, and she was looking forward to meeting more mates.

"We are. When we mentioned it to Helen and Julia, we expected them to shy away from being around so many people, but they both seemed excited to get out of the house for a while."

The back door opened, and Ripley didn't have to look to know it was Glory. Her energy was connected to his in a way he never expected. "I would ask how it went, but I've heard you sing together. You're going to wow them with your talent, or make them find God, if that's what the hymns are designed to do."

"I hope it only takes one time for Julia to get over her nerves," Glory admitted.

"She'll at least make them believe in angels." Branson stretched his legs out and crossed his feet. "What about you? Are you nervous too?" Branson asked Glory.

"No. Singing is such a big part of who I am. It's the going somewhere I don't have good memories of I'm not looking forward to. Church was something forced on me growing up, and then Haven happened. I'd rather go sing, then slip out the door instead of listening to another sermon. I've had enough of those to last a lifetime." Glory propped her butt on the arm of Ripley's chair, and he snaked an arm around her waist. "But like I told Rip, if this helps Julia, then I'm willing to do it."

"You're a good soul, Glory. You and Rhiannon are two of the strongest females I've had the pleasure of meeting. You both were put in bad environments, yet you didn't let it tarnish your hearts."

"Thank you. Now, so I don't burst into tears, I'm going to go help Lynette in the kitchen." Glory smacked a kiss on Ripley's lips before hopping up and rushing into the house.

Branson sighed. "I love my sons, but I think I would have enjoyed having a daughter."

"You're not too old to try for one," Rip said.

"Lynette and I talked about it a few years back, but we decided to put our energy into helping those like Helen and Julia. Glory would have been among them had you not come along and stolen her from us."

Ripley grinned at his friend. "I'm not going to apologize for that. Besides, Glory adores Lynette, so I have a feeling she'll be over here often. And you two are welcome to come visit whenever you'd like once we're settled in our new place."

Branson finished his beer and set the bottle on the ground. "Just so you know, Lynette's going to talk to Glory about helping here at Providence. Julia is a completely different person than before she met Glory, and Lynette thinks it's because of their mutual love of music. Plus, Glory's been there. She knows what it's like behind the compound walls, and she can commiserate in a way neither Lynette nor I can. It was Rory who suggested it. She approached several of the women who've left The Ministry, but none wanted the responsibility. I think most of them just want to get on with their lives and forget about what they endured. It wouldn't be full time, but she would be paid."

"You and I both know Glory never has to worry about money. If this is something she wants to do, I'll back her one hundred percent. Ryot mentioned she should record an album of lullabies, and I think she liked that idea. Whatever she decides to do, I'll be right there by her side. I want her to be happy after all the shit she's endured these past six years."

"That's what we all want for our mates." Branson tilted his head to the side as though he were listening for something. "According to the conversation happening in the kitchen, I'd say you and I are doing a good job."

"Eavesdropping is rude," Ripley chided.

"It is, but I don't give a rat's ass. Besides, it's not like she isn't going to tell me what the two of them are talking about. We share everything."

"Couples goals," Rip muttered before downing his beer. "Want another?" he asked, shaking his empty bottle.

"Actually, I'm going to mow. I won't have time tomorrow with the party."

"Since the women are content, how about I weed eat for you?"

Branson picked up his empty bottle and held it out to Ripley. "I'd appreciate it. Please take these inside and inform the ladies we'll be doing yardwork."

Glory was giggling at something Lynette said when Ripley entered the house. He winked at her as he crossed the kitchen to the pantry where the recycling bin was located. When he returned, Rip grabbed Glory and dipped her, planting a kiss on her plush lips. She giggled again, and it was the sweetest sound, right after her moans of passion. "Branson and I are tackling the yard while you two continue whatever it is you're doing in here."

"We're cooking," Lynette huffed, but her eyes twinkled with mischief.

"Right. Cooking always makes me giddy."

Lynette popped the dish towel at his thigh, and Ripley jumped back before she could strike. He put Glory between them. "Save me, Sunshine." They were all laughing when the front door opened, then closed. Shoes tapped across the tile, and Helen appeared in the doorway.

Ripley kissed Glory on the temple and headed back outside. He didn't dislike Helen, but the less he was around her, the better. Branson had used his Gryphon voice on her and Julia, but Ripley couldn't shake the feeling one of them had something to do with Amos knowing where Glory was. It was the main reason he didn't want Glory going to church without a Gryphon watching her back.

With Rip helping Branson tackle the yardwork, it didn't take them long to get it done, and his parents were waiting on him when they got back inside. His mother was icing a cake, and his dad was sitting at the island peeling potatoes. Glory and Lynette were missing.

"She's upstairs trying on a dress I bought her for Sunday," Regina said.

"I hope it's better than that frumpy thing I found her in."

The knife his mom was using paused, and she arched an eyebrow. "Do you think I'd buy that beautiful girl something frumpy?"

"No, ma'am. I do not. I'm sure whatever it is—" Ripley turned when he felt his mate's presence and nearly swallowed his tongue. Definitely not frumpy. "Holy Zeus, Sunshine. You are stunning."

Glory twirled around, showing off her new outfit. The top fit like a glove, but it wasn't so tight it was indecent. The skirt billowed out around her knees, and the deep blue color suited her. "I feel like a princess. But I'm going to take it off so I don't get it wrinkled." Glory rushed back up the stairs in her bare feet.

"Thanks, Mom."

"You're welcome, Rip. I like having a daughter to buy things for."

Ripley strode around the island and hugged his mother tightly. His parents had tried to give him a sibling, but his mom lost the baby after a couple months, and his father said the pain was too great to put his mate through it again. They talked about adopting, but with them being Gryphons, they didn't want to lie to a human child about what they were.

Conrad dropped the knife on the counter and excused himself. When he returned a few minutes later, his eyes were red, but he continued peeling potatoes as though nothing had happened. Instead, he cleared his throat. "Your mother and I have news." He

271

smiled at Regina as she returned to icing the cake. "We're moving to New Troy."

"Now that's the best news I've heard in ages," Ace said, strolling in from the living room.

"Asher! Come give me a hug." Regina placed the knife down and held open her arms. Ace didn't hesitate to wrap Regina in a bear hug, twirling her around. When he returned her to her feet, Ace walked over to Conrad and embraced him as well.

"Hello, Son. It's good to see you," Con said.

"It's good to be seen. Are you selling your place in Florida?"

"No. We're keeping it as a vacation house, but now that Rip and Glory are ma— uh, together," Conrad amended since Julia and Helen were walking down the stairs, "We want to be closer."

"Awesome. And since I'm due for a vacation..." Ace hedged.

Conrad clapped him on the shoulder. "It's yours anytime you want it."

Lynette, followed by Glory who was now wearing jeans and her biker boots, came downstairs. With everyone gathered in the kitchen, the room was crowded, and Ripley was glad they were leaving. "You ready to go look at bikes?"

"Yes. Give me a second." Glory rounded the island and gave Regina a hug. "Thanks again."

Regina pressed a kiss to Glory's temple. "Any time. We'll see you later for dinner, and bring Asher with you."

After saying their goodbyes, Ripley held Glory's hand as they followed Ace outside. "Where are we eating?" Ace asked.

"Regina wants Mexican, so we're going to Martina's."

"Sounds good to me." Ace had taken a rideshare to Providence House so he could ride with Rip and Glory. When she offered to sit in the back since it was a tight squeeze, he waved her off. "Just pull your seat up a little, and I'll be fine." Ripley knew his best friend would be uncomfortable because the back seat was barely big enough for Major and Marshall, but Ace did it so Glory wouldn't have to.

Rip had already looked online at the Harleys the shop had available. He wanted Glory's opinion since she would be riding with him. His old one wasn't a touring bike, but the one he had his eye on had a wrap-around backrest, and that was important to him. Glory's comfort was important to him.

Less than an hour later, Ace was in the Camaro, and Ripley had his mate seated behind him on a midnight blue Ultra Glide. They followed Ace to his house where he parked Rip's car, then fired up his own bike to ride with them. While he was swapping vehicles, Rip opened one of the hard cases and pulled out his kutte.

"Do you always wear your vest when you're riding?"

"It's called a kutte, and usually, yes."

"I like it." When Ripley was reseated, Glory traced the patch and rockers. Her touch was gentle, but being a Gryphon, he felt it. Once Ace was beside them, they headed to the clubhouse so Ripley could get Havyk scheduled to do a custom paint job soon. The youngest

Lazlo was brilliant when it came to his artwork. While there, Glory got to meet several Hounds, and once they mentioned eating at Martina's, a line of Harleys took off from the clubhouse parking lot.

"I never want to ride in a car again," Glory said, leaning against Rip's back. She had yet to use the backrest, and he was fine with that. Having his mate wrapped around him was all he'd ever dreamed of.

Ripley had called ahead, giving Martina a heads-up about the number of Hounds coming for dinner. When they arrived, she ushered the Hounds, their mates, and Ripley's parents into a back room, where they could enjoy dinner together without having to rearrange the front dining room. Ripley introduced his parents to the ones who hadn't met them over the years, and everyone settled in for the best Mexican food for miles.

Tank, carrying little Patrick, joined them, and when the baby saw Glory, he waved his fists in the air, babbling happily. Glory held out her hands. "Gimme." Tank obliged, and when Patrick was settled in her arms, she sang softly to him. Word of Glory's talent had made the rounds, and everyone stopped talking so they could listen. His mate dazzled the crowd, and Regina wiped a tear. Ripley got it. Seeing Glory focused on the baby, completely oblivious to her surroundings, was something to behold. When his mom caught his eye, she placed a hand over her heart. Yeah, Regina got it. Glory Yearwood was something special, and Rip was the luckiest Gryphon on the planet.

Later, after mounds of food and copious amounts

of alcohol had been consumed, the party broke up. The Hounds gathered in the parking lot to climb back on their bikes. When Sultan let out a curse, everyone turned his way, waiting to see what was wrong.

"The alarm's going off at my cabin. I gotta go." Sultan shoved his phone in his pocket, slammed his helmet on his shaved head, and took off like a rocket. Ripley didn't know Sultan owned a cabin.

Judge, who was close with Sultan the way Ace was with Ripley, rushed to his bike. "I'll go with him."

Knowing there was nothing they could do to help, the crowd disbursed and went their separate ways. Most of them would see each other the next day at the park. Glory hugged Ripley's parents before climbing on the back of their bike, and with a wave at the others, they took off for an evening ride. As they took the backroads through New Troy, Ripley sent up a prayer of thanks for the amazing female wrapped around him.

# CHAPTER TWENTY-TWO

## Glory

LIFE COULDN'T GET any better. Glory was surrounded with new friends and a new family. She missed her sisters, and even if she was able to convince her mother to leave Haven, they more than likely would end up in Florida with Granny. That was okay, though, because they would be away from the evil men. Glory still didn't know how she was going to get in to talk with her mother. She couldn't waltz back into the compound, but that was a problem for another day. Today was about celebrating. The last time Glory had seen fireworks, she was a teen and had to watch from her backyard as neighbors set off small rockets. Their family hadn't gone to the local park to watch the huge display the town set off, and their house was several miles outside of town, so Glory could only hear the booms as they reverberated through the night sky.

The few Hounds who rode their bikes to the park had on their kuttes. Glory tried not to stare too hard at each man, but she was intrigued by their road names. Some made sense, like Ripper and War. They were a play on the person's name. Some she guessed had something to do with the biker's personality. Ones like Sultan? Glory couldn't figure out. The other Hounds who had driven their family to the park were dressed in shorts and tees but were no less intimidating than those who wore jeans, boots, and their club colors. Maybe it was because Glory knew their secret. Not all were as tall as Rip, but they all exuded strength in the way they carried themselves. It amazed her that there were shifters walking the Earth with most humans being none the wiser. Rip said the Hounds had been around since the beginning of time and were created by Zeus. That was another thing that astounded Glory. Zeus was thought to be mythical. If Gryphons and other shifters were real, then why couldn't their god or goddess be real too? Thinking about what she'd been taught her whole life and what she now knew gave her a headache.

The Hounds weren't the only ones at the park. It was filled with families and couples with kids. There were even couples who appeared to be on dates, sitting on blankets having private picnics. Some teens were playing volleyball. Others were throwing footballs and frisbees. This was only a small part of what Glory had missed out on when she was their age. She glanced over at Julia to see how the woman was faring. Having been raised in The Ministry, Julia had missed out too, but she appeared to be having a good time. Helen, on the other hand, was staring off into the distance. Glory wondered if Helen was also thinking of things she missed.

Ripley, Conrad, and a few Hounds were playing football with some teens. The twins, Mateo, and kids their age were enjoying the inflatable slide and playing chase. Females with babies had congregated under the large tent to keep the sun off their little ones. Rhi was there with Daisy, and Ryker stood behind his mate and child, standing guard. Glory imagined a time when that would be her and Ripley.

"Glory hallelujah, save me!" Major launched himself onto her lap. She caught him with one arm while holding her grape soda in the air with the other.

"Who am I saving you from?" she asked. Lynette took the soda and put it in the middle of the table where it would be safe from the little Lazlo.

"Lolly."

"And what did you do to your mom that you need saving?"

Major leaned his mouth against Glory's ear. "I stole her cookie." If the chocolate on the boy's lips was any indication, he wasn't lying, and now that chocolate had been transferred to her skin. Glory couldn't find it in herself to care, he was that cute. Natalia stalked toward her son, her eyes narrowed. "Come on. Let's go slide." Major crawled off Glory's lap and tugged on her hand. Glory stood and silently checked with Natalia to see if she was playing or ready to throttle her kid.

"He's all yours," she said with a wink, taking Glory's seat at the picnic table.

Glory didn't hesitate to go with him after that. Other adults had been flying down the inflatable with their own kids, and it looked like fun. Marshall and Mateo joined them, and for the next half hour, Glory let herself be a kid. Afterward, she joined Ripley at the food tables, and they piled their plates high with all sorts of deliciousness. They found empty seats at the table with Hayden and Sadie, and Ripley dug into his potato salad. Before he took the bite, he sniffed the air and turned to face Glory.

"Are you wearing chocolate?" Rip leaned over and licked her ear. "You taste delicious, but please tell me how you got chocolate on your ear."

"From a really sweet kiss," Glory sassed. Ripley growled, goosing her side. Glory squealed and squirmed. "Stop! It was from Major."

Ripley nodded. "I see. The kid's five and already making moves on the older women."

"He is his father's child," Hayden deadpanned. Sadie elbowed her mate, and Hayden grinned at her. "What? It's the truth."

"You know your brother is devoted to Natalia."

"Yes, but you didn't know him when he was younger." Hayden had them in stitches talking about some of Maveryck's conquests. Glory couldn't imagine growing up the way Hayden and his brothers had. The way all the kids at the park had. Sure, some might not have a great home life, but from what she could see, everyone there was having fun, parents and children alike.

Mateo ran up to the table. "Daddy, I need to pee."

Hayden's face lit up like the boy had given him the best gift in the world. Knowing Hayden wasn't the child's biological father, maybe he had in calling him Daddy. "Then let's go pee." Hayden leaned over and kissed Sadie before standing. The two walked off hand-in-hand, and Sadie watched them go. Her smile was as bright as her mate's.

279

"That never gets old," Sadie whispered, but Glory caught the wistful words. Maybe life *could* get better.

After eating, Glory and Ripley walked around talking to Hounds and their mates to burn some of the calories from all the food. He never let her go long without a bottle of water or grape soda, so when it was close to time for the fireworks, she told him she had to pee. They were standing by the table where Lynette and Branson were sitting with Julia, Helen, and Rip's parents.

"Do you mind if I walk with you?" Helen asked.

"Not at all." The bathroom wasn't far, and Ripley could see the door from where he stood talking to his parents.

"Have you enjoyed yourself?" Glory asked as they walked down the paved pathway.

"Yes. Everyone has been so nice. And the food? Oh my goodness. I'm going to have to eat salad for a week to counteract all the calories."

Glory was going to burn her calories off by having copious amounts of sex with her mate, but she didn't think Helen would care to hear that. The restroom was spacious with two rooms having two rows of toilets each. There was an exit at the other end of the building as well. Once she and Helen finished peeing, Glory was washing her hands when Helen stepped up beside her. She turned on the water and soaped up, lathering for what seemed like an eternity. When Helen finished, she went to the far wall for paper towels instead of the closest dispenser. Glory waited for her to return, but Helen motioned at the door closest to her.

"Are you coming?"

Glory shrugged and walked toward her. It wasn't that far to the other side, so she didn't think it was a big deal. When they exited the block building, Helen went left instead of right.

"It's this way," Glory reminded her. Helen kept walking as though she didn't hear her. Glory hurried to catch up. "Helen?"

"There's someone I want you to meet," Helen tossed over her shoulder.

"What? No, we need to go back."

A man stepped out from behind the men's restroom. "Jacob, this is the woman with the amazing voice I was telling you about. Glory, Jacob is a record producer, and he's interested in hearing you sing."

Jacob held out his hand. "Hello, Glory. It's a pleasure." Glory automatically stuck her hand in his as was polite to do. His voice... it was familiar, but she'd never seen this man before. "I'm only in town through tonight, but when Helen told me about you, I just had to meet you."

"Uh, that's nice and all, but I haven't really decided that I want to produce an album."

"But if you decide you want to, knowing a famous producer will fast track the process," Helen insisted.

Glory tried to pull her hand out of Jacob's grip, but he squeezed. "Let's go somewhere we can discuss this."

Glory shook her head no, but when she did, she felt nauseated.

"What's wrong, Glory?" Helen asked. The other woman wrapped an arm around Glory's waist. "Let me help." Sandwiched between the two, Glory was led in the opposite direction from where Ripley waited.

"*Rip!*" Why didn't her voice work? Her legs weren't cooperating either. Helen and Jacob cradled her weight between them.

"Is she okay?" a woman asked. Glory tried to yell no, but no words came out. She then tried shaking her head, but the pain was too intense.

"Too much to drink. We're taking her home," Jacob said.

No, no, no! "*Rip! Help me!*" They carried Glory to the opposite side of the park from where the Harley was, and Helen opened the door to an old pickup truck. Jacob grunted as he lifted Glory inside the cab. Helen started to climb in beside her, but Jacob stopped her.

"You were wonderful, but now I need you to return to the group and act as though nothing happened. Can you do that, Beautiful?"

"What about us? I thought you were taking me with you," Helen asked.

"I will meet you at church tomorrow, and then we will be together." Jacob dug Glory's phone out of her back pocket and handed it to Helen. "Here, take this and drop it on the ground when no one's looking. Go on now before they miss you." Jacob closed the door and rushed around to the driver's side. Glory couldn't hold her head up. It bobbled to the side, falling against the passenger window.

Jacob pulled Glory toward him so that she was lying on the bench seat, her head on his thigh. "There, there. Everything is going to be just fine," he said, patting Glory on the head causing another jolt of pain.

Jacob started the truck, and Glory cried out again. "*Rip! Please.*" Tears streamed down Glory's face, but with her limbs immovable, she couldn't wipe them. She couldn't do anything but close her eyes and think about her mate. About never seeing him again. About never getting the opportunity to sing or play again. Never having children.

As Jacob drove away from the park, a boom shook the air around them as the fireworks show started. That was another thing Glory was never going to see since she couldn't lift her head. The old truck managed to hit every pothole, and Glory was sure she was going to die from the pain in her head. Jacob didn't speak as he took her farther away from Ripley and her new family. After what felt like an eternity, her limbs began to tingle, and Glory attempted to move the hand beneath her. When it twitched, she wanted to yell for joy, but she also didn't want Jacob to know whatever he'd done to make her paralyzed was wearing off.

She had no idea how long they had traveled when Jacob turned off pavement and hit gravel. The truck stopped, and Jacob rolled his window down. "I'm here to see Brother Thomas. I have something for him."

"Let him pass," a man said.

Jacob eased the truck along the gravel path. He shut off the motor and got out, coming around to the passenger side. He opened the door and grabbed Glory's arms, pulling her to a seated position. "Has the paralytic worn off?" he asked. Glory didn't answer. Didn't move a muscle. She wanted him to think she was still incapacitated. He dragged her out of the truck and tossed her over his shoulder with a grunt.

"Fuck, you're heavy," he muttered.

*"No, you're weak,"* she thought. Ripley could carry her no problem.

Jacob carried her several yards, then stopped and opened a door to a building. As soon as they were inside, Glory had to choke back a sob. She was in the barn where she skinned animals. She was back at Haven. Jacob dumped her on the ground, and Glory bit her tongue to keep from crying out. He stared down at her, his eyes narrowed, then he took a step closer. He pulled his leg back to kick her, but the door opened, and Brother Thomas walked in.

"What are you doing?" Thomas demanded.

"The paralytic should have worn off by now. I was making sure she's not faking."

"Where's the other woman?"

"I left her at the park. I'll get her tomorrow from the church."

"Are you sure that's a good idea?"

Jacob stabbed a finger at Brother Thomas's chest. "Who are you to question me? Do not forget your place."

Thomas bowed his head. "Yes, Brother Jos-Jacob."

Holy shit. She knew his voice sounded familiar. It was one she had heard daily while at Haven. Jacob was Josiah. But how? If he was wearing a disguise, it was a good one. Had Josiah undergone plastic surgery?

"What happens now?" Thomas asked.

"Now we wait for her to come around. When she does, she'll place a call to that thug she's attached herself to. If he cares for her, he'll make the exchange. If he doesn't? I'll find another way to get Anna back. For

284

now, find some rope and tie her up. I don't want her getting any ideas about escaping when she's no longer paralyzed. Oh, and bring her mother. Maybe seeing her eldest daughter will help raise Marjorie's spirits."

"Where will you be?"

"Moving Nadine into one of the single women's cabins. Something you should have already done, unless you've been fucking my wife."

"Hardly, but what do you care? You're bringing the other woman here to replace her."

"I don't care. If you want the cold, dead fish, have at her. Now get Glory tied up. I want to make the trade before morning."

"Yes, Sir." Thomas turned to find some rope as Josiah left the barn. While his back was turned, Glory tested her muscles. They still felt heavy, and before she could test whether her legs would hold her if she stood, Thomas was back with ropes. Glory didn't try to fight the man. Better he thought she was still drugged. After he got her hands and legs tied, he left her alone without a word. As soon as the door was closed, Glory wiggled around until she managed to get to her knees. He had tied her hands in front of her, which was a mistake. Glory placed her fists on the floor and pushed on them to steady herself as she slowly got to her feet. Prickles coursed through her feet and legs, and Glory bounced to work through the sensation. She took stock of the barn, finding it just as she left it the last time she'd been there. All the equipment was as it should be with the knives in their holders. Before she got the chance to grab one, Brother Thomas spoke to someone outside the barn, and Glory dropped back down to the floor, curling up how he'd left her.

"She's in here." The door opened, and Glory's mother gasped.

"Glory of God!" Marjorie rushed to Glory's side, dropping to her knees. She brushed Glory's hair off her face. "What did you do to your hair, child?"

Glory didn't answer. She stared at her mother, then cut her eyes to Thomas.

"What's wrong with her? Why is she tied up?"

"Her paralysis is temporary. It was the only way Brother Jacob could get her to cooperate. She's tied up so she can't escape again. I suggest you use this time wisely to talk some sense into your daughter. Your husband ran off, betraying Haven, leaving you to bear his shame. It's up to you and Glory to right Amos's wrongs. There will be a guard outside the door, so don't get any ideas of trying to leave. Splendor and Majesty are already without a father. What will they do without their mother too?" With that, Thomas left them alone in the barn.

"Oh, Glory. What are we going to do?"

"We're going to get the hell out of here," Glory whispered. Marjorie gasped, and Glory shushed her. "Hush and listen to me." Glory spent the next few minutes telling her mother everything that happened from the time she left for the market until she was drugged and kidnapped. "I have proof that Father and William set fire to Ripley's house. You might have loved him, but Amos was not a good man. Thomas and Josiah are not good men. They use God as an excuse to keep people like me locked away from the outside. I have a new life, Momma," Glory whispered. "I have a man who loves me. Friends who are probably worried sick about me being missing. I can promise you that Ripley will not stop until he finds me, and when he does, Haven won't stand a chance against his wrath."

"You might have a man to take care of you, but I have nothing, Glory."

"That's not true. Granny is making a place for you and the girls."

"You talked to her?"

"I did. She loves you and wants you to come stay with her in Florida. And don't worry about the money. I'll make sure you are taken care of. My man and his parents are loaded."

"But why would they help me?"

"Because they *are* good. They're the kind of people we should strive to be. They help those who need it without asking for anything in return."

Marjorie wrung her hands, her eyes wide. "I don't see how they can help us. Your Ripley doesn't even know where you are."

"Not yet, he doesn't. But Josiah's plan is for Ripley to trade me for Rhiannon. He's going to have me call Rip, and when I do, the Hounds will devise a plan to rescue us."

"Why would he do that? You've known this man for two weeks."

"Because he loves me, Momma. It doesn't matter how long or how short the time has been. His parents bought me a piano before they ever met me. I'm their family now, and you're mine as are the girls. And Hope. I know she's married, but when we tell her the truth about this place, these men, Father, she might not want to stay either."

"I don't know, Glory. What if your father returns?"

"Can you honestly tell me you'd want to stay with a man who tried to kill his daughter? Your daughter?"

"But he didn't. He…" Marjorie shoved a fist to her mouth and sobbed. Glory felt bad for her mother, but with her hands tied, she couldn't comfort her.

"He's not coming back. Ever." Glory didn't understand why Thomas hadn't admitted Amos was dead instead of spinning a tale of him betraying Haven. "He's not coming back, and you don't have to stay. If you don't get out, you're going to be passed off to some other man. That's what they do. Josiah is currently getting rid of Nadine so he can bring in a younger woman to be his wife. That is not Godly. Don't you want to get out of here and live a normal life? Be with Granny and the girls where they can have a normal life too? Please do not do to them what you did to me. Living here at this cult isn't what's best for them. You can take them out in the real world and still teach them about Jesus. Deep down you know what Josiah and Thomas are doing is wrong. They wouldn't have armed guards otherwise. Please, Momma. Please do it for Splendor and Majesty if not for yourself."

Marjorie let out a deep sigh. "Okay. If your Ripley comes to rescue us, I'll do it."

Glory nodded and closed her eyes. Now it was up to her Gryphon to get them the hell out of there. First though… "Mother, you see those knives over there?"

# CHAPTER TWENTY-THREE

## Ripley

RIPLEY KEPT HIS eyes on the bathroom door, waiting for Glory and Helen to return. After several minutes, Helen walked from the far side of the building alone. Glory might have needed to do something other than pee, but when she still hadn't come out of the restroom after ten minutes, he began to worry.

"Mom?"

"I'm on it." Regina stood, and together they strode toward the restroom. She entered the same door Glory had, and when she called out for his mate, there was no response. "She's not in there," his mother said, her eyes filled with worry.

"Come on. I'm going to talk to Helen."

"Rip, remember she's human."

"And Glory's my mate. I swear to Zeus—" His Gryphon tried to break free, and Ripley took a deep breath. "Let's go." When they reached the table, Helen was seated, drinking a diet soda as though she didn't have a care in the world.

"Helen, where's Glory?" Regina asked before Ripley could.

Helen waved her hand in the air. "She was talking to some man outside the restroom about music. I didn't want to intrude on their conversation."

"What man? Who was he?" Ripley snarled. Conrad placed a hand on Ripley's chest, while Lynette and Branson stared at Helen.

Helen clutched imaginary pearls, and when the first firework exploded, she jumped. "He told Glory he's a record producer. He convinced her to walk toward the parking lot so they could discuss a recording contract."

Ripley pushed through his father's hold, stomped to the table, and slammed his palms down on the metal. "Tell me the truth," he demanded, allowing his Gryphon's voice to come through. "Who was he, and how did he know about Glory singing?"

Helen shrank in on herself. "His name is Jacob. I met him at church, and he asked about Glory and someone named Anna. I told him I had recently met Glory, but she'd gone out of town with you. He promised to take me with him if I got Glory to talk to him."

"Take you with him where?"

"H-he lives and works in New Carthage. He thinks I'm beautiful and would make a good wife. H-he doesn't care that I can't have kids. Jacob told me we could adopt. I just want someone to love me. Why couldn't you love me? What does Glory have that I don't?"

The other Hounds and their mates had gathered around at that point. Ryker pulled his phone out, and after a few seconds, he said, "Bishop? I need you to track Glory's phone."

Ripley pointed at Helen. "I swear on all that's holy, if something has happened to Glory, you won't see tomorrow."

Julia turned on Helen. "You would really go with him? Go back to that place? You know what those men are like."

"What men, Julia?" Lynette asked loudly to be heard over the explosions in the sky.

"The men from Sanctuary and Haven. Jacob's one of them."

"How do you know that?" Regina asked.

Julia twisted her hands together. "He's been coming to our church a while now. He calls himself Jacob, but I recognized his voice from when he visited Brother Gideon. He looks different now. Like he was wearing a disguise."

"And you didn't think we needed to know that?" Ripley growled.

Julia's eyes widened with tears as she wrapped her arms around herself. "I didn't want to call attention to myself. I was afraid he'd try to take me with him. I'm sorry."

"Julia, you said he looks different," Lynette said softly. "Who do you think this man really is?"

"Gideon's brother, Josiah."

Chaos erupted. Ripley lunged for Helen, but his father and Branson stopped him from getting to her. "You're the reason they burned my house down!" Ripley's Gryphon was close to the surface again, but he didn't give a shit. "Get her out of my sight," he demanded before he ripped the female's head off.

Lynette pulled Helen to her feet, and Regina went with her friend to take Helen away as he asked.

Ripley didn't understand. Branson assured him he had voiced both Helen and Julia. He turned on his friend, who held his hands in front of him. "Brother, I'm sorry. I asked if she or Julia had informed Amos or William about Glory being with you. I should have pressed further."

Ripley took a deep breath. "No, this isn't on you. It's on her." Ripley jabbed a finger in the direction Lynette and Regina were leading Helen away from the group. Any other time, he would worry about his mom taking revenge on his behalf, but he honestly didn't care what she did to the woman.

Ryker's phone rang, and he held up a hand to get everyone's attention. "Bishop?" Ryker jogged off toward the bathrooms, and Rip followed. "Her phone's around here somewhere." Ripley used his phone to call Glory's, and it didn't take long to find it in a garbage can. Ripley took off running toward the parking lot. He needed to get to Helen before Lynette and Regina drove off with her.

They were closing the back door where they had placed the woman, and he growled, "Move."

Regina whirled on him, her eyes blazing. "I know you're upset, but you watch your tone."

"Glory's phone was in the garbage can, so we can't track her that way."

Regina nodded but didn't move. Instead, she opened the door and asked, "What kind of car was Josiah driving?"

Helen's face was a mess of tears and snot. "An old

red truck."

"Do you know where he's taking Glory?" Lynette asked.

Helen shook her head. "I didn't know he was..."

"He was what?"

"Not who he said he was."

"Helen, where the fuck is he taking Glory?" Ripley demanded.

"He said he was taking her home. But I don't know where that is exactly." Helen turned her head away from them, her shoulders shaking with each sob.

Ripley stalked off to where Ryker was waiting with Branson. "Tell Bishop that Talbert's driving an older model red truck. See if he can get a lock on it." Ripley's shoulders sagged, his eyes growing moist. He couldn't lose Glory now. Not ever, but not so quickly after finding her. When his father approached, Ripley told him, "I'm calling Ace. See if he wants to go flying."

"Do you want me to come with you?"

Ripley didn't want to risk his father getting shot if the guards got trigger happy. "No. Stay with Mom and make sure she doesn't kill the bitch." Ripley had never spoken so harshly about a female, but Helen had betrayed all of them. All for a man who had caused so much pain. He didn't care that Helen didn't know Josiah's true identity. Telling a practical stranger that Glory was with Ripley? That was unacceptable.

Ripley called Ace, and when his best friend answered, he told him what happened. "I'm not waiting on Bishop. I'm headed to Haven to see if Talbert took her back there."

"Where do you want me to meet you?" Ace offered

without Ripley having to ask.

"I'll be waiting at the south entrance to the nature center."

"I'll be there in thirty. We'll get her back, Rip."

"Asher—"

"No, Ripley. We *will* get her back. Your mate's a fighter. See you soon." Ace disconnected, and Ripley leaned his head back, staring at the various colors sparkling above his head. Glory was supposed to be there, enjoying the light show. Staring at fireworks wasn't doing her any good, so Ripley strode to his bike. He stowed Glory's helmet in the tour pack, then climbed on, strapping on his own helmet.

"Lead the way, Brother," Locke said as he, Maximus, Legend, and Shadow all climbed on their bikes. Ripley didn't argue. He didn't question whether the males wanted to ride into enemy territory. This was what they did. The MC was a brotherhood. One where they always had each other's backs. It had been a while since Ripley had ridden with the club when it wasn't for a family outing. He had almost forgotten what it felt like to have his fellow Hounds at his side when something was at stake. While he wanted to share almost everything with Glory, this was something Ripley had that was all his.

Before he fired up his bike, Ripley's phone rang. He didn't recognize the number, but he didn't hesitate to answer. "Hello?"

"Rip, it's me. I'm at Haven!"

"Glory. Oh, Zeus, Sunshine. Are you okay? Did he hurt you?"

A loud slap sounded through the line, followed by

Glory crying out. Ripley was going to eviscerate this human. Talbert said, "Glory isn't hurt yet, but she won't remain that way unless I get what I want."

"And what is that?"

"Anna. You bring her to me, and you get Glory back."

In the background, Glory yelled, "Don't do it, Rip!"

Ripley climbed off his bike, heading back to the group. He had to warn his president that Talbert was gunning for his mate. The other Hounds followed him as he informed Josiah, "Anna, as you call her, is now married with a new baby, so that's not an option."

"It's the only option you have if you want to see Glory alive. I'll give you two hours to get to the market where you took Glory. Just you and Anna. If I see anyone else, Glory gets a bullet to the brain." The phone disconnected.

"Fuck!" Ripley wouldn't hand Rhi over, but how the hell was he going to save his mate?

"What's going on?" Natalia asked. She and Maveryck, along with several others, had gathered around Lynette's car, but Ripley focused on Ryker.

"That was Josiah. He wants me to trade Rhi for Glory. I told him that wasn't going to happen."

"Josiah? How the hell did he get this close?" Hayden asked.

"He's either wearing a disguise or changed his appearance somehow. Julia recognized his voice," Rip explained before glaring at Helen, who was still sitting in Lynette's back seat. "You're going to burn in Hell for this." He slammed the car door, not wanting her to hear any more of their conversation. Julia was standing close by, and when Lynette saw him staring at the young woman, Lynette ushered her into the car with Helen.

"We'll head back to Providence in a few minutes. Please wait in the car."

Julia nodded, but before she slid into the front seat, she turned to Ripley. "I'm really sorry. I hope Glory's okay."

After the door was closed and they could speak freely once more, Natalia said, "I'll go."

Ripley arched an eyebrow at the feisty Russian, who was standing with her own mate. "I appreciate the offer, but you look nothing like Rhi."

"We're close to the same size. I'll wear a wig and her clothes. When the exchange is made, you Hounds can do what you do best."

"No." Regina stepped up to Natalia and grabbed her arms. "We both appreciate you willing to step in, but I'll do it. I won't need a wig, plus I have something you don't." Regina let her Lion's eyes come forth.

"Mom—"

"Natalia has two boys who need their mother."

"And I need *my* mother," Rip whispered.

"Oh, Darling." Regina pressed her palm to his cheek. "You're not going to lose me. I can take care of myself, and with you and your father there as backup, I'm not worried."

"Mom, Josiah has a gun. You're a badass, but even you aren't impervious to bullets."

"No, I'm not, but this will work. I'll voice him before he can pull the trigger."

Conrad stepped behind Regina and pulled her

back to his chest. "Tell us everything."

Ripley stared at his parents. His father was fierce when he needed to be, but most of the time, he had a smile on his face. Conrad enjoyed the simple things in life. His mom though? Rip's gorgeous mother with her long blonde hair and startling blue eyes was the fiercest being he knew as were most of the female Gryphons. Not only were they shifters, but there was something to be said about a mother's protectiveness. And her love.

"When I answered my phone, it was Glory. She told me he was holding her at Haven, then it sounded like he slapped her. When Talbert told me he wanted to trade Glory for Rhi, Glory yelled at me not to do it, so I know she's unharmed. But he said he wouldn't hesitate to put a bullet in her head if we tried to trick him during the exchange. He said for me to bring 'Anna' and come alone. He gave me two hours to bring her to the market where we rescued Glory."

"How far away is this market?" Conrad asked.

"Less than an hour."

"Then we all need to get a move on so we can park far enough away that he won't see our vehicles. We can shift and fly in," his dad said. When Ripley didn't move, Conrad sighed. "Your mother will be fine. I'll make sure of it."

"I need something with long sleeves to cover my ink. A zip-up hoodie preferably," Regina said.

They were really doing this. Ripley knew better than to argue when his mother made up her mind. She was an unmovable force. Rip sent Ace a text telling him the change of plans. They could still meet at the same designated spot since it was on the way to the market.

After a quick discussion with the group, Ripley and the Hounds loaded up once again, but this time, there were more of them. Several stayed behind to watch over the mates and kids of the Hounds riding with Ripley. The fireworks show was coming to a close, and everyone would need to go home. Since Ryker wasn't leaving Rhi and his new baby girl behind, Maveryck took lead, and the rest of them got into road formation. With Sultan out of town checking on his cabin, Ripley took the sergeant-at-arms place in line. His parents brought up the rear in their rental car.

Those of the group who were mercenaries went home to grab their sidearm before meeting up with them at the appointed spot. The rest stopped at one of the big box stores so Regina could purchase a hoodie. After, they continued on to pick up Ace. They lingered just long enough for the mercenaries to arrive. While waiting, Rip gave Ace a rundown of the new plan, and with no time to waste, they were off again. Maveryck led them to the area where they camped before rescuing Glory. Ace pulled his bike to the side and parked so he could unlock the gate. Once everyone was through, he followed, then locked the gate behind them. Maveryck led them deeper into the area so no one would see their bikes if they happened to be walking along the perimeter.

Regina turned her back while the Hounds who were flying to the market stripped out of their clothes, added them to the travel bags, and shifted to their Eagles. Their duty was to take out any guards Talbert brought along. Maveryck squawked, and the Eagles lifted into the air, leaving Ripley with his parents.

"Mom—"

"Stop. I have my two brave Gryphons with me watching my six."

Ripley couldn't help but grin. "Your six, huh?" Regina smirked, and Ripley gripped her hands, kissing her knuckles. "What I was going to say is thank you. And I love you. Everyone should have a mom like you in their corner."

Regina squeezed his fingers. "You're welcome. Now, let's go get our girl."

Conrad held the passenger door for his mate before slipping into the back seat. He refused to be in the sky while she was on the ground. It made sense because Ripley's focus would be on Glory. His dad unlocked the gate, then relocked it once Rip drove through. They were quiet on the ride, but Ripley's beast was anything but. It had been shouting in his head ever since Rip received the call from Talbert.

*As soon as Glory is safe, you can do whatever the fuck you want to Josiah.*

**Get ready for lots of blood.**

Not wanting to risk getting pulled over thus delaying their arrival at the market, Rip kept to the speed limit. Talbert had given him two hours, and Ripley still had twenty minutes on the clock. He backed into a space so he could see someone else pulling into the lot. Twenty minutes came and went, and Rip started to worry. "Something's not right."

"Don't borrow trouble yet," Conrad said from the back seat. He was lying down, covered with a dark blanket so anyone peeking into the car wouldn't notice.

299

After another fifteen minutes, Ace strode up to the car. "There's no one here. We've checked the area for miles, and unless they're holed up in someone's house, they didn't make the trip."

"Fuck!" Ripley slammed his hand on the steering wheel. "What if something happened, and—" Ripley couldn't finish the thought. "I can't wait any longer. I'm driving to Haven. Round up the Hounds."

"We're with you, Brother." Ace raced back the direction he came from, and Ripley started the car. The Hounds could fly as fast as he drove, so he didn't worry about them. He did worry about his mate. Why would Josiah insist they meet at the market, then not show up? His Gryphon wanted to fly with the others, and Ripley thought about it. His parents could fly as well, but when they rescued Glory, he would need the car.

*She can fly with us.*

He shut the car off and turned to his mother. "Are you up for a late-night flight?"

# CHAPTER TWENTY-FOUR

## Glory

WHEN GLORY TOLD Rip she was at Haven, the slap was quick but not unexpected. She had to give her mate every advantage. Josiah ordered Marjorie back to her cabin, leaving Glory alone in the barn. She didn't feel so good, and it had nothing to do with her stinging cheek. Her stomach was a mess, and she chalked it up to nerves. Marjorie didn't have time to grab one of the knives before Josiah reappeared, but now Glory wasn't wasting any time. She clambered to her feet and hopped over to the storage cabinet, grabbing the one she used most often. If it could cut through bone, it could work on ropes. Glory was grateful her hands were tied in front of her. Otherwise, she'd have been screwed. After getting her feet loose, Glory worked on her hands. That was easier said than done. She sat on the ground and gripped the hilt between her thighs. It kept moving as she attempted to slice through the bindings. It was slow-going, but it finally worked. Now free, Glory retrieved another knife and plastered herself to the wall next to the door.

Her stomach rumbled again, and Glory choked

back the bile. She never got sick to her stomach. She would chalk it up to everything she'd eaten that day, but it had been hours since she'd had any food. Using her forearm, Glory wiped the sweat from her brow. She had one shot at taking Josiah down when he entered the barn, and she didn't need her vision impaired. Glory had a moment of doubt about stabbing Haven's former leader, but the man was evil. He wanted to trade Glory for Rhi, and after learning about Rhi's gift, Glory had no doubt the man wanted her friend back for his own gain. Glory couldn't let that happen, especially now that Rhi had Daisy.

The doorknob turned, and Glory took a deep breath. Josiah stepped into the barn, and Glory didn't hesitate. She sliced across the back of his knees, bringing the man to the ground.

"What the fuck?" he cried. Josiah turned and pointed the pistol her way, but Glory had the advantage. She jumped across his body, slashing his arm as she went, stumbling as she landed. He dropped the gun, but he wasn't done. Even with his legs bleeding, Josiah twisted. "I'll fucking kill you!" he raged.

"Not if I kill you first." Glory kicked the gun across the floor. She didn't want to alert the guards with a gunshot, so her knives would have to do.

"You're not going to kill me, Glory of God. You don't have it in you," he taunted.

Glory gripped both knives tightly, but before she could attack the man, her stomach rumbled again, and this time, there was no holding back. Glory threw up, and it landed on Josiah's face. She scrambled away from him as he thrashed about, swiping the mess off his face with his good hand. While he was preoccupied, Glory wiped her mouth with the hem of her T-shirt. She was weak from whatever had been used earlier to paralyze her, but she was still standing. Somewhat. Glory walked behind him, and stabbed him in the side with the hunting knife. Josiah cried out for the guards. He called out to God. He cursed Glory. He grabbed for the knife, but Glory was faster. She used the serrated weapon to slice through his bicep and stepped back. Forward, slash, step back. She continued her assault until he no longer attempted to dig the knife out of his side.

Blood trickled out of the side of his mouth as he glared at her. "Y-you'll go to H-hell for th-this," he stammered.

Jutting her chin, she told him, "Save me a seat." Glory kept an eye on the man as she went to the cabinet and got another knife. Shouts outside the barn had Glory scrambling to the ladder. She climbed as quickly as possible carrying two weapons, but she wasn't waiting for one of the guards to come in and shoot her. Glory had never been in the loft, so when she got to her feet, she looked around. The loft was filled with crates. Glory stumbled over to the closest one, finding it empty. The next three were also bare, but the last one was filled with weapons like the guards used. Glory had never fired a gun, and these large, black rifles were daunting. Ignoring them, she made her way to the window. It was smudged with years of grime, so Glory wiped away a small section so she could see outside, then wiped her hand on her shorts.

The scene before her made no sense. The Haven men, dressed in their black guard uniforms, were on their knees with their hands on their heads. Then the most beautiful sight ever appeared before them. Glory banged on the window. "Ripley! I'm up here!" she yelled. Ripley looked up at the window and smiled, but her joy was short-lived as a rifle blasted behind her, and the window shattered, raining glass everywhere. Glory dropped to her knees, covering her head.

"You'll pay for killing Brother Josiah," Thomas seethed from behind her. Glory was cornered. There was nowhere for her to go, not with the man pointing a rifle at her. Regina appeared at the top of the ladder, and Glory's gasp gave away her presence. Thomas turned, and Glory didn't think. She flipped the hunting knife, catching the blade, and threw it end-over-end at the elder. It hit its mark, embedding into the man's shoulder. The rifle sprayed bullets all over the walls as he went down. Regina leapt to her feet, and Glory sank back on her butt as Rip's mother shifted to her Lion, her clothes shredding, then ripped Thomas apart with her fangs and claws. Glory's stomach lurched, and she vomited again. This time, it was mostly foam.

"Glory! Oh, Sunshine," Ripley cried, his voice full of anguish as he crawled through the broken glass of the window.

"I'm okay," she assured him, but he was lifting her off the floor before she got the words out. Cradling her to his chest, Ripley pressed his face into her neck. Glory dropped the knife she still held and wrapped her arms around his shoulders. "I'm fine, Rip. Look at me." His tear-stained face broke her heart, but she smiled at him. "I knew you'd come for me." Glory kissed him on the cheek, mindful of her breath. When she pulled back, she looked over his shoulder at the bloody Lion. "And thank you for saving me."

Regina swished her tail, huffing at Glory.

"I'm sorry you had to see that, Sunshine."

Glory ran her fingers through Ripley's hair. "I'm not. Thomas was going to kill me."

"But you threw up."

"Not from that. My stomach is wonky. I also threw up on Josiah's face."

"Glory, who saved you from Josiah?"

"I saved myself."

Ripley narrowed his eyes. "You killed him?"

Glory shrugged one shoulder. "If he's dead, then yes. He was going to force Rhi back here, and I couldn't let that happen. What's going on outside?"

"We voiced the guards and took their weapons. I'm so sorry we missed that one." Ripley tilted his head toward Thomas.

"I'm just glad he couldn't aim," she muttered. "Can we get out of here? I want to check on my mother. She agreed to come with us if you managed to rescue me."

"Anything you want." Ripley set Glory on her feet, and when she wobbled, he gripped her elbow. "Are you sure you're okay?"

"Yep. Just weak from tossing my cookies. Josiah somehow paralyzed me, and I'm still a little wonky."

Ripley pressed a kiss to her hair. "I want to hear all about what happened, but we can talk later." When they walked toward the opening leading downstairs, Regina's Lion stood and pressed against Glory's legs. Glory ran her hand over the silky fur of the Lion's head. "Best mother ever," she whispered. The Lion nuzzled Glory's hand before looking up at Ripley.

"I'll send Dad up with some clothes," Rip told his mother. Regina chuffed in agreement. Ripley went down the ladder first and helped guide Glory the last few rungs. When they were on solid ground, Glory glanced over at Josiah. Someone had covered him with a tarp, and for that, she was thankful. She didn't feel like vomiting again.

Glory expected chaos outside, but it was quiet. All the guards were still on their knees, and the Hounds were holding the rifles. "What happens now?" she asked.

"Sutton comes in and talks to the members. Anyone wanting to leave can. Normally, the cops would be called, but with both Josiah and Thomas dead by our hands, we'll voice the entire community and tell them one of the guards killed Josiah. It won't be a stretch considering Abraham, his father-in-law, was adamant about Josiah not returning to run things. As for Thomas, we'll take his body and dump him in the woods where your father and William were dropped."

"About that. Why wouldn't Thomas have told the community about their deaths? My mother thought my father was in hiding."

"That's a good question. One we may never know the answer to. Are you sure you're okay? Taking a life isn't easy."

Glory plastered herself to Ripley's side. She searched her heart, then told him truthfully, "I am. It was him or me, and I like to think I have more to offer this world than an evil man does. Will I have nightmares? Probably, but I'm counting on you to be there when they happen."

"Always."

"I'm almost positive Helen was the one who told Josiah you and I were together. She introduced him as Jacob, a record producer."

"She admitted to it after I voiced her. He promised her a future with him, and she bought it."

Glory almost felt sorry for the woman. All she wanted was to be loved. "What'll happen to her?"

"Don't know and don't care," Rip snarled. Yeah, Glory could understand that too.

Ripley led Glory over to Conrad, who grabbed Glory and wrapped her up tight. While he was hugging her, he asked, "Where's my mate?"

"In the loft of the barn waiting on you to bring her clothes. She was something fierce," Glory told him.

Conrad was still hugging Glory when Marjorie called out, "Glory?"

Conrad kept his arm around Glory when her mom approached. "I told you Ripley would come for me."

Marjorie eyed Conrad. "Thank you for taking care of my girl."

"Oh, no. I'm her father-in-law." Con gestured toward Ripley. "This is her husband, my son, Ripley."

Marjorie did a double take. Seeing the two men together was surprising considering they could pass for brothers. "Oh, uh, well, thank you. Glory told me you and your wife bought her a piano. That's very nice of you."

"It was nothing. Glory deserves everything this world has to offer, and we were more than happy to provide for her. Now, if you'll excuse me." Conrad took off toward the barn with a bag in his hand.

Marjorie watched him walk away. Her eyes were misty, and Glory wondered if Conrad's words caused the tears. Glory wasn't sure if he meant them as a dig to Marjorie, but if the shoe fit…

"Glory, I talked to Hope. She and Scott want to come with me and the girls to Florida, that is, if my mother has room for us all."

"We'll make sure you have a place large enough to accommodate all of you. If Hope and her husband want a place of their own, we'll make that happen too," Ripley said. "If there are things you want to take with you, pack them now. We'll be heading out as soon as my boss arrives with transportation."

"We have nothing of importance here. I'll go gather the others." Marjorie shuffled off toward the cabins, and Glory sighed.

"Six years and nothing to show for it. That's sad."

"It is, Sunshine, but now they have a chance at a better life. You and I will make sure they have whatever they need."

"You're the best," Glory whispered, swaying on her feet. Ripley lifted her into his arms once again, and Glory rested her head on his shoulder.

When Sutton and Rory arrived, Sutton convinced one of the guards to have all the members of Haven meet in the church. Glory was bone tired, but she wanted to be there to see Sutton in action. When they entered the building, Ace stood at the back of the room next to them while the other Hounds took up spots along the perimeter. Melinda and Lisa Ann entered together, and when Melinda noticed Glory, she rushed over.

"Glory! Oh, my god. What are you doing here? Sandra said you ran off from the market," Melinda asked, eyeing Ripley while doing so. Then she did something weird. She sniffed the air, and her head snapped over to Ace. If Glory didn't know better, she'd think Melinda was a Gryphon. Then again, Glory didn't know better. She knew next to nothing about the other woman.

"I did run off, and now I have a new family. This is Ripley." Glory patted Rip's stomach. "And this is his best friend, Ace." Glory thumbed Asher's direction.

Melinda took a step toward Ace, and her eyes widened. She quickly schooled her features before holding out a hand. "Melinda. It's a pleasure."

Ace gripped Melinda's hand. Instead of shaking it, he held it between both his. "The pleasure's mine."

Sutton got everyone's attention, and Melinda excused herself to find her seat. She turned and looked at Ace over her shoulder right before she sat down, and she gave him a smile. Glory still felt there was something about the woman... something off. Instead of dwelling on it, she watched as Sutton did his thing.

It took about a couple hours for Sutton to talk to the community and round up those who no longer wished to remain at Haven. The number wanting to leave was small, but Glory didn't judge those who stayed. For most, this was the only life they knew. When her mom, sisters, and Scott were loaded into one of the vans, Ripley and Glory climbed in behind them. He had already explained how the others were flying back. Glory was sad she and Ripley weren't joining them, but she wanted to be there for her family. Instead of going to a hotel, Rory drove them to Providence since it was equipped with clothes and essentials.

When they arrived, Lynette and Branson were waiting to escort everyone inside. First, they hugged Glory after checking for themselves she was okay. When they were satisfied she was fine, they turned their attention to the newcomers.

Glory spent time with her family, but she didn't have the energy to stay long. Ripley promised they would return the next day after getting some much-needed sleep. Before they parted ways, Glory gave her granny's number to Marjorie and told her to call her mother.

Helen was nowhere to be seen, but Julia stood off to the side while her new housemates were shown where they would sleep. Once the room was cleared, Julia approached Glory. "This is all my fault. I recognized Josiah's voice, but I was afraid he'd try to take me back to Sanctuary."

"Did you tell him where to find me?" Glory asked.

"No. I swear I never talked to him. But I should have known he was up to no good having changed his appearance."

Glory reached out and brushed a hand down Julia's arm. "I forgive you."

With tears in her eyes, Julia whispered, "Thank

you." She wiped her face and asked, "What happened tonight?"

"The good guys won," Glory hedged. "My mother, sisters, and brother-in-law will be moving to Florida to live with my granny, but everyone else is going to need guidance. Your guidance."

"Mine?" Julia squeaked.

"Yes. You have been at Providence a while now, and you'll be able to help Lynette and Branson get the new tenants settled. Listen, I know I promised I would go to church with you tomorrow, or today rather, but I'm wiped. If you still want to sing, I'll go with you next Sunday."

"You'd do that? After everything that's happened?"

"Absolutely." Glory's energy was zapped. She gripped Ripley's arm, and he understood what she needed.

"Glory's had a long night and needs to get some rest. You can talk more about this tomorrow." Julia gave them a little wave before rushing off upstairs. He wrapped a strong arm around Glory's waist and helped her to the Camaro Ace had brought for them. Glory was asleep before they made it out of the driveway.

The brush of lips on her cheek woke Glory, but she kept her eyes closed. Her brain was foggy, and she wanted five more minutes before facing the day. The next time she woke, soft voices carried from the living room of the hotel suite, and Glory rolled to her side. Her sleep had been dreamless, and for that, she was grateful. Glory chalked it up to how tired she had been when they got back to the hotel. That and the Gryphon holding her tightly all night. When her stomach rumbled, Glory sprang out of bed and rushed to the en suite, barely making it before spewing bile into the toilet. The water turned on, and soon a cold, damp washcloth was pressed to her forehead.

"How long have you been sick?" Regina asked.

"Since yesterday. I think it's from whatever Josiah used to paralyze me."

"Hmm."

Glory wondered what the non-response meant, but she was too strung out to think on it too much. Once her stomach was no longer waging war, Glory pushed to her feet and brushed her teeth. Regina remained by her side until she was finished, then guided her to the living area.

"Where's Rip?" she asked after plopping down on the sofa.

Regina rummaged in the refrigerator, but came back empty handed. "He and Con left to go to your new house. The furniture arrives today." Regina picked up the hotel phone and asked for some crackers and ginger ale to be delivered to her suite. Glory was starving, but she was also afraid to eat. Vomiting was the worst.

Glory leaned her head back and closed her eyes. "Is it wrong of me to be glad we don't have to go to church with Julia today?"

"Not at all. Even if you hadn't been kidnapped, fought for your life, and rescued, you shouldn't do anything you aren't comfortable with." The sofa cushions dipped, and Regina took Glory's hand in hers. "You were so damn brave, Glory. I'm in awe of you."

Glory rolled her head toward the female and opened her eyes. "What's your middle name?"

Regina's eyebrows shot up. "Grazia. It's Italian for Grace."

"Grazia. That's pretty, but you don't look Italian."

Regina grinned. "I'm not, but my mother loved an opera singer named Grazia Russo and named me after her. My father's name is Reginald, thus Regina. Why do you ask?"

Glory squeezed Regina's hand. "Ripley is going to fill out the paperwork to change my middle name. Would you mind if I choose Grace? You did save my life after all."

"Oh, Glory. I would be honored." Regina slid her arm around Glory's shoulder and pressed her cheek to Glory's hair. They sat in companionable silence until someone knocked on the door. Regina patted Glory's leg before standing to retrieve the items she'd called for. Regina took the soda to the kitchen, added it to a glass of ice, then brought it along with the crackers to Glory. She took a sip of the cold drink and nibbled on a cracker. After keeping both down, she ate several crackers and finished the ginger ale.

"When you feel up to it, why don't you shower, and then I'll drive us over to your new home? Since we aren't going to church, we might as well help our males."

Glory liked that idea. She would much rather help wash bedding and put away their new dishes than sit around doing nothing. So that's what they did. When

313

they arrived at the house, a couple vans were parked in the driveway along with several cars. Regina maneuvered around them to park close to the door.

When they entered the house, Glory's heart swelled. All the living room furniture she and Ripley picked out was in place. Boxes were stacked against the walls, on top of the dining table, and on the kitchen island.

Branson emerged from the laundry room, grinning when he saw Glory and Regina. "The washer and dryer are hooked up and ready to go."

"Thank you. Where's Rip?"

"I'm here, Sunshine." Ripley strode to her and kissed her softly. "How are you feeling?"

"Still shaky. I threw up again, but your mom got me some ginger ale and crackers."

"Maybe I should take you to the hospital."

"Why? I'm sure it's nothing," Glory said. She didn't want to miss out on getting the house set up.

"Or it could be something. We don't know what Josiah used to paralyze you. I'd at least like to have Rev check your blood."

"How about this? If I'm not feeling better tomorrow, then you can call him."

Ripley cupped her cheek. "Against my better judgment, I'll agree to those terms, but if you throw up even one more time, we're going."

"Deal."

"Want to see the bedroom?" Rip wiggled his eyebrows, and Glory giggled.

"Lead the way."

The house looked completely different with

furniture, and the bedroom was no different. A king-sized bed filled the far wall with nightstands on either side. A tall armoire and dresser with mirror sat opposite the windows, and the wall across from the bed held a wooden chest topped by a flat-screen TV. Next to the chest was a door leading to their en suite bathroom where two walk-in closets bracketed the jetted tub. The tiled shower was large enough for them to comfortably bathe together. A couple of boxes sat atop the counter waiting to be unpacked. The bed still needed linens, so Glory put their new sheets in the washing machine before helping Regina unpack boxes. The men continued placing the rest of the furniture.

When they stopped for lunch, Glory asked Ripley to take her to Providence. "I need to get my driver's license so you don't have to play chauffer all the time," she said when they were on their way.

"I don't mind driving you, but I understand. Since your old license was issued in a different state and has expired, you may need to retest, so I'll do some checking to see what the requirements are this week. If you choose your new middle name before then, I can have the paperwork drawn up. That way when you get your license, you won't have to get a different one later."

"Oh, I know what I want my new name to be. I chose Grace after your mother."

Ripley kissed her knuckles. "Glory Grace. That's perfect. Just like you."

# CHAPTER TWENTY-FIVE

## Ripley

THE TRIP TO Florida didn't happen immediately. When they visited Providence House, Marjorie told Glory she needed time to think. Glory gave it to her, and during the next few days, she spent time with her sisters. She also agreed to visit Rev and Bethany to have blood drawn. She didn't vomit again, but her appetite was gone, and her energy hadn't completely returned.

When Glory asked Marjorie for a decision, they got into a heated discussion regarding the kind of man Amos had been. Glory asked Hope to watch over their younger sisters, and she dragged her mother to the car and had Ripley drive by his old house. Without a body to bury, Marjorie was adamant he might still be alive, and therefore she was still his wife, so while sitting out front of the remains of his house, Rip voiced her. Not about Haven because now that Josiah and Thomas were dead, the compound would get new leaders. There was every possibility Abraham would send in someone else equally as bad, but that was a choice Marjorie would have to live with. Ripley didn't care one way or another about the woman, except Glory did. Marjorie hadn't been a good mother, but she had two daughters who needed her to step up for them. He did convince her Amos was never coming back, but still, she hesitated.

Marjorie didn't fit in with the others who were glad to be away from Haven. Meanwhile, Glory and her sisters spent several hours together every day, becoming closer as time went on. Four days after arriving, Marjorie decided she was returning to Haven. She had no control over Hope since she was married, but Majesty and Splendor needed a guardian. Being away from Haven, the teens had been allowed to watch TV, listen to music, wear regular clothes, and eat good food, so when Marjorie mentioned returning to Haven, the two younger sisters pitched one hell of a fit, yelling at their mother and threatening to run away. After lots of angry words and tears, Marjorie agreed to let the teens live with Leona.

When deciding what Helen's punishment would be for betraying Ripley and Glory, they sat down with his parents, Sutton, Rory, Branson, and Lynette. The three couples gave their opinions. His mother wanted to eviscerate the woman. Rory felt the same way, but Lynette had a gentler solution. They left the decision to Glory and Ripley.

Glory questioned the woman herself, asking about her motives, also asking if Helen had been in her room. Helen told Glory the same story about wanting someone to love her, and yes, she was the one who hung Glory's jacket the wrong way. She admitted to trying it on, but there was nothing sinister behind it. Ripley voiced the woman, so she was telling the truth.

Regardless, he was on team annihilation, but Glory made her case.

"I say we send her to Haven with my mother. Helen planned to go with Jacob, and he was taking her to Haven. Why don't we give her what she wanted? Josiah's gone, but there are plenty of single men there who will gladly take her for a wife." The gleam in his mate's eyes hinted at the type of men Helen would find. Once it was decided, Ripley voiced the female, making her forget about everything she'd seen or done over the last year. He had her call and quit her job so no one would miss her. When all was said and done, Helen thought she was being moved from Sanctuary to Haven. Marjorie was voiced with the same information so their stories aligned. The two women were then taken to the cult and dropped at the gate. Later, when Julia asked about Helen, Lynette told her Helen had taken off in the middle of the night.

Rip leased a private jet and flew Glory's family to Florida. The reunion was a happy one. Leona was a hoot, and Ripley could see where Glory got both her attitude and singing chops from. Hope spent all her time in the kitchen whenever Leona was cooking, soaking up every bit of love her granny offered as well as her expertise. The woman could cook, and Ripley loved to eat. For the first couple days, Majesty and Splendor clung to Glory, but after seeing how fiercely Leona loved, they warmed up to their grandmother and were behaving like normal kids.

The teens took their mother returning to Haven in stride, both happy for the opportunity to live far away from Haven. Leona acted as though she'd won the lottery. In a way, she had. She was getting acquainted with the girls she barely knew and would soon have her first great-grandchild in her life as well. Glory offered to take her sisters with her and Ripley, but Leona assured them she was thrilled at having a houseful.

After much discussion, Ripley convinced Leona to let him buy a house big enough for her, the three sisters, Scott, and the baby when he or she arrived. Rip bought Scott and Hope a new vehicle so they wouldn't need to borrow Leona's. Bishop ordered the sisters' birth certificates, since none of them had a copy. One afternoon, Scott had a heart-to-heart with Ripley about his fears of not being able to provide for Hope and their child, but Ripley promised to help anyway he could, whether Scott wanted to go to college or get a job that suited him.

It took a week to find the perfect house, and Ripley got the ball rolling on the purchase. While he was in Florida, Ripley filed the paperwork to have Glory's middle name changed to Grace. He called on one of his parents' friends who was a judge, and he pushed the petition through for them. Rip and Glory flew down to New Boca for a few days of alone time, relaxing on the beach and loving each other at night. He shifted into his Gryphon in the privacy of the back lawn, and he relaxed in his Lion so Glory could cuddle her "big guy." Ripley didn't mind since he got belly rubs.

They flew back to visit Leona and crew, and Ripley signed the paperwork on the house as well as added money to Leona's bank account to pay for movers and anything the sisters and Scott needed. He also set them up with medical insurance since Leona was the only one with coverage. Before leaving, he and Glory promised to come back before summer was over to help get the teens enrolled in school.

The next few months flew by. Bishop located Sheri, and Rip took Glory to visit her former best friend. Glory got to hang out with Sheri and her parents, catching up on lost time. Sheri was married with three kids, who took to Glory like all other children did. Glory talked to her family daily, and Ripley flew her to see them whenever she needed to put eyes on them. His mate missed her sisters and grandmother, so Rip made sure she saw them as often as possible. Once the teens were settled in their new school, Glory decided to get her diploma. As expected, she passed the exam with flying colors.

Ryker's idea to record an album of lullabies was something Glory decided she wanted to do, so Ripley got in touch with Desmond Rothchild, who happened to be a half-blood Gargoyle. The larger-than-life rock star brought his mate, Simone, to meet Glory. Once Desi heard Glory sing, he was determined she was going to be a star in her own right. Even though Ripley offered to pay for everything involved, Desi insisted on footing the bill. The two males came up with a contract that was beneficial to everyone involved. Not only was Desi a god behind a microphone, he was also a shrewd businessman. He hired songwriters and lyricists since Glory had no desire to do either. She only wanted to sing and play the final products.

It didn't take long before they had enough music for Glory to record. A rough demo of the album was sent to Glory so she could learn the songs on her own piano. When she was ready, Ripley and Glory flew to California where Glory recorded her part of the album. A violinist and cellist added backing tracks, and their portions were added later. What resulted was nothing short of amazing. They spent a few days after her time in the studio with Desi and his mate, Simone, whose father was a Gryphon. They also met Desi's father, Sixx, who was a Gargoyle, and his mate, Desirae. Before leaving California, Glory had two more females in her growing sisterhood.

"I had such a wonderful time, but I'm glad to be home," Glory said when they walked in the door leading from the garage to the kitchen after the return flight. "I've missed your parents. I need a few days to recharge, but maybe we could host a party. Your birthday is coming up, you know."

"I'd like that. We can get mom and dad to help with food and decorations. How about Saturday? That gives us a few days to relax and send out invites."

"Sounds perfect." Glory followed Rip upstairs, and she got busy with a load of laundry while he rounded up dinner. They had been too busy in the back of the jet on the flight home to eat.

The rest of the week, Glory and Rip shared lunch with his parents, regaling them with every aspect of recording the album. Con and Regina had found a house not too far away, and that suited Ripley fine. Glory and Regina were thick as thieves, and Ripley loved his mother more every day for being the kind of mom Glory should have had all along. She and Conrad asked Glory to call them Mom and Dad, and Ripley held Glory tight as she cried tears of happiness.

Saturday arrived, but instead of getting ready for the party, Ripley's Lion was lying on the living room floor with his massive head on Glory's lap as she rubbed his belly. His tail swished back and forth, his eyes were closed, and he rumbled low in contentment. Until he didn't. His Lion tensed and turned its head, paying close attention to Glory's stomach, which had Ripley tensing in turn. Rev had been able to determine the paralytic Josiah used, but in the long run, it didn't matter. Glory had bounced back with no long-term side effects.

*What's up with you?*

**I hear a heartbeat.**

*I would hope so.*

Before Ripley could ask what his Lion was going on about, someone knocked on the door. Ripley's Lion growled low, and Glory giggled, patting his nose.

"Put your clothes on, we're coming in," Regina called out.

"It's unlocked," Glory responded, not bothering to get up.

Regina entered the house and made a beeline for the kitchen. "Glory, I need your help in here."

Glory brushed a kiss to the Lion's nose, then pushed against his side. When he moved out of the way, Glory rose and followed Regina, leaving Ripley to shift and get dressed. "What, no hello for your son?" he called out.

"Hello, Rip," Regina answered after a few seconds.

"The party's not for an hour. Right?" Ripley asked Con as he entered the still open door.

Conrad's arms were loaded with cases of beer. "Right, but we wanted to come early and make sure everything was ready." Ripley took the top two cases and led the way to the kitchen. When he entered the room, his mother and Glory, who had been whispering about something, froze.

"What?"

"What, what?" Regina asked.

After placing the beer on the island, he gestured between the two of them. "What are you two conspiring about?"

Conrad entered the kitchen, placing his beer down. "Did you give her the pregnancy test?"

"Con!" Regina chastised at the same time Glory said, "Dad!"

"Pregnancy test? Who's…?" Ripley grabbed his chest. His Gryphon was trying to break free with joy. His Lion wanted out to rub against their mate.

*That heartbeat,* his Lion informed him.

"How is that possible?"

Regina rolled her eyes. "It's called biology, Rip. And with all the unprotected sex you two have been having, it's not only possible but highly probable."

"Mom!"

"What? You asked, and I answered. Glory didn't get on birth control after leaving Haven, so unless you were using condoms, the probability is high."

Glory crossed her arms, uncrossed them, and crossed them again. "I missed my last period, and the one before that only lasted a couple days, so I called Mom and asked her to pick up a test on the way." When Glory had been sick during the Haven fiasco,

323

Ripley had a moment of hopefulness that she was pregnant then, but her stomach settled, and they chalked her sickness up to whatever Josiah used to paralyze her.

"Where's the test? We need to take it now," he told his mother.

"*We* need to take it? Son, it doesn't work that way," Regina joked.

"You know what I mean. Now, gimme," he demanded with his hand out.

Regina dug in her purse and presented the box to Glory. Ripley snatched it away, tossed his mate over his shoulder, and strode down the hallway with both Glory and Regina yelling at him to put her down. He did set her on her feet when they reached their bedroom, and Glory sank down onto the floor.

"Sunshine?" Ripley squatted next to her. "Do you not want children?"

"Yes, but…" Glory placed a hand on her stomach, her eyes searching his.

"Talk to me, Love."

"I'm scared, Rip. I want this with you. I think about little Patrick, Daisy, the twins, Mateo, and Sheri's children. I remember helping my sisters. Loving them when our parents were too busy. Then I think about how selfish my mother was. I don't want to be selfish."

"Oh, Baby, you don't have a selfish bone in your body. You will be a terrific mother, and you'll have all the other mates who have kids as a support system."

Glory held out her hands to Rip. "Help me up. We have a test to take."

He followed her into the bathroom, and she didn't

324

bother to ask for privacy. Sure, peeing on a stick wasn't glamorous, but this was his future too. He closed the door behind them, opened the package and read the instructions aloud, then handed the plastic stick to her. Glory grinned at his reflection in the mirror when he turned his back while she peed, but he couldn't help watching. He was too excited to miss one second of the process. As soon as she was done, he took the test from her and stared at it while she wiped and pulled her shorts up. Glory flushed and then washed her hands, studying Ripley in the mirror. He studied her back, taking in the blue stripes in her hair to the way she filled out her T-shirt. She was stunning. When she continued staring, he winked at her.

"I take it you want it to be positive?" she asked, leaning against the counter after drying her hands.

"Yes. I want that, Sunshine. I want everything with you. But if it's negative, we'll just have to keep trying. We have many years ahead of us."

"I know I'm getting ahead of myself, but I've been thinking about names."

"Yeah? What did you come up with?" Ripley darted a glance to the window on the stick.

"I couldn't think of a female name that went with Ripley, so I chose Andrea after Anders, and Grace for your mom. We could call her Gracie."

"And if it's a boy?"

"Anders Blaine." Blaine was Conrad's middle name. His girl wanted to honor both his parents.

"Those are both amazing. You know what else is amazing?"

"What?" Glory asked, trying to look at the test

Ripley was holding away from her.

"You are. My amazing mate, and now, the amazing mother of my baby."

Glory gasped. "It's positive?"

"Yes, my love. It is." Ripley placed the test on the counter before kissing Glory with more passion, more love than he'd ever shown, and that was saying something.

"Well? Am I going to be a grandmother?" Regina called from the bedroom.

Rip tore open the door, and said, "Hello, Grandma!"

Regina covered her mouth with her hand, her eyes filling with tears. Conrad stepped up behind her and pulled her to his chest. "Nope. This is your baby's Gigi."

Glory grinned. "And what about you?"

"I kinda like Big Poppa."

The four of them burst out laughing, and soon they were a mess of tears and hugs.

"Where the hell is everyone?" Ace called out. Glory passed out tissues, and that's how Ace found them all, wiping their faces. "What's wrong?" he asked.

"Nothing's wrong. You're going to be Uncle Asher in about seven months."

Ace grabbed Ripley and wrapped him in a bear hug. "I'm so happy for you both." He released Rip and held out a hand to Glory. If it was anyone else, Rip would threaten to tear his hand off, but this was his best friend. His brother of the heart. Glory placed her hand in Ace's, and he kissed her knuckles. "Congratulations, Glory. You're going to be a fantastic mother."

"And I'm going to be the best Gigi who ever Gigied," Regina crowed.

"Come on, Gigi. Let's get ready for the party," Conrad said, leading his mate out of the crowded room.

"Yes, Big Poppa."

Ace choked at Regina's reply. "Are they…? Nope. Never mind." Shaking his head, he followed them down the hall, leaving Ripley alone with his mate.

He took advantage of the quiet and kissed his mate gently while pressing his hand to her stomach. His baby was growing inside, and Ripley was overcome with gratitude. "Thank you, Sunshine. You have given me the best gift imaginable."

"You're most welcome. Let's go celebrate with our family. Later, we can have a celebration of a different kind."

The next few hours were spent eating, drinking, laughing, and celebrating life. Glory radiated joy with every smile. She spread that happiness throughout every room she entered. She shared her talent by playing and singing. If there was an embodiment of sunshine, it was his mate. She never asked for anything, yet Ripley longed to give her the moon and stars.

When the last guest was gone and the doors locked behind them, Ripley led his mate to their bedroom. Wordlessly, they stripped out of their clothes, and Ripley made love to his female. Their coming together was slow, tender, and so full of everything Ripley never knew he needed. He couldn't believe how much his life had changed over the last few months. One day, he was a sad Hound, sitting alone while surrounded by friends at the campground. That fateful day, he met the one being he never imagined finding, and he thanked Zeus for his blessing. His Glory Grace.

# THE END

# A NOTE FROM THE AUTHOR

If you've made it this far, dear reader, thank you. Thank you for your patience as I waded through the murky waters of life. Being an author means your thoughts have to make sense, and you have to have time to put those thoughts down in a cohesive manner. The last year has been rough, but things have finally leveled out. So thank you for waiting, patiently or not, for this Hounds book. Without my core group of friends, Candy, Jennifer, Katie, Kerstin, and Nikki, I couldn't have made it through each day. Thank you all for being my sounding boards. My shoulders when I needed to cry. My strength when I was flailing. I love each one of you.

I had this gorgeous photo of Soj for a while. I first bought it to use as Kayos, but he just didn't fit. When I started writing Ripper's book, he did. Thank you to Wander for shooting these fabulous men who make my covers special. And to Jay for giving me another stellar cover I am so proud of.

If you read the author's foreword, you know how I came about the character of Glory. I have to give another shout out to the real Glory for being such a bright light and allowing me to use her name. Her story is her own, and it's nowhere near as crazy as the one in my book, but it was a doozy.

I always thank the man, but during the hardest

months of my life, he was there every day, defending me, cheering me on, and basically holding me up. He really is my rock.

# ABOUT THE AUTHOR

Multi-genre author Faith Gibson began writing in high school, and through the years, penned many stories and poems. As her dreams continued getting crazier than the one before, she decided to keep a dream journal. Many of these nighttime escapades have led to a line, a chapter, or even a complete story.

"Love is love, and there's not enough love in the world." This belief she holds strongly, and it's the prevailing theme in her works, all of which come with a happy ending.

Faith believes her purpose in life is to entertain the masses, even if it's one person at a time. Living just outside of Nashville, Tennessee, with the love of her life and her American Staffordshire pup, when she's not hard at work writing her next adventure, she can often be found reading, listening to live music, or off on an adventure of her own.

www.ingramcontent.com/pod-product-compliance
Lightning Source LLC
Chambersburg PA
CBHW072343020726
47506CB00004B/983